# THAT DARKENED DOORSTEP

## AN ANTHOLOGY

EDITED BY
CATHERINE JORDAN

HELLBENDER
BOOKS

an imprint of Sunbury Press, Inc.
Mechanicsburg, PA USA

**HELLBENDER BOOKS**

an imprint of Sunbury Press, Inc.
Mechanicsburg, PA USA

For information about special discounts for bulk purchases, please contact Sunbury Press Orders Dept. at (855) 338-8359 or orders@sunburypress.com.

To request one of our authors for speaking engagements or book signings, please contact Sunbury Press Publicity Dept. at publicity@sunburypress.com.

FIRST HELLBENDER BOOKS EDITION: September 2022

Set in Adobe Garamond Pro | Interior design by Crystal Devine | Cover by Lawrence Knorr | Edited by Jennifer Cappello.

Publisher's Cataloging-in-Publication Data
Names: Jordan, Catherine, editor.
Title: That darkened doorstep / Edited by Catherine Jordan.
Description: First trade paperback edition. | Mechanicsburg, PA : Hellbender Books, 2022.
Summary: When faced with a darkened doorstep, think before you walk through. Feel our dread, grief, anxiety, and fear at an unopened door. This anthology encompasses diverse viewpoints and a wide interpretation of the theme.
Identifiers: ISBN 978-1-62006-948-6 (softcover).
Subjects: FICTION / Horror | FICTION / Short Stories | FICTION / Thrillers / Supernatural.

*Product of the United States of America*
0 1 1 2 3 5 8 13 21 34 55

*Continue the Enlightenment!*

This anthology is dedicated to the memory of a dear friend, Carol Lauver, artist, writer, actor, humanitarian, and elementary school teacher.

Carol was one of the earliest supporters in my writing career. She came to every class with me, to every reading, and attended every signing. On April 12, 2022, Carol passed away suddenly, shortly after she completed her final short story, "Funeral Pyre."

*Footfalls echo in the memory*
*Down the passage which we did not take*
*Towards the door we never opened*
*Into the rose garden.*

— T. S. Eliot, *Four Quartets,* "Burnt Norton, Part I"

# CONTENTS

Introduction / *Catherine Jordan* ix

Seeking a Good Woman / *Jacque Day* 1

Black Metal in a White Room / *S. J. Townend* 18

Primal Scream / *Mia Dalia* 32

Lab Test / *Dianna Sinovic* 37

Clerks and Convicts / *J. L. Royce* 50

Dismantled / *Vickie Fernandez* 58

Where the Elk Roam / *Amanda Headlee* 66

Locks and Promises / *N. M. Brown* 85

Seal of Solomon / *Fred J. Lauver* 93

Funeral Pyre / *Carol A. Lauver* 112

Room 333 / *Lori M. Myers* 121

Ashes to Ashes / *Diane Sismour* 128

Lonely is the Desperate Heart / *Catherine Jordan* 146

The Last Kiss / *Alyson Faye* 155

Meeting the Monster / *John Kujawski* 161

Doors of Death / *Thomas M. Malafarina* 163

Children of the Goat Man / *Douglas Ford* 174

That Shade Next to You / *Sergio Palumbo* 188

A Face to Die For / *Amie DeStefano* 196

Editor's Note 212

Lost in a Pyramid, or the Mummy's Curse /
    *Louisa May Alcott\** 213

Acknowledgments 224

\* "Lost in a Pyramid, or the Mummy's Curse," by Louisa May Alcott, originally published by Frank Leslie in 1869, sourced from Project Gutenberg of Australia, eBook No.: 0603041h. This work is in the public domain.

# INTRODUCTION

've been a fan of anthologies ever since I can remember learning to read. A short story is easy to absorb, and it makes for a good time-filler when I don't have much to spare. They're perfect for airplanes, appointments, mornings on the porch, and summer days at the pool. I especially like reading tales from a new or unknown writer. I'll never forget the first time I read Shirley Jackson's "The Lottery", W. W. Jacobs's "The Monkey's Paw", and Edgar Allan Poe's "The Tell-Tale Heart." Then I discovered collections from Flannery O'Connor, Matthew M. Bartlett, and Joyce Carol Oates. And I always appreciate a theme, like *Charles Keeping's Book of Classic Ghost Stories*, and *Scary Stories to Tell in the Dark* by Alvin Schwartz and originally illustrated by Stephen Gammell. Another favorite of mine is the serial novella; consider Stephen King's *The Green Mile*. I remember buying *The Green Mile, Part 1, The Two Dead Girls—The Serial Thriller Begins* at my local grocery store, devouring it in one sitting, and waiting impatiently for part two, *The Mouse on the Mile—The Serial Thriller Continues . . .* ; part three, *Coffey's Hands;* part four, *The Bad Death of Edward Delacroix;* part five, *Night Journey;* and part six, *Coffey on the Mile—The Serial Thriller Concludes!*

I love to write short stories for publication within themed anthologies. Mostly, I enjoy curating them. Someday I'll publish my own collection, but until then . . .

The idea for this anthology came about during a meeting with the Hive Writing Group, a spinoff from the Pennsylvania chapter of the Horror Writers Association, comprised of five women authors—Diane Sismour, Amanda Headlee, Jacque Day, Dianna Sinovic, and me. We connect monthly and take retreats and conferences together. One evening during our monthly chat, Day mentioned her Cape Cod-style house with its small doors that lead to dormers—and in particular, one she had never opened! After I picked my jaw up off my lap (because who has a door in their house that's never been opened!?), I said to Day, "That would make a great story." Then I thought, *that would make a great themed anthology.*

Within two days, I got the green for go from my publisher at Sunbury Press. With contributions by Day, Headlee, Sinovic, Sismour, and an exciting slate of known and unknown authors, this anthology explores the broad theme of its darkened doorstep including the grief, anxiety, and fear when faced by an unopened door.

Day has since opened her door. She says, "I expected to find a cubby or a crawl space. Instead, the door opened into a blank slate of a space outfitted with an overhead light, nearly ten feet deep and with enough headroom to (nearly) accommodate my 5'9" height." Anticlimactic— yes, but not so with this book! I offer you stories that I think conjure the flavor of an unopened door and its doorstep, dark and quiet and exposed unto dread.

# SEEKING A GOOD WOMAN

## JACQUE DAY

Nicole Livengood navigated the sunless dirt road for what felt like an eternity. The gears of her 2004 Chevy Tracker had managed the ascent of Winch Hill with only the occasional groan thus far. But, she thought with dismay, if the last few bumps were any indicator, it would take a miracle for the aging vehicle's suspension to survive the trip.

As if on cue, the right tire plunged into a pothole, and the Chevy lurched downward. Its undercarriage scraped something hard, and Nicole winced as the car shuddered from the impact. She glanced into the rearview mirror, bracing herself for the very real possibility that some vital metallic guts lay ripped away on the road behind her. Sparky, haunches on the passenger seat and nose pressed to the window, let out a soft whine. But, seeing nothing out of the ordinary in their wake, only the road and its cavernous, godforsaken ruts, Nicole exhaled, reached over, and patted her companion reassuringly. "It's okay, boy."

Finally, the road plateaued. She drove into a clearing, and her breath caught hard in her throat. Before her, like something out of a Thomas Kinkade painting, a picturesque farm capped the mountaintop. The nineteenth-century Victorian farmhouse was immaculately white with red trimming. Its slated roof pointed to the sky at a steep pitch. Beyond the house, a barn presided over the vista. Nicole had come across dozens of barns since moving to Vermont the previous summer, and most looked as if a good wind would blow them to matchsticks. But this barn, fortress-like and red as the trimming on the house, stood strong and sturdy.

But the flowers; oh, the flowers.

Stretching beyond her field of vision as far as the eye could see, acres and acres of purple blooms blanketed the hilltop. A path of high green grass, wide enough for a vehicle, cut through the meadow like a river, snaking up to the house and past it, to the barn. But the grass path, the house and its picturesque barn, even the blue sky overhead, seemed dimmer somehow in the wash of the hilltop meadow's bright-purple glow.

*It's . . . so . . . beautiful.*

Sparky's urgent bark yanked Nicole's wandering mind back into focus. She gasped. The car was still moving.

"Sorry, boy," she said, letting off the gas and coasting to a stop. She took three deep breaths, and her racing heart calmed. "This place is some sight, isn't it?"

Sparky pressed his paws on the dash and sniffed the air, then offered a staccato "Yip!"

"Well then, we're in agreement."

Nicole peered over the steering wheel and craned her neck, trying to see if any human stirred on the property. She turned to Sparky. "Should we just drive up through the grass path?"

As if that sounded like the best idea in the world, Sparky turned and placed his paws on the passenger door, sniffing again at the air.

"You catch a scent? Want to get out and go exploring?"

Tail whipping back and forth, Sparky looked ready to leap as soon as the door opened.

"Just how much English do you understand?" Nicole asked, shifting the Chevy into park.

Still, she stopped short of killing the engine. Nicole didn't share Sparky's enthusiasm to exit the vehicle; not just yet. The Chevy's onboard thermostat put the outdoor temperature at just above fifty degrees, far, far too cold for this time of year by Nicole's Mid-Atlantic sensibilities. Being a relative newcomer to Vermont—a flatlander, as born-and-bred locals called her with a mix of welcoming affection and proprietary pride—Nicole had committed herself to a "when in Rome" attitude about the little state's peculiarities. Many traits of the Green Mountain State she absolutely loved. Tops on her list was Vermont's statewide ban on billboards. Having grown up in a part of Pennsylvania where ads loomed over every imaginable roadway, hawking anything from food to legal services to political messages to warnings that "One day, you will meet God," Nicole found the plain highways of Vermont, free of the clutter of ads, refreshing.

But when it came to the interminable lingering of chill air into May, Nicole's appreciation ended. Not even the intoxicating allure of the lush meadow before her could quell her resentment over having felt cheated out of spring. Yet even then, despite the cold outside, it was a far deeper cold within her that froze her in this moment.

Just a week before, in the early morning hours on the first Saturday in May, Nicole had stepped out of her rented cabin on Turkey Hill into a dusting of snow—not a heavy blanketing, just flurries, but still, *snow*. Later that afternoon, Kyle, her boyfriend of a year, sent her a text message, dumping her.

At the fresh memory, a knot formed in Nicole's stomach. She gripped the steering wheel and braced herself for the inevitable gut punch, that unavoidable whoosh of pain that stopped all time and sent the earth beneath her crumbling away. The wave crashed into her, and the pain of losing Kyle consumed her every sense. She saw nothing. Nothing at all ahead of her, not the beautiful farm or the endless flowers, not even her faithful canine companion. Only the years without Kyle stretching out like a highway to nowhere. She clenched her eyelids shut. "Do not cry," she scolded herself. "*Do not* cry."

Eventually, gradually, her sense of time returned. A soft weight pressed on her legs. Moisture lapped at her cheeks. Eyes still tightly shut, she let go of the steering wheel and wrapped her arms around Sparky, who had climbed onto her lap. She buried her face in the nape of his neck, and her breathing slowed. "You're a good dog," she said, her voice muffled by his fur. "The goodest boy."

She took a deep breath and reached into the visor. "Give me a minute to figure out if we're even in the right place. Then we can go exploring."

Satisfied, Sparky resumed his place on the passenger seat and turned again to peer out the window.

Nicole flipped off the heat and shut off the engine.

In the visor, her fingers snagged the flier she'd swiped from the library bulletin board the day before. She pulled it out and unfolded it. The letter-sized poster bore all the characteristics of a home job done on an inkjet printer, complete with a gaudy all-caps headline reading: FOR A GOOD WOMAN SEEKING A GOOD MAN. Below the headline appeared a photo of a tiny camping trailer with the name "Gertrude" painted across the side. Nicole ran a finger over the surface of the paper. Parchment, with flecks of purple.

Sparky sniffed at the paper. She raised it to her nose and did the same. "You're right. It does have a smell. What is it, do you think?" She dropped the flier onto the passenger seat. The aroma lingered in the air, its soft scent faintly enveloping her. Absently, she scratched behind Sparky's ears and tried to think of what to do next.

If Kyle were here, he'd point out the obvious problems with this scenario. *Look*, he'd say. *There's no name listed on the flier, no email, and barely an address. Do you even know who you're going to see? And you don't even know how long that poster was up on that bulletin board.* In the argument now blooming in her imagination, Nicole spat back, *And why was I in the library in the first place? Why was I there every day last week, checking out rom-com movies like the pathetic loser that I am?*

Sparky placed a paw on the flier, and Nicole smiled in spite of herself. "You damned dog," she said, picking up the wrinkled paper and smoothing it out. "Let's see if we're on a wild goose chase." She cleared her throat and read from the description, "*Ideal for a single woman.*" She grunted. "As if there's anything ideal and not at all pathetic about being single and alone."

Sparky whined.

"Okay, okay," she told him. "I'm not alone. I know. No more editorializing, promise." She continued, "*Lightweight, easy to hitch and easy to tow, Gertrude, the one-of-a-kind teardrop camper makes the perfect travel companion for a good woman looking for a good man. Enjoy satisfying meals in the rear galley surrounded by wondrous natural scenery. When night falls, snuggle up in the cozy interior and stargaze through the generous windows. Gertrude is a necessity in a world where good men are hard to find.*"

She paused and winked at Sparky. He perked up. "And here's the bonus: "*Gertrude never met a dog she didn't like.*"

Sparky's ears shot up. He sniffed vigorously. Letting out a triumphant bark, he scratched at the door handle. His paw landed on paydirt—the window switch. Air gusted into the Chevy as the window lowered, and Nicole braced for the invading damp chill. Instead, a warm breeze surprised her, and when the light wind hit her face, the aroma of the purple paper washed over her, only far, far stronger. Outside, a zephyr caught the field of flowers. They swooshed in unison and seemed to rise up in song, as if possessed by a chorus of human voices.

Sparky scrambled out the window's opening. Nicole reached for his collar, barely hooking it with her index finger. But Sparky wriggled free and took off airborne, landing in a gallop and bolting up the grassy path toward the farmhouse.

"Sparky, wait!"

Nicole fumbled with her seatbelt and flung open the driver's side door. As she lunged from the car the seatbelt looped her arm, jerking her backward. Her legs splayed out in a comical "v" as she landed hard on her rear end in a patch of high grass. She rolled onto her knees and dug the toes of her Skechers into the ground, springing into a wobbly sprint. After a few uncertain steps, she regained her footing and ran after her galloping canine.

Sparky reached a small outbuilding and banked left, disappearing around the corner. Thirty seconds later, Nicole turned the same corner, breath burning in her lungs. She found Sparky seated, begging-style, chomping away at something. Before him stood a slender, attractive older woman. Sparky swallowed in a gulp and looked up at the woman, expectantly.

"Amazing," Nicole panted, hands on her knees. "Six months of obedience training and he won't as much as sit on command. But I show him once how to roll down the car window and a monster is born. Sorry about that."

"Not at all." The woman winked. "Sparky is most trainable. It helps to have the right incentive." An elegant hand disappeared into the pocket of her immaculately white, knee-length apron. Adorning the garment, Nicole noticed, were patterns of the same purple flowers that grew in abundance on the farm. From her pocket, the woman produced a biscuit in the shape of a bone and held it out to the dog. "Sparky, lie." He took the treat and flopped onto the grass, gnawing and contented.

"How did you know his name?"

"You must have told me over the phone, dear."

"I guess I did," Nicole said. "I don't even care what's in those treats. I'll buy a dozen from you right now."

The woman laughed and extended a hand to Nicole, who reached out and shook it. "It's just a plain old dog biscuit in the shape of a bone. Dogs do enjoy bones, don't they?" The woman patted Sparky's head and turned to Nicole. "Now, you've come about Gertrude. Follow me."

As they walked, Nicole lagged a few paces behind and studied the older woman's body, taking note of sleek, muscular legs beneath impeccably starched and ironed black trousers. She wondered what this woman did to maintain such a toned figure at her age. Was she a dancer? An equestrian? Or was the day-to-day work of maintaining a farm enough to keep the muscles firm and fit? Self-conscious of her own fleshy curves, Nicole breathed a mental sigh of relief that she'd donned baggy jeans that morning. She pulled her loose-fitting windbreaker down over her hips and caught up with the woman. "Funny, when I first drove up, I noticed the house, and the barn, and the . . ." Nicole's voice fell to a near-whisper, ". . . and the flowers. But I didn't see this building."

The woman stopped, brushed Nicole's cheek with her fingers, and smiled. "Sometimes we see things when they're ready to be seen."

Nicole, who usually flinched at the touch of strangers, relaxed under this woman's caress. Another warm breeze filled the space between them, carrying with it the aroma of the meadow. Nicole gasped at the pleasure of it. "The flowers on your farm are breathtaking."

"Lavender," said the woman, turning and continuing around the building. "You'd be surprised what people are willing to pay to make their worlds a little bit more peaceful." The woman stopped at a massive set of barn doors, lifted the latch, and swung them open wide.

The moment Nicole saw Gertrude resting in the shade of the building, she *knew*.

"It's even prettier than in the picture," she said, approaching the camper and running a hand over its smooth exterior. "And it really is shaped like a teardrop."

"Many a tear shed in this old girl," said the woman, smiling affectionately. "She was just the right medicine for me, at a time in my life."

Nicole's hand found the door handle. "May I?"

"I can already see that she's yours," the woman said. "Go ahead."

Nicole lightly pressed the lever, and the door slid open. She stepped into a surprisingly spacious interior, the bed neatly made with white blankets and pillows with purple trim. Far from the musty odor Nicole might expect from an old camper long in storage, Gertrude's interior smelled of fresh linens, and, to Nicole's delight, lavender.

"When you're ready, I'll show you the exterior features," called the woman from outside. Sparky leaped through the door and bounded onto the bed. Nicole ran a hand over the comforter. She lowered herself onto the mattress, wanting nothing more than to disappear into its softness. She sighed blissfully and closed her eyes.

"You will be most pleased with the galley."

Nicole scooted to a sitting position. How long had she lain there? Had she fallen asleep? She scrambled outside to find the woman at the rear of the camper, gripping a handle.

"This," she told Nicole, "is where the real magic occurs." The woman hoisted the hatch, revealing an opening as wide as Gertrude's full width and half as tall. "Here is your outdoor galley kitchen. A full stove, a deep sink with a faucet, storage, and refrigeration." With a wink, the woman went on, "This galley is a place for great meals. Great meals, indeed."

The appliances gleamed. Pots, pans, and cooking utensils hung suspended from hooks. Along the wall panel, a full stainless-steel cutlery set clung to a magnetic strip.

Nicole's eyes widened. "Is that a meat cleaver?"

"Yes, and a butcher knife, a boning knife, and a half dozen steak knives," said the woman. "Polished and sharp, ready for service."

Nicole touched the handle of the butcher knife with the tip of her finger. A chill ran from the knife into her fingertip and up her arm. She jerked her hand away. "I . . . I won't have much use for such a beautiful knife set," she said, reflexively backing away from the row of downward-pointing blades. "I'm a vegetarian. Well, mostly."

"You never know what you'll need, or when," the woman said, playfulness dancing in her tone. "Nevertheless, they come with the unit."

Nicole rubbed her finger. As the warmth returned to it, she relaxed and couldn't help admiring the galley. "This is nicer than the kitchen in my rental," Nicole said and meant it.

The woman nodded, more than a little pride glowing in her eyes. "It won't take long for Gertrude to feel like home."

A glint of color caught Nicole's peripheral vision. She stepped forward and squinted. Tucked into the corner of the galley, nearly out of view, stood a glass jar. "What's this?" Without waiting for permission, she lifted it and turned it in her hands, peering at the miscellany inside: coins, assorted pens, keys, buttons, what appeared to be a man's money clip, a Zippo lighter, a bottle opener, and several rings. "Looks like you left this here."

The woman took the jar, peered through the glass, laughed softly, and placed it back where Nicole had retrieved it. "Every kitchen has an odds-and-ends drawer. Think of this as Gertrude's odds-and-ends jar. It also comes with the unit."

"Okay, well . . ." Nicole trailed off, not knowing what more to say about that subject. "Um, speaking of jars." She dug deep into her pockets as if trying to find something that wasn't there. "That jar has more cash value than I do right now. I came here thinking . . . I don't know what I was thinking." Nicole bristled at the realization of this truth. "This camper—Gertrude—is way out of my price range. I'm sorry to have wasted your time."

Nicole turned to leave, but the woman's soft grip on her arm stopped her. "Don't go, please." Their eyes met, and the older woman's gaze bore through Nicole, her unwavering smile revealing teeth as white and pristine as porcelain. "I thought you understood, dear. The advertisement states plainly that Gertrude is free to a good home."

Nicole's jaw went slack. She quickly snapped her mouth shut. "It does?"

Sparky, up from his nap on Gertrude's bed, bounded out the camper door and trotted up to them. Tucked into his collar was the purple slip of paper. Nicole pulled it free, patted Sparky's head, opened the flier, and scanned it. Beneath the photo of Gertrude, in small print, read the words: FREE TO A GOOD HOME.

"Funny, I didn't notice that before."

"Sometimes," the woman repeated, "we see things when they're ready to be seen."

While they hooked Gertrude up to the Chevy, the woman admired the old car. "I can see you take care of it," she said. "A good mate for Gertrude. Well loved."

"It was my father's car. He—he was a mechanic. His name was John, but everyone called him Sparky, you know, because he was like a spark plug. If there was an ounce of life left in a vehicle, any glimmer of hope for it, he could keep it running. He died, and the Chevy went to me, and now I don't know how long it will last. I'll hold onto it as long as I can." Nicole bit her tongue to keep from saying any more. "I'm sorry for rambling. Kyle says I ramble."

"Not at all," the woman replied, waving off Nicole's apology. "Sparky was a good man, I can tell, and he passed his name to a worthy gentleman." She patted the dog's head, reached into her pocket, and produced another treat. Sparky took the bone-shaped biscuit gingerly in his teeth, careful not to graze the woman's skin. He dropped onto the dirt floor and began gnawing. The woman stood up and brushed her palms on her apron.

Nicole knelt to stroke the dog's back. "Sparky was a rescue. Well, it's like they say—it's more like he rescued me. He just . . . wandered up to my door one day. My dad had died recently and, well, I just had a feeling about this one."

The woman's smile reached her eyes. "When we're lucky, in our moments of greatest need, help finds its way to us. Sparky found you. Gertrude found me once. Now, she found you."

Nicole looked up at the woman. "People . . . well, Kyle . . . said it's creepy to name a dog after my dead father."

"Kyle, I take it, is the reason for your sad eyes?"

Nicole stood, shoulders slumped and head down. "Is it that obvious?"

"Been there myself, dear."

"Kyle is the reason I'm broke. I sank all my cash into this cross-country trip that we were going to take together. We were supposed to leave tomorrow. Then, a week ago, he dumped me."

The woman touched Nicole's chin and turned her face upward. "No more hanging your head. You have Gertrude now to look after you. And let's not forget your faithful Sparky."

Nicole ran light fingers over the name emblazoned on the camper. "Gertrude. How did you come by that name?"

The woman gazed past Nicole. "Gertrude was her name when she came to me," she said. "It means 'strength,' or 'spear.'"

"Which one is Gertrude, strength or spear?"

"A little of one, a little of the other," the woman answered with a wistful chuckle. "Once, a man suggested I change her name to Christine. He didn't last long."

Nicole kicked at the ground, fighting the question that burned on the edge of her tongue. "Forgive me, ma'am, but nothing is free." She stammered, "What . . . what's the catch?"

"Just take care of Gertrude," the woman said, a slight edge creeping into her voice. "Take care of Gertrude, and Gertrude will take care of you. That's the catch."

The wind struck Nicole, far stronger and chillier than the breeze from earlier. It cut through her windbreaker. Shivering, Nicole opened the Chevy's passenger door. Sparky leaped in. "If I haven't thanked you already, thank you," she said. "Hey," she said, turning back around. "I never got your name."

But the woman was gone.

It was Kyle who had convinced Nicole to rent the cabin on Turkey Hill. The idea was, he'd move in with her as soon as he settled things with his ex-girlfriend, who still held half the lease on his apartment in town. At first blush, it looked like the plan would work. Kyle moved his things into the cabin—well, some of his things. Nicole didn't press Kyle for rent while he maintained his apartment. That wouldn't be fair to him. Plus, everything would change when his lease expired. He would move permanently into the cabin, and they would share a home, the first of many steps toward cementing their lives together.

When that time came, however, Kyle renewed his apartment lease. He explained that they'd have a place in town to crash and a remote cabin in the woods for a getaway. As the months progressed, Kyle spent fewer and fewer nights at the cabin. Eventually, he decided to stay at his apartment during the week and spend weekends with Nicole, reasoning that his commute to work was just a short walk from his place in town—never mind that Nicole had to drive down the mountain every day for her own commute. Come winter, a month sometimes went by between his visits.

Yet still, Nicole clung to the idea of the future that awaited them. Their future together.

And there was, of course, the late-spring/early-summer trip in the works. They had spent part of winter and all of spring planning it. By heading out in mid-May, Kyle had reasoned, they'd beat the Memorial Day crowds. They could pitch a tent and eat on the cheap. Kyle had the fuel-efficient hybrid SUV with built-in navigation. He had the camping gear. He had, she more-than-a-little hoped, a ring that would erase the ache of the lonely winter in the cabin and transform their cross-country trip into an engagement trip.

Then, last week—seven days before their scheduled departure—it all came crashing down with seven words in a text message from Kyle: "Let's just be friends. Can't do trip."

But, Nicole was to learn, there was more. There always is.

Kyle's ex-girlfriend was not, in fact, an ex at all.

On a normal day—on a day when her heart beat whole in her chest—Nicole might have worried over the Chevy's ability to haul Gertrude up a steep incline like Turkey Hill. On a normal day, the two-decade-old truck would bump and groan all on its own, needing no help from any extra weight on its tail. With Gertrude firmly attached, the Chevy should have struggled mightily. Yet now, the Chevy felt lighter. It took the hill smoother. Potholes that once made Nicole's teeth chatter passed beneath as if pillows lined the rutted road.

On a normal day, Nicole may have noticed this. She may have remarked that Gertrude lightened the load for all of them, even the decrepit old Chevy.

But today was no normal day, and Nicole's heart did not beat whole in her chest.

On the climb up Turkey Hill, Nicole seethed.

Why hadn't she cut Kyle loose when he renewed his apartment lease? With the writing on the wall, why hadn't she *suspected*? Why had she accepted every excuse without argument or complaint? Certainly, Kyle had been two-timing her with his ex long before his mortifying breakup text. And how lame was that, breaking up with her over a *text message*? Yet, despite every abuse and humiliation he had heaped upon her, still she spent the past week watching romantic comedies, checking them out by the dozen from the library, all the while pining for him like a limp dishrag, hoping against hope that he'd show up at her door.

Today, he did.

Kyle leaned against the door to her cabin, casually, as if returning from a trip to the grocery store. Cowboy boots poked out from the ankle cuffs of his Levi's, and in spite of the chilly weather, he wore only a white T-shirt.

"Well, you've been busy," he said to Nicole as she pulled up. He eyed Gertrude. "Where'd you get this?"

"She was a gift."

"*She?*" Kyle hopped down from the front stoop and trotted toward Nicole. In just a week, he had already changed. During their time as a so-called couple, Kyle never went without a clean shave. Now, a soul patch sprouted from the divot between his lower lip and chin. But the most marked difference was the earring, a small gold loop gleaming from his left earlobe.

As he closed the distance between them, Nicole thrust her hands into her pockets. No outstretched, open arms would do for this occasion. She nodded upward toward the earring. "That's new."

He touched it. "Yeah," he said absently, clearing his throat. "Still planning to take that cross-country trip?"

"Of course."

"Want some company?"

"What happened to your ex-ex?"

"Went back to New Hampshire."

"Smart girl."

"Nice camper," he said. Without invitation, he strode over and ran a casual hand across Gertrude's side, tracing a finger through the letters of her name. "Gertrude," he said, snorting. "Kind of an old-lady name, isn't it?"

"I like the name just fine."

Kyle snorted again. He tried the door. It didn't open.

He tugged harder.

"Door's stuck," he said. "I'll bring over some WD-40, lube her right up."

He moved around to Gertrude's rear end. "Hey, it's got one of those kitchen galleys. These are great." He yanked at the handle. The hatch didn't budge. He yanked harder. "This one's stuck, too," he said. "You know," he said, grunting as he tugged, "I always thought these galleys looked like big gaping mouths." He opened his maw wide and chomped down, laughing uproariously at his own sense of humor while he continued to pull, the muscles in his arms bulging from the stress of his effort.

Just as Kyle let go, the hatch clicked open.

He stared, awestruck, as the door rose and he beheld the galley's gleaming interior. "Wow, Nikki," he called to her without looking up. "This is amazing. It's . . . it's so much bigger than it looks from the outside. Hey, what's this?"

Kyle leaned into Gertrude's galley, disappearing from the waist up. Nicole's arms erupted in goose flesh. Her breathing quickened. She fought the urge to run to him, grab him around the waist, and yank him away. Instead, she cleared her throat. "What's what?"

Kyle emerged with the glass jar of trinkets. He held it up to the light and turned it one way, then the other, studying it.

Nicole, herself, had first held the jar just a little while ago. She knew its contents. Still, she wanted to know what *he* noticed. Crossing her arms across her chest, she called out, "What's in it?"

"Someone just gave you this old camper with this jar of stuff?" Kyle held it over his head. "Some of this looks pretty valuable. That there," he pointed to something inside it, as if Nicole could actually see the object. "That's a man's diamond ring, two carats at least for the stud, and smaller diamonds crowning it. Depending on the metal it's cast in, this ring alone could be worth a few grand. Someone loved the guy who got this. Or he loved himself enough to buy it for himself."

"Imagine that," she said. "A man in love with himself."

"Hey," he said, as if she hadn't spoken at all. "I bet you have a drawer full of souvenirs like this hidden away. I bet it's filled with things you've swiped from some guy or another over the years. Though," he said, shaking the jar, "you wouldn't have *this much* stuff."

Nicole's fingers tapped her crossed forearms. "Why wouldn't I?"

"You know, because you're so . . . young."

"Oh, sure. Young."

"This camper's a real piece of junk, but you hit the jackpot with this jar," Kyle said. "We could sell that diamond ring, take the trip in style. Hotels all the way, classy restaurants. Leave this clunker at home. The mutt, too."

Next to Nicole, a low growl rumbled in Sparky's throat.

"And Gertrude," Kyle snorted. "What kind of a name is that? You know what we should call her?"

"What?"

"Christine."

The butcher knife caught him first.

The blade lodged in his neck. It happened so quickly and stealthily that, initially, all Nicole saw was a glint of light streaking through the air. Kyle dropped the jar. It landed on the soft earth with a thud—miraculously, it didn't break. His hand went to his neck, his face a mask of surprise as if he'd been stung by a wasp. Blood trickled from around his fingers.

Kyle mouthed, "What the . . ."

But no words came out, just a meager gurgle followed by a gush of fresh blood that turned his white T-shirt red.

Later, Nicole would come to understand the butcher-knife-in-the-neck as Gertrude's pre-performance warmup, her soft open, if you will. The knife's long blade severs the vocal cords. Clean and efficient, so the prey can't scream. It simultaneously slices through the jugular vein. Not so clean and efficient, but the sudden blood loss weakens the prey and provides a little bit of theater, a visual shock for the benefit of the audience. Nicole would appreciate Gertrude's—*methods*—in time, during long journeys across the continent's highways and byways, with other prey.

But now, thrust into the novel shock of it, Nicole barely processed the scene before her. She heaved, gulping at the air. Her legs turned to rubber, threatening to give out and send her body tumbling into the dirt. Her vision blurred. "Kyle," she wheezed, her voice barely a whisper. "Oh, God, Kyle." She covered her face with her hands.

A soft nuzzle, so faint she barely noticed, grazed her fingers, followed by a gentle lapping at her neck. She peeled her hands away from her face, and Sparky covered her with wet kisses. She opened her eyes.

His gaze stopped her cold.

Sparky's eyes bore deep into her, reading her in a way that no person, nor any creature, had ever done before. The message in his unblinking stare unfolded in her mind's eye like parting clouds. She understood.

*Finish him.*

By some miracle still on his feet, Kyle extended his arms, reaching for her, and she knew that if she did nothing to stop him, he'd try to come to her. She inhaled.

"Gertrude," she said, barely recognizing the voice as her own. Like the pull of gravity, Nicole felt Sparky's eyes on her. She felt Gertrude waiting.

She gave a slight nod.

The knives flew.

The steak knives, as it turned out, were for show. By themselves, they produced only surface damage. Still, their pincushion effect as they found purchase in Kyle's flesh—hitting their mark six for six, even as he tried in vain to dodge them—did heighten the spectacle. They also laid the groundwork for the job of the boning knife.

The less said about that, the better.

The meat cleaver made the final appearance. It sailed from Gertrude's galley in a grand arc, burying itself neatly in Kyle's forehead. He lurched forward and slumped into Gertrude's sink, unmoving.

The galley door closed over him.

And Gertrude began chewing.

Kyle's bones crunched and snapped as Gertrude consumed him, his legs lurching off the backside of the camper like the lower half of a rag doll. A fresh burst of blood exploded from Kyle's body as Gertrude bore down on his vital organs. Soon, only his cowboy boots protruded from the lip of the galley. With a final heave, Gertrude sucked in what remained of Kyle, and the galley slammed closed. Gertrude rocked for a few moments more. The galley opened with a lurch. Gertrude made a sound—before today, Nicole would never believe a thing made of metal and wood could *gag*, but that's precisely what Gertrude did—and spit something forward onto the ground. The galley closed gently, and the world fell silent.

Nicole approached Gertrude, slowly, as if treading on a field of land mines. She ran a tentative hand across the handle that opened the galley kitchen and looked at her palm, expecting the slick wetness of bloodspatter. But her hand was clean and dry, and the metal of the handle gleamed as if brand new. She pressed the latch lightly, and the hatch sprang open. The stainless steel of the sink and stovetop shone, spotless, as if nothing at all were amiss. The knives clung to their magnet, perfectly aligned, neat and spotless.

*Ready for service.*

And, something new. To the right of the stovetop hung an apron, perfectly starched and immaculately white, embroidered with fields of purple flowers.

*Sometimes we see things when they're ready to be seen.*

Something glistened in the grass at Nicole's feet. She bent for a closer look and picked it up. It was Kyle's earring. She removed the lid from the glass jar and dropped the earring in, placed the jar back in the galley, unhooked the apron, and tied it around herself.

Nicole rose to her feet, a new and unfamiliar feeling expanding within her.

She felt free.

"Oh, and by the way, Kyle. It's not Nikki. My name is Nicole."

Nicole strode to the door of the sleeping compartment. It opened for her, letting loose a warm gust of fragrant air. She stepped inside. Sparky sat on the bed, waiting for her. She ran a hand over the bed—Gertrude really was so much bigger on the inside—and sank into its luxurious softness. Sparky settled in next to her, lapping her face. "Just you and me, the way it was meant to be," she cooed, hugging him to herself.

He closed his eyes, satisfied.

As Nicole fell into peaceful rest, a thought floated into her waning consciousness. *When we wake up, we'll drive up that mountain and return Gertrude.*

But already, the memory of the woman, and the farm, were fading from Nicole's mind, as do the images of a dream. As she drifted away, sheltered by one faithful companion and nuzzled by another, she dreamed of fields of lavender.

**Jacque Day** writes about stuff she finds too perplexing to figure out any other way. She served as the longtime managing editor for the *New Madrid Journal of Contemporary Literature* and has zigged and zagged as a book and magazine editor, radio correspondent, TV producer, journalist, motion picture crew member, and occasional comedy writer and producer.

**Author Website:** jacqueday.com

**Social Media Handles:**
Facebook: https://www.facebook.com/jacquedaypallone
Twitter: @jrevolver

# BLACK METAL IN A WHITE ROOM

## S. J. TOWNEND

"**M**r. Monkton? Answer the door. The door."

I hadn't wanted to answer the door. At all. I knew full well who it'd be: one of the Empties, collecting. No one else had the nerve to bang on so hard and so fast for so damn long. Their clinical scent of industrial bleach and hospital corridors hit me long before the sound of their knocking.

"We're after one pint today. One pint."

They'd been rude and insistent ever since they'd taken over. I detested the way they spoke, too, echoing everything, cacophonous enough without the additional reverb. Their voices hurt. Their words ricocheted in the air like orchestral gunfire, like shards of glass, like black metal. And I am not a black metal fan. I like classic rock. But I didn't dare say anything or ask them to drop their volume—the Empties were not beings to be messed with, and they sure as heck didn't handle requests with pleasantries.

"Yeah, sure. I know. I'm coming," I said. I switched off my screen, grabbed my bag, and shut my front door behind me on my way out.

— —

Everything had changed the day the Empties came to Earth. No one really knew what they were or where they'd come from, but they weren't looking for friendship or seeking to embrace our culture, that was for certain. The newsreaders said they'd "slid down a moonbow" in the middle of the night. No one had seen them arrive per se—due to their invisibility—but many claimed to have seen their ominous shadows bounding down from the night sky under lunar light.

We couldn't see them, but we could always hear them. Everyone heard them all right, with their distorted foghorn sounds and their ear-splitting wah-wah voices and their tone of Cradle of Filth. The racket they made was the opposite of music to the ear, enough to make your windows rattle, your molars hum.

———

He, or it, or whatever it was that'd disturbed my gaming session by knocking on my door that cloudy morning led me to the train station once more. I tagged along behind it, a knot of apprehension making a pretzel of my innards, all the while trying to avoid placing my foot directly on all I could see of it, its trailing shadow of black static. Distracted by a feral cat darting from behind a bin, I stepped within the hazy prickles its presence scattered on the pavement. My toe barely grazed it, but the Empty let out a bloodcurdling scream. I apologized profusely, fear bubbled beneath my skin, and I padded with caution for the remainder of the journey. I knew full well I'd be of no use to them with curdled blood.

It was taking me to make a transaction. Each payment journey to the old church hall in the next district was always chaperoned, despite the escort being totally unnecessary. We all had a damn good idea about what happened to people who didn't obey, and it wasn't pretty, yet still, each week, a knock at the door and a waft of chlorinated disinfectant would pull me away from my VR screen and a satanic shadow would be hovering over my coir doormat, waiting to take me away.

At least it felt pleasant to be outside for a while, away from the four ever-pressing walls of my own front room where I'd been cooped up since the Empties arrived. A moment of weak autumnal sunshine broke through the cloud, hit me on my cheek, and gave me a little hope. A little vitamin D stirred in my cells.

———

As far as I could gather, all of the Empties were cruel, but some of them were rogue and took more than just the odd donation. People had gone missing. Society had broken down; most people had decided to stay in, watch mindless television shows, or join the virtual reality gaming realm, all existing on the just-about-adequate provisions our uninvited guests trundled about not quite regularly enough. (I'd had to make an extra hole in my belt.) Still, we had the internet to communicate through: chat rooms, email, FaceTime, and so on, but for those of us without close family or friends, existence was paramount to isolation.

My VR escape stage—*Classic Rock Concert Pro*—had become the main source of joy in my life. I definitely wasn't happy, what with the apocalyptic invasion on the other side of my black curtains, but at least I had entertainment to help pass time. An innate urge to survive powered me onward each day. We were all hopeful things would get better.

I hopped onto the train, glanced across the carriage at another man who also sat under the veil of a doom-shadow. Poor guy was probably heading to the same place I was. Too tired to make conversation—the payment I'd made last week had knocked the stuffing out of me—I simply raised my eyebrows and nodded at him, a gesture that he, looking equally as exhausted, returned. I rubbed my sore arms and contemplated asking the Empty escorting me if it'd be possible to make my prospective payment from a vessel in my leg instead this time. I had more track marks than a heroin addict, and some of them looked infected. I decided against asking it while sitting on the train—I'd wait until I arrived at the payment center. This decision was partly due to my lethargy and partly because I didn't want to inflict the sound of its horrible, shuddering, thrashing voice on the chap sitting opposite me. Not unless I had to.

———

An hour later, the shadow wrapped me up with a roar and shoved me through the door of the payment center. I rolled up the length of my trouser and pointed to the back of my knee.

"Any chance we could take it from here today?" I asked and placed my fingers into my ears. The hideous noise from its invisible gob thundered out; a chill skittered down my spine.

"Yes. Yes. If we can find a vein. A vein."

I felt a revolting pressure, the tangible equivalent of a fork scraping down a blackboard or a guitar string snapping as the Empty pushed me back and groped and shuffled its invisible parts all over my body, searching for a suitable blood vessel.

I have no idea which part of its body it used to jam the needle into my groin, but it did so with the bedside manner of Dr. Harold Shipman. The sharp steel spike entered my skin and the vein beneath it, causing me to let out a yelp. Red stuttered out at first in dribs and drabs and then gushed down the plastic tubing, eager to escape. It filled up the bag on the end of the line, which appeared to be floating in front of me, suspended somehow by the invisible, rough-handed monster. As my blood collected, the Empty jabbed another needle—this one attached to a syringe full of black static—into my thigh. "In exchange, exchange," it hollered. I dug my grubby fingernails into the palms of my balled fists, channeling the sharp pain through and out of my limbs. Dang. What the heck was being pumped into my body in exchange for my blood?

I was left to pull the cannula needles dangling from my groin out myself once my blood had filled the pint sack. It had what it wanted and immediately lost interest in my de-juiced body.

———

How long would a pint take to replenish? The internet told me it'd take forty-eight hours to top up the volume of liquid I'd lost, a further four to eight weeks to manufacture and replace the red blood cells. This was my seventh payment. They'd come every week, like clockwork, to march me to the donation center, to drain me like the dregs from an upturned bottle of Merlot. No wonder I felt like death warmed up.

On my way out, I glanced back to see the bag of my blood arc through the air—a crimson-sailed boat bobbing along unseen wave crests—until it stopped in the corner. There, it was tipped up and emptied into what I can only presume was the feeding organ of an Empty. I watched the red dripping down, shifting, glugging, becoming momentarily an out-of-focus polygon of sorts. The vermillion shape throbbed in time with my own heartbeat as if the liquid were still present within my viscera. Then, the air-puddle faded away to nothing and the bag dropped like a stone.

Were the bastards drinking it? A crisp burp—a violent duck-quack oddly echoless this time—came from the corner above the emptied blood bag, which lay discarded on the floor.

Disgusting.

Whatever these invisi-beasts were, they had appalling table manners. The belch was followed by a series of smaller burps and a satanic shriek of a giggle. The sound ripples hit my eardrums. A wave of vomit thrummed against the walls of my esophagus, eager to escape my fragile body—as eager as I was to get the heck away from the slovenly, blood-drinking toads.

Dizzy with blood loss, I legged it back to the station and caught a train back home.

At least the payment covered me for another week. A pint a week— that seemed to be the going rate for internet. A pint for internet, a half for electricity, and a half for food, water, the essentials. It was rough but manageable. After making a payment, rehydration was key, and maybe a couple of biscuits, then back I went, into my virtual-reality game. I was okay with a pint each week.

*They'll get bored,* I thought. *They'll go home soon.*
*Things'll get better. Life'll return to normal.*

———

The next day, the familiar excessive knock at my front door came again—albeit a little earlier than I'd anticipated. A whole six days earlier. I was mid-performance.

I paused my game, inhaled deeply, and admired the faux view. Jack Bruce stood to my left. He repetitively shifted from side to side, his bass guitar hiccupped in and out of virtual existence, his microphone stand flickered on, off, on, off. I glanced behind me—Ginger Baker, head tipped back, a pair of drumsticks hung blurred in the air in front of him mid-paradiddle. I lifted my foot from the special-effects pedal, slung my Gibson Les Paul behind me, and waved goodbye to my incandescent glitching audience of thousands.

The sound of the unholy transparent beast knocking and screaming at my front door had drowned out the song anyway. Dang its pungent aroma. Only an unearthly creature could handle the constant, eye-burning bark of sodium hypochlorite. I pulled my nose away from the center of the large wall-mounted screen, and the device switched *off*—the blank canvas hung, desolate, on the wall of my otherwise sparse living room, a rectangular body draped from the gallows of my white wall.

I'd been center stage at Wembley Arena from the comfort of my own living room, but the knocking and screaming and all-penetrating stench had grown more persistent.

I grumbled to no one and yanked my body up from the couch. The puncture wound in my puce groin oozed a translucent yellow pus that dripped down my inner thigh like sour tears from heaven. On exploration of this disgusting body juice of mine, I found it hummed like stale cheese. The gloop, sticky between my fingertips, was difficult to wipe onto the lip of my sofa cushion. My body still ached heavily from the abuse endured the day before. They must've made a mistake knocking for me again so soon.

I fumbled for my bag and coat and caught sight of myself on the reflective black screen; a walking disaster. Drawn cheeks, waxen skin pale as my white walls, undereye bags dark and inky as my black curtains. I must've lost ten kilos since the arrival of the Empties. Loose skin hung, almost dripping from my slouched frame.

It knocked again with its dreadful hand of nothingness. "I'm coming," I shouted and pegged my nostrils tightly with my fingertips before opening the door. Dirty shadows scuttled on the floor by where I imagined its feet might be—or the base of its hexagon or polygon or tesseract or whatever the heck its true form was. Draped over its rippling nothingness, a cloak! Akin to some kind of horrific *Emperor's New Clothes* role-reversal parody, a black, hooded cape was suspended over my doorstep, a menacing shadow flitting about beneath.

"Hurry. Hurry," it said. Its voice shook dust from my windowsill, filled my boots with dread.

"I made a payment yesterday," I quivered.

"Rate increase. Increase. Increase," it replied with extra distortion. I wanted to ask why, why me, why again, why more blood? But I needed its thunderous, searing voice to stop.

I marched behind it to the station, hopped dejectedly onto the train, and waved goodbye to my house through the window. As home shrank into the distance, its black roof became small and insignificant, and then, like the Empties themselves, invisible.

———————

We reached the payment station. This time, instead of instructing me to sit and wait my turn in a loop of seats pressed against the internal perimeter of the old church hall, the shadows were leading people off into side rooms with gusto. Scratchy, irksome black patches flitted back and forth, tired humans like sad sheep following with their fingers rammed into their ears in a useless quest for silence or with their noses pegged to avoid the extreme-clean scent. The mass of black static chaperoning me pooled on the floor by my feet and screeched, "*Follow.*" So, follow I did. Through a side door, down a corridor I rushed. Unseen claws shimmied me into a tiny, makeshift cubicle and instructed me to lie on the narrow bed within.

"Left or right. One, two, three, four, five. Four or five. One, two, three, four, or five?" Christ alive, why did it have to manifest such hideous sounds and speak in echoes?

"I'm sorry, I'm not sure what you mean," I replied, my index fingers thrust as plugs in my ears.

"Left or right finger. Or toe. Finger. Or toe."

Sweet Jesus. I looked down at my hands and realized what it meant.

It wanted more than my blood—it wanted a digit too.

It wanted my fresh flesh and bone.

I stood up and moved to the door. I needed out. This was one step too far. The seemingly vacant unit shifted through me, glided from behind me to the door in front. This penetration of my core felt like a wave of acidic hellfire riding through every cell of my body. I gagged as its antimatter gushed through my muscles and bones. It reached the door before I could, and I watched in despair as the bolt slammed across.

"Fingers or Toes. Left or Right. Right," it said again, its voice hammering my eardrums, spattering me with the tang of bleach. A leather fedora hat, which had been sitting atop a small corner table, flew upward and came to rest midair, shoulder height. I watched, frozen to the spot, as the hat floated back across the room. "You must choose. Internet fee gone up. No tissue payment, no internet, no life."

I sat back down on the gurney bed, my heart bashed like a jailed bird. No life? Did it mean this in the literal sense? Was I to die today if I didn't succumb to its demands? Or was it somehow aware of how much I valued my gaming time, how trivial my existence would become without my virtual stage? Either way, the door was locked. I was trapped. I could feel its revolting nothingness brushing up and down against my thigh, keen for my answer. I had no choice. It wasn't going to let me leave, and I needed the internet—I spent over sixteen hours a day doing virtual gigs, touring the world with Cream, performing to massive crowds, all from the comfort of my living room. I had nothing else, no one else. Without the internet, would I even exist? Betwixt a rock and a hard place was where I was wedged—I just hoped it, the Empty, wasn't going to *use* a rock and a hard place to take this heavy payment.

I shuffled my butt back onto the loose sheet of blue medical paper towel atop the wheeled bed, braced myself, and through gritted teeth, replied: "Left toe."

I clenched my fists, held my breath in preparation. Imprinted on my retina, before I screwed my eyes closed, was the snapshot of a floating, dipped fedora hat and a levitating hacksaw.

———

I screamed for ages, bled for ages. The Empty tossed a bunch of bandages at me, unbolted the door, and left. Stemming the flow of blood from my foot with my shaking hands, I watched a floating hat escort away my toe on a small dish.

I wrapped my foot. The bandage became red-soaked in an instant. I grabbed another roll from the medical trolley and wrapped and re-wrapped the wound until the bleeding eased. I hopped back to the

station that day, through sideways sleet, onto the train, a mess of blood
and rain and tears, and made my way back home.

———

I immersed myself in my VR performances for the rest of the week,
my pain alleviated slightly by being on stage. I wondered how long a toe
would buy me. Weeks? Maybe a month?

Ten days after the Empties first mutilated me, another knock came
at my door.

This Empty was wearing a necktie with the symbol of an upturned
cross on it. I followed its scuffle of a shadow, its hovering black noose,
down the road, onward, toward the train station. I psyched myself up to
say goodbye to the little toe on my right foot this time. My left foot's toe
stump had started to dry and scab over. Four toes per foot wasn't the end
of the world. I could deal with that. In a couple of hours, I'd be back at
home, in my living room, on stage at Glastonbury Festival thrashing out
"Deserted Cities of the Heart" and "Sunshine of My Love" to thousands
of virtual smiling fans.

This time, though, they kept me overnight. Paralyzed by the medication they'd forced upon me, yet able to witness and feel every scrape and
cut the floating scalpel made, I had no option but to watch them hack off
my entire foot and imbibe bag after bag of my lifeblood. Each time one
of them downed a gulp, I'd see an evil body cloud up, become vermill-
lion fog before my eyes. Some of them started to look a little less empty.
Instead of shadows cast beneath spaces of nothingness, through drugged
eyes I swear I saw fleshy, flitting geometric shapes. Organic. Fluid. Peach,
pink, brown, and cream. Edges, angles, corners, and planes. Dustings
of rose. Blockish, translucent organic apparitions sloped from room to
room as I bawled in agony. Was the pain making me delusional? Many of
the shapes were wearing black baseball caps, black beanie hats, studded
leather jackets. One had draped over its shifting image a Darkthrone
t-shirt held together with safety pins.

My entire leg throbbed. Pain pinballed up my left-hand side from
where my foot was once attached. Shock punched me in the gut. I yelled
a hopeless, "*Help me*" from the hospital bed, but of course I received no

help, just a hard, thick slap around the jaws from a flush-tint, cuboid Empty appendage.

"Shut up. Shut up. Shut up," it screeched, echoed by tenfold more of its allies. Fear stapled my mouth closed. "Be quiet or no anesthetic next time. Next time."

Next time? I yanked out the pouch and needle, which had been drilled into a vessel near my groin. It seemed to be replacing my body fluids with something dark, something made of nightmares, something I knew I didn't want or need inside of me. I lobbed it onto the floor and then vomited hard into a cardboard kidney dish.

———

And there was a next time. Against my will and from a pit of unimaginable pain, I bid goodbye to my other foot. That debilitating loss bought me a knock-free month. But then they came again. They broke into my home, pulled me out from under my bed where I'd hidden. I was petrified, still feverish, battling an infection from the last amputation. They dragged me to the payment center, knocked me out for twelve hours. My last memory before that surgery was of a floating chiffon Victoriana evening gown, matched velour gloves, and a disposable medical mask screeching orders at me in tones of death while tethering me down to the wheeled bed. That time, they told me they'd removed a kidney, half of my lung, my right eye, and a large section of my liver.

When I came around, I was on the train. Propped up in a wheelchair, I regained consciousness, seated under the semi-clothed, black-gray cloud of an Empty—the Darkthrone fan. The train rolled to a stop, and it pushed me along, all the while whistling a shrill, gut-splitting note from its invisible lips. Each toot it made felt like a woodpecker hammering on my eardrums. Disharmonious vibrations emanating from it shook and irritated each throbbing part of my sore, pained body. I was a shell of a man. It wheeled me back home and tipped me out onto my sofa with a bag of medication and comestibles.

"Aftercare package, package," it hollered and left.

I felt like I was dying. The reek of slow death, of summertime roadkill, soured my living room, irritated my nasal passages with every slow, pained inhalation. Was the near-intolerable stench emanating from me? I did nothing but sleep and clamber to the kitchen for water for what felt like eternity, all the while spinning in and out of consciousness until, at some point, I managed to muster up the energy to haul my frail body over to the VR screen. I pressed my nose up against the cold black mirror and switched it on. Thank God for VR, an escape from my world of pain. Within a second, I was back on stage, my boys behind me, able one more time to belt out the classic rock hits. Performance euphoria washed over me. The myriad of injuries and incisions the "surgeons" had left all over my body, for a moment, fell numb.

Three long months passed before they called again. An Empty knocked, screeched at me in power chords, and wheeled me to the train station. Another Empty with a hint of peach to its nebulous form knocked me out with its Luciferous knuckles and a syringe of black static. When I came around, one of the b'stards told me they'd taken everything that was left to take from within the cavity of my abdomen. I screamed and screamed. It whipped and thrust a horrific, leather-gloved limb out at me, which struck me solid. I recoiled in further pain, silenced.

They didn't understand—organs did not replenish as blood did. Yes, the liver had the weak ability to regenerate partially, but not as fast as they had been reaping slices of it from me. I felt like death warmed up. My hair had all fallen out. I had just one eye, I could feel no teeth were left. My arms were like drumsticks, bare bones. My hands and feet were long gone. I felt like a tipped-up sack.

In my delirious state of agony, as an Empty wheeled and tipped me out, back into my front room, I noticed something. The Empty—it appeared to have a human shape. A humanoid outline, human legs dressed in human trousers, peachy arms and hands, a torso wearing something woven, soft, possibly angora, in a shade of bruised blue. Under the cap perched on what I imagined must've been its head, was a writhing bonce of tangled long, midnight-black hair that whipped about like Medusa's snakes, and a pair of soulless eyes filled with loathing. And the odor of this beast—which had once reeked of cleaning chemicals and sanitized sanatoriums—the pong of it now overrode the stench of death my own self seemed to be secreting. Its bouquet now packed a honey-and-cinnamon punch. Was this evil cloud, dressed and fleshed out now as an earthling, also wearing my ex-girlfriend's favorite *eau de parfum*?

"Cheerio," it said, its voice no longer resonant, no longer overly loud, no reverb—just human. I didn't have the strength to reply; every breath hurt. I swear, as it left, it winked at me and smirked.

I collapsed on the sofa and slept. When I awoke, I scrabbled about, half on, half off the sofa, to retrieve the bag of pain relief and rationed food and water it'd hurled into my home as it left. Days passed; I felt weak, feverish, certain that death was near. Had I given up? I felt sure my end was nigh. Despite this overwhelming feeling of impending doom, I wanted, needed, to spend my last few days, hours, doing the one thing I loved before dropping off for the Big Sleep. Doped up on pain relief, I hauled myself to my screen. Could I muster the energy to check in on my band? See the boys, hear the crowds cheer with joy just one more time? I pressed my nose up against the black screen and stretched for the *on* button.

Nothing. Nothing happened. After flicking the button back and forth several times, I realized something was wrong.

It can't have run out already, the internet. I'd only just made a payment, and that payment had been a rather substantial one judging by how terrible I felt. I'd a vague memory of bartering with the Empty surgeon. I'd allowed it to take the last meter of my intestine, the final lobe of my liver, the other one of my kidneys in exchange for infinite internet. That's when I realized. That's when it clicked. I hadn't thought it through. Silly, foolish me. *What an idiot,* I thought, sitting there in my white room, drowning in tears of pain and pure frustration—I hadn't made a payment for electricity.

It'd been cut off. And I couldn't delve into my online VR world without electricity. I couldn't stand on stage, complete, with all my virtual organs, limbs, appendages, and drill out Cream classics to baying crowds of fans. Ginger Baker would bang on his drum skins unaccompanied by the thrashing of the battle ax. Jack Bruce's lyrics would sound hollow without my guitar melodies accompanying him. I pressed my nose again and again against the black mirror of my VR entertainment system, hopeful I was mistaken. Again and again, harder and harder. Frustrated, furious, throbbing with pain, fear, anger. I opened what I felt was my one remaining eye and looked into the black mirror of the dead VR set in front of me—

—to be met with no reflection.

No face.

No sallow, concave cheeks; no glazed, tired eye; no strands of hay-wire, desperate hair sticking out from my scalp. No scalp. No neck, no shoulders. Biting down on the inside of my cheek to hold in screams of anguish, I drew myself up onto my bleeding, oozing sore stumps—and could not see any of them. I could see none of me in the dark reflective screen, none of me at all. I was nothing. I had become nothing. I was gone, empty.

I threw the space where my body should be back onto my sofa and screamed an acidic scream that echoed and bounced around the four ever-pressing walls. I sat my nothingness down in a pile of misery, invis-ible and alone. Through no nose, I inhaled nothingness, a scentless air, like an empty blanket of midnight sky, devoid of any stars or light.

My living room walls were painted white. My ceiling, which stretched out above me, was as white as a bed sheet, and the floor below was all whitewashed boards. It was the whitest room in my house, yet, in the fi-nal moment before I lost my mind completely, it felt exponentially dark. It was as if a three-foot-deep, thick padding of virgin snow surrounded me, made a death's row prisoner of me. I wish I'd never opened my front door.

Almost incandescent and with the weight of infinity, my own four white walls pushed in.

And, trapped within them, I have become nothing but a thunderous shadow, an eternal black metal scream.

---

Reprint Acknowledgement: "Black Metal in a White Room" also appears in *Hunted*, an anthology published in 2022 by UK-based Grave-stone Press.

**S. J. Townend** is the odd, dark twist you never expected. An author of contemporary romance, horror, sci-fi, speculative, and dark fiction, she has published with Brigids Gate Press, Ghost Orchid Press, Gravestone Press, *Gravely Unusual Magazine*, and Timber Ghost Press to name a few. She is the winner of the 2020 Secret Attic short story contest and the 2021 Tortive Literature story contest and was shortlisted for the HG Wells Short Story Competition, also in 2021. Right now, the Bristol, UK-based writer is compiling her first collection of horror stories under the working title, *Sick Girl Screams*, so she may not answer the phone if it rings. *Looks across to ringing phone . . . notices ringing phone is unplugged at wall.*

**Author Website:** www.sjtownend.com

**Social Media Handles:**
Twitter: @SJTownend
Amazon Author Page: https://www.amazon.com/SJ-Townend/e/B086H51N7C

# PRIMAL SCREAM

## MIA DALIA

Every evening at approximately the same time my neighbor lets out a scream.

No, that's really me underplaying the situation.

Every evening at approximately the same time, my neighbor lets out a scream that rattles my world, sends shudders down my spine, and—for just a moment—rips apart the very fabric of my existence.

No. Now I'm thinking maybe I'm overdoing it.

The thing is, it's too bizarre an occurrence to describe adequately and too frequent to ignore. I thought about reporting my neighbor to the rental company, but what exactly would I report? Besides, this is a perfectly good neighbor otherwise, quiet (other than the daily bloodcurdling scream), not a smoker from what I can tell, never threw a party that I know of. Good neighbors are tough to come by these days.

I would know.

I've lived in this building for ages, longer than any other tenant. Possibly longer than the rest of them combined. It wasn't originally built for apartments. Once upon a time, it was a proper mansion, a single-home residence for someone wealthy and fancy. I'm sure then it was a nice place. But it's long since been sold and subdivided, quite shabbily I might add, into a number of small units. Short-term living for college kids, single people going through a transitional period in life, newcomers to the city. I'm none of those.

I'm in a decent enough situation to move on—except for a lack of more suitable options. I've been in this city way too long.

My mother always used to say, "Life is stormy, so save for a rainy day."

And so, I did. I have. I'm always saving—not an easy thing to do on the salary of a desk jockey. The thing I long ago discovered about money is that if you can't make more of it, you spend less. That's how I ended up in my apartment in the first place. It was cheap then. And it is still cheap, relative to the area. The smallest unit in the building. A box, really, with amenities.

But when I think about it, life is a series of boxes. I go from my box of an apartment to a smaller box of my car to my tiny box of a cubicle. Rinse and repeat. All to eventually end up in the tiniest box of them all. It's depressing to contemplate. I try not to.

I've thought about moving, but the practical details always bog down the grand plan. I'm all about details. Ask anyone at work. 'Meticulous' was what they put down on my last two annual reviews.

And yet I do not know much about my neighbors. They come and go on a yearly rotation. Just anonymous numbers on lobby mailboxes. Could be anybody. We travel like ghosts through this building, on different schedules, different parallel lives.

We're all stuck here in our tiny boxes, sharing thin walls with strangers.

The neighbor in question, the screamer, I don't know a thing about either, except I think it's a woman because of the heels clicking on the hardwood floors. But who knows? The scream tells me nothing, the same as the heels. It's rendered genderless by its pitch, by its volume.

It haunts me, that scream. I occasionally lie awake at night, trying to imagine scenarios that would lead someone to express themselves that way. The pent-up rage, sadness, powerlessness, frustration, the claustrophobic feeling of the walls closing in on you, the slow and steady crush of the weight of life.

To tell the truth, I don't have to stretch my imagination all that far. I think my neighbor screams the scream I hold inside every day.

———  —  ———

I've grown too curious. I'm no longer satisfied with my imaginings. I still haven't met my neighbor and don't know if I ever will and I have made peace in my mind with the fact that I'm about to do something unseemly, unthinkable, really.

I'm going to spy on her (assuming the screamer is a "her").

I place great value on privacy, but sometimes you have to act outside your moral code.

Technically, this won't be a difficult feat. There's a system of metal stairs attached to the back of the building so tenants can escape in case of fire. A noble idea that's long been appropriated for smoking balconies. With a small degree of contortion, I think I can get to my neighbor's window. Just to sneak a glance. That's all.

———

I pick a nice evening, reasonably mild with clear skies. Nighttime comes early these days, providing the much-needed cover of darkness, and I'm wearing all black to blend in further. No one should notice me, unless they're looking for me.

I have a pretty good idea of her schedule by now. Whatever her job is, it usually sees her home by six o'clock.

By 5:55, I'm stationed on a small metal grid landing outside her window, gently rubbing my knee, which I bruised getting there.

She enters her apartment. It appears I was right about the gender. She's a plain-looking woman in her thirties. No one you'd give a second glance to on the street. Business-casual, smart, low heels, a black leather bag. She kicks off her shoes by the entryway, a nook far too small to merit the title of "foyer," and hangs up her long woolen coat on the wall hook. Discards her bag to the floor. Pushes her hand through her shoulder-length brown hair and exhales.

She seems even smaller now. As if whatever inflated her to buoy her through the day has now abandoned her. She goes into the kitchen, washes her hands thoroughly, then pours herself a glass of water and drinks it.

I wait, feeling like a creep. About a decade ago in this neighborhood, a serial rapist spied on women just like I'm doing now. Big difference—he'd break in and do his worst. All I'm after is an explanation behind a single, bizarre daily occurrence. And then I'll leave. Back to my box. Never to be seen or heard or noticed.

Her drink finished, she enters the sparsely furnished living area and lets out another sigh.

Then, she lifts her arms and does the single most disturbingly unforgettable thing I've ever seen. She reaches behind her back as if to unzip a dress, but what she really undoes is her skin, from the base of her neck to her tailbone. And then, she proceeds to peel it away.

As her skin comes off, she screams that scream.

It is so much louder out here. I slap my hands to my ears but the sound travels straight through my desperately clutched fingers.

I can't help but listen. And I can't help but watch.

She takes off her skin like one would shed their clothes at the end of the day—if those were sewn onto a person. And beneath the skin, there's no bloody mess of muscles, none of the things you'd expect from anatomical charts.

Beneath the skin is pure fire.

It looks like lava—molten, powerful, alive, impossibly bright to look at directly. And yet I can't turn away.

Out of this inferno unfolds a pair of wings. Beautiful, fiery wings. Like nothing I've ever seen or imagined.

She is a mythical phoenix trapped in an ugly, small apartment. A stunning, incongruous thing.

She approaches the window now, and finally, I come back to myself enough to move, scramble, flee. I make my way back down the fire escape as quickly as I can.

The screaming has stopped. Now, the only sounds in the night are the oceanic swoosh of blood in my ears and my panicked, gasping breath.

I watch from below as she opens the window and contorts her body to step outside, then straightens out, a brilliant incandescence against the darkness of the night.

There's no scorching wave of heat to blast me for my sin of proximity. No smoke. The conflagration is odorless, heatless, impossible. My neighbor is considerate to the last. I can't believe that no one else sees it—that I live in a world where such a thing can go unnoticed.

And then she opens her wings and takes to the sky. Gone in a moment. Too soon to register, almost. And now that she is gone, none of it seems real. Plausible. Possible.

I stare at the night sky, but she isn't coming back, I know, not any-time soon. I won't hear her footsteps until much later in the night or even early morning. Where does she go? What does she do? I can no longer speculate on such things. She is an impossibility, a dream.

Now that I'm in the beat-up armchair inside my apartment, a place so plain, so soul-crushingly bland, it seems impossible that what just happened, happened at all.

I get up, turn the chair around so it faces the window instead of the TV.

I think, what would I do, where would I go if I could flee this life, if only temporarily? Tomorrow she'll be back in her business-casuals, in her nine-to-five routine. No one would ever suspect; no one would ever know her incandescent secret.

No wonder she screams. Trapped in this split existence. I'd scream, too, to shed this skin, to get out of myself for a while. I'd scream too.

**Mia Dalia** is an author, a lifelong reader, and a longtime reviewer of all things fantastic, scary, and strange. Her short fiction has been published by Night Terror Novels, 50 word stories, *Flash Fiction Magazine*, *Pyre* maga-zine, and Tales from a Moonlit Path. Her short story "The Last Interview" will be produced for a Bane episode of Grey Rooms podcast this summer. She'd like to give you nightmares . . . the fun kind.

**Social Media Handle:**
Blog: https://advancetheplot.weebly.com/

# LAB TEST

## DIANNA SINOVIC

The door to the lab was closed . . . yet Jacie was sure she'd left it propped open when she went to retrieve the tray from the walk-in cooler.

She shifted the tray of test tubes, cold in her gloved hand, right to left, so she could push open the door, but it held. Tight. Which was even more odd, since the door was new; the lab building was only two years old.

She scanned the lab's interior in her memory: the tables, sinks, equipment, her project, the lab tablet open and blinking and awaiting her return. She pushed again on the door, refusing to accept its solid state, but paused. A clink? She heard a second clink, then a third—as if glass were being slammed down on the stainless steel lab table but not breaking.

She put her ear to the door to better hear and sensed a whistling; high-pitched air screaming around the door's edges. The cold blasts blew her frizzy hair in streamers from her face.

Jacie looked down the hallway for Peter or Meg, but the area was quiet. She finally looked down at her sample tray. It was alive with movement, each test tube flashed and glinted, the contents in motion. Instinctively, she dropped the tray, stepping back from the door as the tubes hit the white linoleum of the hallway, and she felt the liquid splash her face, her hair, her gloves. Her safety glasses were still on the lab table inside the door, which now stood ajar.

———

The morning Jacie got the news of her promotion was the same day she had a flat tire on the way to the lab and misplaced the tiny, bejeweled silver star her mother had passed on to her when she graduated from Cornell. She'd spent ten minutes searching in vain for the pendant, but it wasn't where she usually put it. Then driving too fast to make up for lost time, she ran over a nail, and within a block, she had to pull over and call AAA to put on the spare.

Brock Smithton, the CEO of Planisphere, called her into his office on the third floor of the corporate headquarters in the Malvern office park, and, with her father standing beside him, shook her hand and congratulated her. The lab ribbon-cutting ceremony was scheduled for the following week, and she would oversee a staff of twelve researchers.

"Dr. Clemens," Brock had said, speaking to Jacie's father, one of the founders of Planisphere, "we are so fortunate to have your daughter working for us."

Her father smiled that smile of his, the one taking credit for all things whether he did them or not. "I always knew she was a keeper," Matthew Clemens said.

Jacie tried not to let her annoyance show. It was nothing new. The daughter of a brilliant but self-centered man, she always found herself trying to stay out of his shadow.

The best route to make her own way was to jump into her new role, which she did by putting in ten or more hours a day, sometimes working weekends. She inherited some staff from another Planisphere division and hired the rest. Most of them worked hard alongside her. Then there was Peter Norris, who'd been moved over to her department when the new lab opened. Three years younger than her at thirty-two, he wore his resentment on his face and in the slouch he favored when he walked through the labs.

"How many doctorates does *she* have?" she overheard him sneer one day not long after he joined the team. "That promotion was mine. *I* should be running this lab."

Jacie had considered requesting his transfer out, but Peter was a top-notch researcher. She wanted his skills, needed his nimble mind to accomplish the ambitious goals she had set. He could easily have been named head of the lab—except that his father was not a co-founder.

In the two years since the lab opened, they had accomplished a lot, including four patents for novel molecules. One of those had already been turned into a treatment for Alzheimer's disease. A few colleagues murmured that Jacie might be headed toward a Nobel, an award that even her feted father had not yet garnered.

Then, three months ago, Peter had come to her one afternoon with an idea.

She was sitting in the breakroom, nursing a cup of house blend from the Keurig while she mentally churned through her latest project, searching for the next step. He made himself a cup of coffee and sat down across from her. They were alone, and she prepared herself for snark.

"I need a favor," he said. His words were lazy, matching the way he sprawled in the chair, but his dark eyes looked right at her.

Jacie kept her face unexpressive. He seldom asked for anything directly, usually funneling requests to her through others. Even after two years, she assumed his resentment of her still festered.

"For what?" she said. She couldn't look away; his gaze demanded her attention.

"I need a small sample, just a few millimeters. Enough to mine the DNA or whatever it is it's got."

Pulling her mind back from the puzzle she'd been contemplating when Peter walked in, Jacie parsed his words and drew a blank. "Sample of what? I thought you were working on the GEN2 sequencing."

"Something better." His lazy words seemed to tease her.

"Okay," she said. "I still don't know what sample you're after. Or how it will help."

He dropped his gaze and looked around the breakroom, then leaned forward. "From Stardust." He whispered it, but still she flinched.

"How do you know about that?"

"Who doesn't?" he said, his words slipping back into a lazy rhythm.

Her father's project. Even she didn't know a lot about it.

"If I *could* wrangle a sample for you—and I strongly doubt it—what are you proposing?" Just like Peter to march down a path that diverged from the rest of the lab. "We've promised the board we'd deliver on that new agent. Trials could start as early as next year."

She closed her eyes briefly and scolded herself. *I sound like my father.* Matthew Clemens became so intent on his latest project that nothing else mattered, even if a breakthrough shimmered for another researcher. He didn't want to hear about it.

Sighing, she nodded at Peter. "Have your project outline on my desk by tomorrow morning, and I'll see what I can do."

———

What he planned was so audacious Jacie chuckled. *Who was he kidding?* Her father would never approve the release of a sample based on the fantasy Peter had written. She closed the folder and pushed it to one side of her tiny desk. Turning to her computer, she opened her emails to begin her morning's prep. A knock on the door interrupted her.

Peter didn't bother to wait, walking in and glancing around briefly. Still sizing up the space, she speculated, and once again she steeled herself to face him. It was a lab office, barely room for one person, especially when cluttered with stacks of journals, folders, notes, and a whiteboard covered with molecular equations. Her desk was tucked in the back corner next to the lone window. A Planisphere emblem—the blue globe swirled with the company name—hung from the curtain frame. A feeble winter sun etched the outline with gold.

He slid into one of two empty folding chairs and handed her a mug of coffee.

"You read it?" He sipped his own coffee and leaned forward. "What do you think?"

Jacie tried to sense if he was serious or mocking. His face revealed little, but he seemed so earnest. Despite her misgivings, she opted for serious. But how to begin without laughing?

"You are one of the best researchers on this team," she started. "No, let me change that. You are the best." She paused and noted that his eyes had flickered briefly at that. "But . . ."

"You think it's too far out there." He stated this without a hint of a smile.

Here it came. He would criticize her for playing the cautious hand when what he had in mind would change the future of the world.

"It's just . . ." She tried to assemble something more than a knee-jerk response. "Your idea, *if feasible*, holds enormous potential. But it's such a long shot, and we already have several strong lines under development. The board is fully behind what we're doing. You know funding is never a sure thing in this industry."

Peter frowned and looked away from her. When he spoke, he didn't meet her eye. "If I had an in with Matthew Clemens the way you do, I would leverage it this very moment to push ahead with my plan. You need to trust me, but I know you don't." He held up a hand when she started to protest. "But what about Tau?" He took the folder from her. "With Tau, you took a chance, a big chance, because in your gut you knew it would pan out. And it did. That's what this represents for me."

Jacie's face grew warm. She had gone head to head with her father over that project. When Matthew Clemens said no, she'd pushed back—the first time since joining the company—and her father nearly got her fired. She'd learned that later, after he'd acquiesced, thanks to a last-minute maneuver by Peter.

"I'll give you that." Her research led to the first of the novel molecules, beating the 300-to-1 odds that Tau had represented. She picked up Peter's folder again, opened it, leafed through the pages. "How is this even possible?"

"I *know* this will work. But I can't move forward without that sample."

After a moment, she nodded. "You've convinced me. Now, I just need to convince my father."

Peter leaned back in his chair, arms embracing his folder, and that lazy pattern of speech from earlier returned. "Maybe what he doesn't know won't hurt him . . ."

Jacie gasped. "I hope you don't mean that."

Peter grinned and stood to leave, half-saluting her. "Just saying . . . think about it." At the door, he turned back to her. "You, me, Meg—let's keep our group to a bare minimum, at least until we have the basics figured out. We can bring in the others later."

Then, he was gone, while Jacie's mind raced through a scenario that put her on the far side of breaking and entering.

Matthew Clemens had secured the Stardust sample, shortly after it made its way back to Earth, by pulling strings and cashing in on favors owed him. That much Jacie knew. Once she'd gone off to college and then was on her own, her father shared very little of his research with her. Yes, he'd invited her to join Planisphere, but she wasn't sure if that was because she was his daughter or because he was making a corporate investment based on her expertise, family be damned.

So, she had no insight into what if any research he'd done on the sample. He kept it in his own lab, in the adjacent building in the complex. Maybe having the sample was enough for him. That he had obtained it might have been the only coup he was after. If so, then Jacie agreed with Peter: Time to put it to use.

Looking back, Jacie marveled at her brazenness. She sweet-talked her way into the lab, using her family tie as the key. The story she concocted wasn't far from the truth: Her team really *was* going to use the sample for research. But the part about her father being onboard . . . a full-out fairytale.

And then her own instinct for research took over. Gazing at the chilled tissue, she felt electrified with excitement. *This* was why she had chosen this field: the mysteries to solve, the unknowns to unwrap, the possibilities to explore. Settling herself, she refocused and used the laser cutter to slice off the minute sample they needed. Then she made sure to insist on secrecy from that lab: The sample was part of a top-secret project, something only her father and a few others knew about.

* * *

"Peter!" Jacie shouted in the empty corridor. "Meg! Anyone!"

The hallway was silent; the lab room through the now-opened door also lay silent, though moments before she had heard the loud thumps and felt the arctic breeze whistle past her face. The tray that had slipped from her hands lay on its side, and the floor glittered with the shards of broken test tubes and the streaks of the liquid that had splashed out. The liquid moved—not simply the kinetic motion set in place by the fall, but on its own, Jacie was sure.

Her arms itched, her face burned. Thank God she had closed her eyes when she dropped the tray. With a start, she connected her skin reaction to the holes the liquid had burned through her lab coat and the sweater she wore beneath it.

And the empty lab beckoned.

Gingerly, she picked her way through the glass and splatter and through the lab door. Puzzled, she surveyed the room. It was indeed vacant. Moreover, nothing seemed amiss. She looked in vain for broken glass, beakers overturned, equipment flashing red warning signals—but all looked tidy and organized, just the way she'd left it.

She went to the sink and rinsed her hands and face quickly then wiped down her shoes and pants with a cloth. She pulled off her lab coat to better inspect the holes that had burrowed through her sweater, the red skin on her arms and face already blistering. Uneasy at what material might have breached her skin, she gently washed the wounds and applied ointment and bandages from the first-aid kit they kept for emergencies.

*I'll live*, she said to herself. *I hope.*

Too unnerved to resume her work, she stared at the mess in the hallway. She tried the lab phone to call Esteban, the complex's all-purpose handyman/janitor, but the line was dead. Donning a fresh pair of gloves and a spare lab coat, she moved to the hall for the dropped tray. And stopped.

The floor was as dry as though Esteban had already cleaned up the mess. Not a trace of the spilled liquid. Glass still littered the area, crunching beneath her shoes.

"Peter?" she called again. And then because it seemed to make more sense, "Esteban?"

With a sigh, she picked up the tray and went back to the lab for a broom. Sweeping up the shards into the dustpan, Jacie blinked at the debris. Etched into the glass, the dried residue drew her attention. She could see the pattern left by the cells . . . on a microscopic level, yet she was using just her naked eye. *Impossible.* Was this an illusion?

When the alarm siren started, she jumped. Someone had triggered the howling noise to alert the staff to evacuate: A biohazard had gone rogue. From *her* lab?

The tinny voice over the PA repeated in two-second bursts, "Sector IV."

*I'm in Sector IV.* She knew security would lock down the area in a matter of minutes, trapping her along with whatever threat had been reported. Jacie ran back into the lab room and put down the broom and pan.

The clearance team met her just before she reached the exit. Fully suited up, the three people surrounded her, blocking her way.

"Dr. Clemens, you'll need to go through the decontamination unit," one of the suited figures said. "Rachel will escort you there."

"What happened?" she said. Distracted by the minute details of their suits—the sealed seams, the layers of rubber—she almost missed the suit's reply.

"We're not sure," the same figure said. "But getting you out of here ASAP is the priority."

"Peter Norris and Meg Walker are also working in this sector," she said, wondering again why neither had responded to her earlier shouts. "Did they get out?"

"They're safe." The suit waved her through the exit door with an identically outfitted Rachel.

In the decontamination room, Jacie pulled off the lab coat and removed her sweater; her pants had been spared the worst of the splatter, so she kept them on. Tossing the sweater into the biohazard bin, she examined her arms. They no longer hurt, and she peered under one of the bandages. The skin beneath was smooth and unblemished, yet no more than fifteen minutes before, she had to grit her teeth as she dressed the wounds.

Opening the supply locker, she found a clean tee emblazoned with *Planisphere*, and went to find Peter and Meg. To find out what went wrong.

In the lab building's reception area, she was welcomed by her staff, who had dutifully evacuated when the alarm sounded. Meg gave her a hug.

"I'm so glad you're okay." Meg's voice quavered. "We were so worried when they said you were trapped in there."

Jacie patted Meg on the back and pulled away from the embrace. "I'm fine. They've contained it, whatever it was."

The emergency medical team arrived and began to evaluate staff members one at a time.

Peter stood away from the group, his face noncommittal. When Jacie walked over to him, though, his glance told her everything she needed to know.

"You too." When he inclined his head slightly in the affirmative, she added, "But your exposure was intentional."

"Yes," he said. "You would never have agreed to take the dose." He paused, and Jacie kept any reaction hidden. "I wanted you to feel the rush as I did."

"So you set up my 'accident'?" She stepped forward, arms up to shove him. "You endangered the entire lab."

He took a step back. "Sometimes it's necessary to take risks."

"I could fire you for what you did." She wanted to, in that moment, but firing him couldn't reverse the damage done—to her, to him.

"You and I are in this together now." He spoke lazily, as though she was the prey watched by a coiled rattler.

"Which means you got what you've always wanted—to run this lab."

Their almost-whispered argument had drawn the attention of the rest of the staff. The room quieted, most all of them trying and failing not to stare.

Turning to the group, she stepped slightly away from Peter, reinforcing, she hoped, her position at the helm.

"I'm glad to say that no one was injured in the incident." Speaking calmly although she felt anything but calm, she continued. "We are investigating the circumstances to find out what happened. Since there may be issues we haven't yet identified, I'm shutting the office for the rest of the day. We'll send out an email to all of you regarding tomorrow, but I fully expect we'll be back in action by then. Once you've been cleared by the medical team, you're free to go."

People murmured and slowly dispersed, picking up their belongings and exiting through the glass front door. The last two people were walking out when Jacie's father strode into the building, followed by Brock Smithton and three other men.

"Trouble," Jacie breathed, but when she looked for Peter, he had gone.

Matthew Clemens's mouth turned down as though he'd just bitten into something unsavory. "I just found out that you raided my lab, removing top-secret materials without my permission."

The CEO stepped forward. "I'm sure you had good reason," he said, directing his comments to Jacie.

Surprised at this conciliatory gesture, she felt less at sea. "We did, Brock. Dad, I knew you wouldn't agree to it, but the possibilities we are exploring could have far-reaching effects. They could prove even more profitable than the novel molecules or the GEN2 project." The more she talked, the stronger she felt. "This could change the world."

Her father laughed. It was more of a bark, but it stripped the seriousness from her statement; deflated it, as so many of her ideas had been punctured by him over the years. Why had he even hired her? Maybe, she thought, it was to make him look better.

"My naive little girl," Matthew Clemens said, shaking his head and continuing to chuckle. "It's been in top-secret storage because to let it out would change the world indeed."

A shiver ran up her shoulders. *And now we've set it free.* She remembered the moving liquid drops on the linoleum hallway floor. Drops that had vanished.

"We've got it under control." Peter, suddenly at her side, came to bat for her once again. "The cleanup team has contained the threat. They'll incinerate whatever they've gathered and do a thorough decon sweep of the entire building."

Peter held up something in his hand, passing it to her. The star pendant on its filigree silver chain, the one that had gone missing for two years. It twinkled in the spring sunshine streaming through the lobby windows, bedazzling her. "One of the decon team found it."

"Thanks," she said, surprised at the catch in her throat.

Her father's face softened as he recognized the necklace. "I remember that." His gaze turned dreamy for a moment. "Your mother . . . God rest her soul." He seemed to gather himself, straightening back into the co-founder of Planisphere. "I'll want a full report on the contamination incident by eight tomorrow."

Jacie tried to listen but was drawn to the elaborate pattern of skin cells on the CEO's nose, cheeks, and chin. The blemish on his right cheek was malignant. A diagnosis that no one could make without a biopsy and a microscope. Except . . . *she* could see it. Just as she'd seen the cell residue in the hallway. Another illusion?

Her father turned to leave but stopped. Looking at Peter this time, he added, "And I'll want the results of your study up to now." He spoke to Brock as the two of them walked away with their henchmen, "Might as well, since they've already done it. It's worth a look."

Jacie's face burned for a moment at her father's slight, and he stumbled, almost falling. She had wanted to push him away from her, but she hadn't moved, hadn't touched him. The illusions were piling up, and she fought a bout of dizziness. To focus herself, she fastened the pendant around her neck, feeling the small, bright star on her collarbone. Where it belonged.

The lobby was now empty except for Jacie and Peter. They stood in silence for a few moments.

"Thank you for overseeing the cleanup," she said finally. "I'm hoping they found it all."

Peter's smile put her on guard. "They won't."

"What do you mean?"

"It's well hidden now."

"But the liquid—I saw it moving, Peter. And then when I looked minutes later, it was gone. We've got to contain it."

"Why?"

"You can't be serious. You heard my father. He said it had been locked up on purpose. And we—"

"Shannah is pregnant." He spoke quietly, serious. "With our first."

Jacie searched his face. The abrupt change of subject baffled her. "Congratulations. I mean, I'm really happy for you." Shannah was his second wife. The first walked out on him, she'd heard.

"We just found out for sure yesterday."

"How nice." She blew out a breath. "But the lab—"

"I took the dose a month ago. Shannah is about three weeks along."

Jacie wondered if he were trying to rub in the fact that she was single, no significant other, no family beyond her irritating father. Then the math clicked. "Oh my God."

"We're planning for three if we can."

"And you're not worried? Birth defects, your wife carrying who knows what?"

"It's a brave new world, Jacie. And you're a part of it now. That was you who made your father stumble as he left. Just as it was me who made your tray fall in the hallway."

"Telekinesis?"

Peter threw open his arms, gesturing at the empty lobby. "That and more. Your eyesight, for one."

"Brock has basal cell carcinoma. I saw the cells dividing."

"Now think about all those sample units that disappeared after you dropped them."

Without effort, Jacie sensed the alien cells in the building. They were linked to her—and to Peter—as though one organic entity. "Fascinating." She was no longer concerned or frightened at the prospect. They were of her blood, as she was of theirs.

Laughing at her expression, Peter said, "Give it time, and you'll live up to your name at last, I'm betting."

Her mother had told her about the days-long argument over her name, but Matthew Clemens won, as he always did. And his daughter was named in jest after the superstar of the New Testament.

"The report I turn in tomorrow will give the old doc enough information to make him salivate," Peter said, "but he won't know the whole story. Not at first anyway. And by the time he realizes what's up, it will be much, much too late."

She smiled at him, and he smiled back.

**Dianna Sinovic** is an author, certified book coach, and editor based in Bucks County, PA. She writes short stories in several genres, including paranormal, horror, and speculative fiction. She is a member of Sisters in Crime, the Horror Writers Association, the American Medical Writers Association, and the Bethlehem Writers Group.

**Author Website:** www.dianna-sinovic.com

**Social Media Handle:**
Twitter: @dianna_sinovic

# CLERKS AND CONVICTS

## J. L. ROYCE

The girl stared through the shatterproof glass at the man outside. He held a tablet in one hand, clutched the doorknob in the other.

"Read this." He raised the screen. "Out loud."

"Fine." She squinted and cleared her throat.

"I, Jodie Tyler, a minor ward of the State, aware of the risks, permit Frank Jophers, a certified technician, onto the premises for the purpose of servitor repair; said risks including exposure to infectious agents, damage to property, robbery—"

"That'll do." Frank turned the tablet and flicked the document to the end. "Read the numbers in the signature box to sign."

Jodie did. The tablet blinked; a green checkmark bounced up. The lock clicked open, and Frank turned the knob.

"Disables the counter-measures." He grinned. "Like inviting the Devil into your house."

Jodie stepped back.

Frank walked in, though slowly. "Can't be too careful around these older doors. Sometimes they bite." He nodded to her. "Name's Frank."

"I *know* . . ."

"And you're Jodie."

She rolled her eyes.

Frank gave her an appraising glance: thin arms and legs, a face losing its baby fat.

"You look healthy. You're what, fourteen?"

"Twelve." She put her fists on her slim hips. "Look, are you going to haul it away?"

"Your Mother?"

"That *thing* lying in the kitchen. It's busted, and I don't need it." She stalked off.

Frank followed. "Well, you can't be emancipated until you're sixteen. Until then, it's a Mother or a group home."

They passed through the living room, a disaster of dirty dishes and food packaging scattered around the immersive projector. The kitchen was in a similar state, with a female form sprawled amid the clutter.

Frank squatted beside the inert servitor and activated his tablet.

"Power's low; diagnostic logs indicate . . . a variety of damage. Won't know how serious it is until she's online again."

He snuggled a recharger from his kit into the curve of the Mother's belly. Its lights flashed *active*.

There was an unsavory-looking puddle next to its face.

"She's vomited up some unprocessed food. You know they only pretend to eat, right? This green stuff . . ."

The chemical aroma was familiar. Frank looked up at the girl, but Jodie simply shrugged.

"How long?"

The girl, studying her mobile, ignored him.

"I asked, how long has she been lying here?"

"I dunno . . ." Jodie continued playing her game.

Frank stared, employing the adult's ultimate weapon: patience.

"A week?" No answer. "Why did you wait to call?"

"I was *busy*."

He panned his tablet around. "Ah. The refrigerator wouldn't open?"

"I thought the house would help if I screamed loud enough. All *right*?"

"No; it just called me. The house knew you were fine." Frank scrolled through the logs. "You haven't eaten for two days?"

Jodie stared at her feet. "I had some snack bars in my room."

Frank pulled the refrigerator's handle: locked.

It said, in a friendly voice, "*Please contact Mother for access!*"

He overrode the lock and peered inside. "I'll make something to eat while she charges. Protein scramble?"

The girl shrugged. "A fruit smoothie?"

"*Jodie would benefit from some kale and ancient grains,*" said the appliance. "*She tends to put on weight when allowed to*—"

"That's not true!" the girl cried. "I'm stressed about school. Stop *shaming* me all the time!"

"Grades?" asked Frank.

"My social scores. I'm trying for early in-person Academy placement. Anything to get away from *her.*"

Frank cleared a space on the counter. "That's ambitious," he said, searching the refrigerator. "This juice should be fine."

The washer was still full of clean items. Frank laid out place settings and poured drinks.

"I *prefer* milk."

"The milk's gone off, sorry. Even non-dairy doesn't last."

Frank put the loaded plates into the microwave and started it. "I'm surprised you're not sick, living in this filth."

"I thought the house—"

"You don't get it, do you? The house would rather starve you than release you into the wild."

The oven pinged. Frank slid the hot plates onto the counter, waved his stinging fingers.

The girl sat down and set to devouring the meal. Frank rummaged in his bag and placed a chocolate bar at her elbow.

She stared at it greedily, then at him. "Why?"

"The chocolate? I just thought—"

"No—why won't the house release me?"

"For your protection."

"What was it like?" Children always want to know whatever adults wish to forget.

Frank stared at his food. "At first it was just another crisis. Then the hospitals were overwhelmed, and the military triage centers. Then there was just mayhem when the police got sick, until the mob died too. The stench must have been awful. All the servitors were repurposed to burial details: MilSpec, Joy-bots, Retail. Then it was just . . . quiet."

Jodie sat wide-eyed. "I meant *before* the Big V—when there were people everywhere. I've done immersives, but . . ."

"You couldn't walk a city block without meeting strangers. You'd go to a bar and could barely move or hear, there were so many people, their voices were so loud, all laughing, talking." Frank stared off, out a window at the empty street. "Stores packed with people. Transit cars crammed."

Frank glanced at the body on the floor. "What was it?"

"Hmm?" Jodie concentrated on her lunch.

"The poison—what did you use?"

She chewed slowly, eyes wandering across the ceiling. "Drain cleaner."

Frank shook his head. "She'd reject it from the scent."

"I put a little in her tea, every day a little more, for a week."

He pondered this. "Probably fried her olfaction. The diagnostics wouldn't call for service since taste isn't considered critical to caregiving."

She twirled her fork idly. "Then I gave her a big serving."

Frank snorted. "Corroded the cervical network. They'll make you pay, add it to your tuition."

Jodie studied him. "Why aren't *you* dead?"

"What?"

"You're an adult, not a machine; why didn't you die with the rest of them?"

It was Frank's turn to concentrate on chewing.

"Well?"

"There was a movie, once."

"A what?"

"Like an immersive, only flat. And you can't interact."

Jodie rolled her eyes: *So 20c.*

He went on. "So, this movie is about avoiding the end of the world."

"Like, the Big V?"

"No, nuclear war."

"Oh." She wiped her plate with the last of her flatbread.

"A character says that after the war, there would be two factions left: the lowliest of clerks, working deep in company files; and the worst of the convicts, in solitary confinement."

"Charming." She popped the flatbread into her mouth, then casually dropped her hand into her lap, clutching a knife. "So, which were you, Mr. Frank?"

"I was institutionalized, in solitary—for my protection. I only had two years left in my sentence anyway."

"Protected from what?"

"The other inmates."

Their conversation was interrupted by a chime from his tablet. Frank swept the rest of his meal into his mouth, chewing rapidly.

"She's ready to reboot," Frank said. He pushed his plate toward Jodie. "Clean up?"

He knelt beside the lifeless figure. "Yeah; her charge is high enough to run diagnostics." He pulled aside the recharger and studied the Mother.

"You know, I think I recognize this model—a Rosie."

"A what?" Jodie tossed the knife back on her plate and stood behind him.

His eyes wandered over the Mother's long legs, broad hips, and bullet breasts.

"Yeah, a Rosie."

"What's *that*?"

"Never mind. She's ready."

Frank lifted the Mother's head and wiped her face with a damp towel, then propped her up against the cabinets.

"I have to do a manual reset." Frank reached under Mother's skirt but paused to look up at Jodie.

"It's nothing personal. And she may act a little . . . confused." He fumbled between the servitor's legs.

She sat bolt upright, staring blindly. "*Restart.*" In a husky voice, she recited a litany of subsystems, running through self-diagnostics.

Jodie slid back into the shadows of the hallway.

The servitor held out her hand. "Help me up?"

Frank assisted her to her feet.

"Rosie?"

She smiled. "Hello! I apologize for the service disruption." Rosie glanced down at herself and then studied Frank.

"Looks like we haven't gotten very far."

"No, we—"

"I'll make drinks, and we'll talk about what you'd like." Rosie glanced around. "I don't see the bar. Not very romantic spot, though if the kitchen's what you want . . ."

She unbuttoned her blouse. "Don't be shy; relax, and let's just have some fun."

She leaned forward to kiss Frank. Jodie muttered, "*Eww!*"

He evaded the servitor. "You need to brush your teeth."

"Of course." Rosie patted her hair. "If you'll just show me to the little girl's room, I'll freshen up."

The servitor stepped around Frank and came face to face with the girl lurking in the hall.

"Not in my room!" Jodie said. "And I'm not a *little girl.*"

"It's an expression," Frank said.

Mother's face twisted and froze. "Jodie!" Rosie's whiskey-and-cigarette voice grated harshly in Mother's stentorian tones.

"It was an accident!" the girl said.

"You've not done your chores in *days*. The house reports your health metrics are low. And I require maintenance—"

"The repair guy is already here!" the girl replied, exasperated.

When Mother saw Frank, she reacted immediately.

"Jodie! Did you let this *man* into the house? Go to your room."

Her charge snorted. "So you and Frankie can do the dirty on the kitchen table? Gross!"

"Go to your room and lock the door!"

"I can't lock it; you—"

"Barricade yourself in then! He is listed on the Sex Offender's Registry."

Jodie's eyes went wide. "You're a dirty old man? I ate your candy bar!"

The girl disappeared around the corner.

Frank raised his voice. "It's not like that—"

With Jodie gone, the servitor refocused and relaxed, cocking her hips. "Where were we?"

He faced the servitor. "Rosie, why don't you sit down until I figure this out?"

"She's role-challenged," Frank called out, for Jodie's benefit.

"Whenever you're ready . . . Frankie." Rosie sauntered over to the counter and perched on a stool, crossing her legs.

He stepped into the hallway.

Jodie retreated toward her room. "I'll scream . . ."

Frank kept his gaze steady. "It was wrong, and I was punished—"

"Until they let you loose! Gave you a deal, right? Risk taking the V-Killer, and if you survive, serve the government?"

"Yes," he nodded. "I couldn't live in prison, so I took the chance. But my record follows me like a bad smell. When I'm not working, I'm locked down in a dorm where everyone hates me."

"Frankie . . ." Rosie's voice beckoned from the kitchen. "I'm lonely . . ."

"And you're going to leave me with that *thing*." The storm of Jodie's anger was about to break into tears. "I may just run out the door when you go."

"If you leave now, I'll be blamed and sent back to prison regardless of my vax."

"She's broken anyway. Can't you order a replacement?"

"No, there aren't enough servitors. They'd probably just send you something worse." Frank paused. "There's another way though."

"Which is?"

Frank licked his lips. "Adoption."

Her eyes went wide.

He quickly added, "Hear me out: I move in, we keep Rosie—Mother—out of your way, and I'll emancipate you—if you qualify for an Academy."

Jodie wrapped herself in her arms. "Invite a *perv* in to live with me? You must think I'm pretty stupid."

"No, I don't. There aren't enough guardians. The authorities will watch the household. You'll have a bedroom with a lock."

"*She'll* be able to get in."

"No, she won't—I'm an adult; she'll take commands from me."

Jodie grimaced. "Eww."

Frank shook his head. "Not what I meant."

The girl pondered the proposition. "And what can I eat?"

The refrigerator said, "*I've got a nice selection of sustainably grown greens!*"

"Shut up," they said.

Frank said, "Whatever you want. Know why? Because it's time somebody let you learn to be an adult. The world's going to be hard, you need to learn now how to cope. But I'll order the groceries, so you'd better get used to curry."

"What's that?"

"You'll see. I'll still work out there, which means you'll have to study on your own—more responsibility. But I can help. I was a teacher once . . ."

"Yeah?" Jodie narrowed her eyes.

"Yeah."

They nodded at each other.

"Family." Frank walked into the kitchen.

"Mother . . ."

**J. L. Royce** is a published author of science fiction, the macabre, and whatever else strikes him. He lives in the northern reaches of the American Midwest, exploring the wilderness without and within. His work appears in *Allegory, Fifth Di, Fireside, Ghostlight, Love Letters to Poe, Lovecraftiana, Mysterion, parABnormal, Sci Phi, Strange Aeon, Utopia,* and *Wyldblood,* among others. He is a member of the Horror Writers Association and the Great Lakes Association of Horror Writers.

**Author Website:** www.jlroyce.com

**Social Media Handle:**
Twitter: @authorJLRoyce

# DISMANTLED

## VICKIE FERNANDEZ

This is how it starts.

The debilitating need to retch with no release. I count backward, trying to remember the last time I bought tampons. I can barely squeeze out enough pee to saturate the thing between my legs. As I set the blinking time bomb on the bathroom sink, I already know the answer.

I won't be able to hide it. He'll know. I wear it on my face like a contorted veil.

Pregnancy transforms me into this asexual vessel; swollen, torpid, and dreading the looming horror of the finale. Those laboring hours of agony culminate—I split open and expel my contents, wet and bloodied. Relief intermingles with utter despair when that unknown part—cultivated for months—is cut out and whisked away.

What follows is a true suspension of self.

There's a moment within the undoing that you are able to take a breath and admire your work, but it's simply a moment. Agonizingly perfect tits swollen with milk, followed by guilt when your son is unable to latch. The relief and shame of mixing that first bottle of formula—failure-laden freedom. Bits of yourself emerge through the exhaustion, but you're not the same. Never yours, always needed, always nurturing and not nurtured. Then postpartum depression rips you from who you were, turning you into a thing not worth knowing. How do you explain this to a man who thinks he wants to share this god-awful miracle with you?

I made the appointment before I even bought the pregnancy test.

No one ever wants an abortion. But my decision is easy—with two kids running around, I'm tired of being the vessel. All the good and love left in me is channeled directly from my heart to my boys like a conduit. There's nothing left to give, not even to myself.

Mathew would beg me not to do this. That this could be our last chance. He is kind but incapable of understanding. Before I can rip myself off the bathroom floor, I hear him.

"Len, I went ahead and got Chinese on the way back from . . . Len, are you, are you . . ."

The pink and white stick sits on the counter. Silently, yelling . . . PREGNANT!

He beams. "Holy shit! Seriously?"

He takes me in his arms, tobacco and cologne enveloping me. All I can think is, How do I get out of this?

He holds my face in his big, soft hands and kisses me.

I kiss him back and force a smile. "I can't believe it. Crazy, right?" I sob what he perceives as tears of joy.

———

I tell him I'm going to the OB.

Matt wants to come, to be there for me and our baby. I lie and say he can come to all the other appointments.

At the clinic, there's a herd of protesters outside.

"It's not too late, they are liars in there," one says to me, a wild look in her eyes. When I keep walking, her tone roughens: "You're a fucking murderer and you are going to hell!"

I totally am, but not for this.

The waiting room is bright, the walls intense with obnoxious slogans of empowerment. I'm weak—my hands shake as I fill out the stack of consent forms. I pay in cash and wait for my name to be called.

"You're going to feel some pressure," she says.

The room is warm and low-lit. My socked feet dangle while I sit bare-assed on the examination table's crinkly paper. "Please lie back and try to relax," the tech says, her buttery voice muffled by the pink surgical mask she wears to match her scrubs.

"Do you want to see the baby?"

Baby? The minute I refer to this as a baby, you can bet I won't go through with it.

"No," I whisper—she taps at a keyboard while moving the probe inside me in a circular motion. I'm sifting through lists in my mind of all the things I'm supposed to be doing right now. This is not one of them.

"Eight weeks."

"Huh?"

"You're eight weeks along, Lennon. A perfect candidate for the pill."

The pill. It sounds innocuous enough, like it's not an actual abortion, right? This is the lie I'll later tell myself.

The next day, I leave work early, pop two 800 mg of ibuprofen, and pray that this shit works. I don't want to go home, and it's too early to pick up the boys.

I park two lots away from Target's entrance, giving myself a moment.

As I walk through the automatic doors, I hit play on my phone, Tiffany belts her '80s mallrat anthem through my earbuds, and I'm transported to a world all my own. My pulse quickens. I'm weightless, thrust into the distant past when I first heard this song—I was eight and wanted nothing more than to grow up and be a woman.

I'm singing in the aisles, filling my reusable bags as if under a spell. The song ends, and I'm spent like the day after a bender.

When I walk out of the store, the sky looks bruised by the threat of a storm. I stand there, the smell of exhaust, humidity, and McDonald's clings to the air. Then it hits, the whip crack of thunder, the fragmenting jigsaw of lightning, the deluge. I stand there and take it, every drop.

My guts contract and fracture—the bleeding starts.

———  ———

By the time I get to Parker and Oliver's school, the car pick-up line is around the block. I'm soaked, mascara runs down my face, and my eyes are red and puffy from crying. I'm sure the other parents think I'm insane. They aren't wrong.

A distinct person once existed within these layers of flesh and bone. She was full to bursting with desires, dreams, and fantasies that she felt could materialize simply because she wanted them to. Alchemy fueled by whiskey. Songs shook her to climax. Ashtrays brimming with lipstick-kissed butts and journals filled with stories and ideas.

Now, I've been reduced to that moment, right before I walk out of a store. That metallic taste of adrenaline in the back of my throat, heart pumping in tandem like when that first bump of cocaine hits followed by the descent. Each time it becomes harder to get back up.

The bags full of things—not sure what the hell I even stole—are stuffed into the space where a spare tire should be. This time I didn't even bother with the payment at the self-checkout. I looked straight at the gum-chewing, red-vested menagerie of teens loitering by the doors, and walked out.

I don't know if it's the hormones or if I am just trying to stir up my feelings, but I can't stop fucking crying.

I admire my beautiful boys in the rearview mirror. Their dad tucked into every crevice of their faces. They are so much happier without him. Safe from the turbulence that was his orbit. They never ask about him or where he went or why. Matt is their father now, and that is the reality we have created for ourselves.

Parker and Oliver are only one year apart, barely toddlers when their dad died. I met him through a mutual friend, our dealer. We did coke together, drank together, obsessed about art, books, and movies, but then he started doing heroin alone. He hid it well for a while, or I was so in love that I refused to see the track marks, the lapses of time where he'd vanish for days, sometimes weeks. When I got pregnant with Parker, I quit everything. That's when I started to notice that the soon-to-be father of my child was collapsing in on himself.

Parker was born and didn't meet his father until he was two months old, when he resurfaced—changed, his face no longer gaunt and sallow. He went to meetings and gave up everything to his higher power. We picnicked in the park with his sponsor. Parker loved his dad.

I loved my family. When I got pregnant with Oliver, he started having wine with dinner, then a six-pack, then vodka. Then I started carrying Narcan in the diaper bag. Among the bottles, sippy cups, and goldfish crackers, was the small antidote capable of tearing a person from the callous hands of death.

I revived their dad five times in three months.

There is nothing more terrifying than watching a soul re-enter its body after death. The initial reaction is not gratitude, it's fucking rage. Every time he'd come back missing more parts and feeling more resentful. That last time I just stood there, fingers wrapped around the base of the nose spray, like Jesus to his Lazarus. Life drained from his face like a blanched fruit—pale, then blue.

I thought of the boys, the way they adored him, and how that love would burn to ashy hate when they became old enough to see this version of their father. I sprayed the elixir into the air, dropped the empty canister, and dialed 911. Relief wrapped itself around me in a thick swaddle as I wept into the phone.

When I met Matt, I wasn't looking for love. He felt like shelter, a warm place to unpack the blistering trauma. We cobbled together a family out of bits of hope and slivers of joy. Time smoothing out our edges, like shards of glass toiling through sand in the ocean hoping to one day look like treasured crystal.

———

The siren in my head wails. How much time has passed? It's been 48 hours since I lay on my son's bed, legs splayed. Held my breath, careful not to lose any of the eight tiny pills they gave me at Planned Parenthood in the folds of his dinosaur print sheets. Matt and the boys in the next room a cacophony of child takeover and adult surrender.

The bleeding wasn't too bad the first day. Then, suddenly, gushing like the liquid remains of a blown-up life. I spent so long fighting, screaming "Pro-Choice!" Now, I'm calling a mass of cells with no brain or heart a life. Who the fuck am I? I'll tell you who I am. I'm a mess of hubris and sentimentality. A hollowed vestige of what once was.

I must've done something wrong. This doesn't feel right. I'm saturating a pad every ten minutes. There is no way I can hide this. I tie a flannel around my waist and run downstairs,

"I have to go to the store."

I don't wait for a response and bolt out the door.

I can't go back home like this. My pants are soaked through with blood. I can't go to the ER—he'll know, they'll know from the meds in my system. When I was a kid, my mom and I would play this game: I'd tell her where to turn until we were lost. She always knew where she was and how to get home but went along with it anyway. This weightlessness came with the possibility of losing your tether to the familiar. I turn erratically, left, then right, then left, trying to lose myself until I come up with a plan. There is so much blood, the seat of the car saturated with the dismantling.

On a stretch of road I'm not familiar with, I press the gas, hit play on the song queued on my phone, that same damn Tiffany song, saccharine and rambunctious, pushing me to speed up. Eyes closed, I take my hands off the wheel and let go. In the freefall—I am alone.

———

A voice calls out, small. "Ma'am, ma'am. Can you hear me?" I wince, the taste of blood in my mouth, smoke in my eyes. I hear a count off, "One, two, three!" Dislodged for a second, I feel nothing, then pain. Everything is pain; until this point, I have never experienced this level of ache, at least not in the physical sense.

"What happened?" I stutter, my broken body strapped and in motion.

"Just stay calm, ma'am." I try to hold on, look around. Objects are strewn across the small stretch of road among the debris. Shoes, cosmetics, bras, dresses, buttery leather purses, notebooks all bearing price tags and covered in soot. Hundreds of dollars' worth of stolen merchandise flank the wreckage; my car totaled and smoldering.

Of course, I already know what happened. What I don't know is the extent of the damage. I think it was a Buddhist monk who once said, "There are a million ways to be dead without dying." Or maybe it was Dorothy Parker.

I want to make one thing very clear: I wasn't trying to kill myself. At least not consciously. It's hard to hold onto my thoughts—they trickle down from my skull in an erratic rhythm like an eroded faucet.

*Fuck, am I dead? Why is it so quiet? Did I say that out loud?*

———

I'm not dead but I might as well be. I sense bodies coming in and out of the room. The hum of the TV, the sound of monitors. I blink my eyes open; I try to open my mouth but can't.

"It's okay, Len. You were in an accident. Your jaw is broken. They had to wire it shut. Just try to relax. Everything is okay."

I look up at Matt, his soft eyes dark and tired.

He starts to cry and grabs my hand. "We lost . . . we lost the baby. I'm so sorry, Lennon."

I'm the one who's sorry. I am sorry I'm a garbage person who doesn't know how to express her feelings. I am sorry I steal everything I can get my hands on because it's the only time I ever feel anything. I killed your baby, crashed the car, and destroyed your life and my face.

Nothing comes out of my mouth but garbled whimpers and the sting of bitter tears.

It is at this moment that I decide to just let go.

I close my eyes and loosen the reins. I'm dizzy, my heart pounds in my ears. I hear Matt scream, the nurses shuffle in, they are saying something, but I can't hear them above the throbbing heart in my ears. I think of Parker and Oliver, and I'm jolted back into my body. I can't leave them. I decide to fight. Not for myself, not for Matt, but for my boys.

I wake up to Matt's face looking down at me shattered, his green eyes squinting in my direction as if I were an equation.

"You had an abortion?"

I blink, motioning at his phone so that I can type up an explanation. I open a new note and start to type. "I was afraid. I don't have the strength to have another child. I'm a mess. I love you. I am so sorry."

"What about the crash, Lennon? The cops say it was intentional. And all that shit you stole? What the . . . I mean, who the fuck are you? You could've died. What about the boys? Did you even think about them? About me?"

I gesture for his phone.

"No. I don't want to hear anything else you have to say." Matt storms out of the room. I feel that same relief I felt when I watched the paramedics wheel the sheathed body of the boys' dad out of my life.

———

"Hello everyone, my name is Lennon and I'm . . . I'm a kleptomaniac." That word used to taste like self-betrayal in my mouth, but now, it tastes like freedom.

"It's been ninety days since the last time I stole. I've always taken things. Since I was a kid, I had this sense of entitlement like my life sucks and the world owes me these trinkets at the very least. After my husband died, the compulsion progressed. It became a need, not a want. I stole to grieve, to feel, to regain power. With the stealing came the deception and secrecy. What people don't get is that with any addiction comes the creation of a world, a world made up of deadbolted doors inside you— behind every door a behemoth of shame longing to be released."

The room is bright and warm. The radiator hisses in time with the drip and gurgle of the coffee maker. The smell of cigarettes, perfume, and sweat fills the air. From an open window, I hear a car come to a stop, the radio blaring that '80s incantation that served as the sonic catalyst to my self-destruction, now just a vapid pop song. I smile at the people looking up at me as they nod.

There are gaping holes where roots once swelled and fragments of bone swimming in my jawline. I blew my life up out of sadness and boredom. It's true. It is all true: sometimes among the wreckage and fault lines, you find slivers of self you'd lost or abandoned. There are a million ways to be dead without dying; this time, I chose to live.

**Vickie Fernandez** is a writer, storyteller, and comedian. She cut her story-weaving teeth in Ariel Gore's Literary Kitchen. Her stories have appeared in various literary journals including *Akashic Books* and the *Rumpus*. She has also contributed to Red Hen Press's *Two-Countries: US Daughters & Sons of Immigrant Parents Anthology* and Lit Star Press's *The People's Apocalypse*. She writes between diaper changes, tantrums, and red lights. Vickie is a mother of two wildly gorgeous boys, a serious coffee drinker, and a lover of Vans sneakers.

**Social Media Handles:**
Facebook: @vickiefernandezwrites
Email: vickiefernandezthewriter@gmail.com

# WHERE THE ELK ROAM

## AMANDA HEADLEE

"People are Strange" echoed off the outer walls of the empty buildings. The Doors song, stuck on repeat, transmitted haunting lyrics far past the resort, through the valley, and into the mountains. That should've been their sign to leave. Sara couldn't stand another second of this torture. "Do you know how to turn this music off?"

Dags ignored her. She scratched nervously at her arm and looked around. This song had always disturbed Sara. Every time she heard it, she felt as though she were going to be kidnapped by a strange group of lunatics that looked like they fell out of an Edward Gory drawing.

"Hey, I know we're here to bag your big trophy and that you only brought me along to mind the camp. But, *please* . . ." The looped song began to drive her mad as they unpacked the truck. *Someone must've forgotten to turn the music off when everyone vacated*, she thought. However, she found that quite hard to fathom given it was just this one song playing on repeat. *Leaving on the music had to be intentional. Maybe to scare the elk away from the center of the resort . . . or to scare away poachers, like Dags.*

After the truck was unloaded and all their gear laid in a heap upon the ground, Dags opened the driver's side door.

"What are you doing?" Sara asked.

"Moving the truck to the far lot so that if anyone gets past the main gate's barriers, they won't see it. Don't want anyone finding us here."

Sara shook her head. "No one's going to come. Everybody knows the resort is closed. Dags, please. The music."

He grumbled and slammed the door shut hard, making Sara jump. She was on edge, and not only because of the music.

It was illegal to be at the resort this time of year. Like clockwork, between September and October, a herd of elk—nearly 2,500—migrated from the forest, through this resort, and continued to the town of Estes Park. The game commission shut down the resort when the herd moved through due to the danger to humans. Elk during rut could go on a murderous rampage.

While the hunting season in the surrounding area outside of the migratory path was open, Dags would be in double trouble if caught, as here they were on private property. Plus, rifle season didn't start until next month, and a rifle was the only firearm he'd brought along. Dags couldn't be bothered with a muzzleloader or archery. Too much work. A rifle was simpler.

"Let's turn that shit off," Dags said.

"I bet we could turn it off from in there." Sara pointed toward the ski resort lodge.

"Like that would be open."

"Never hurts to try." She brushed past him and walked toward the rustic two-story lodge. All the buildings in the resort felt oddly out of place among the Rockies. A Nordic essence inspired the heart of the resort's design, possibly to lure those bored of the Colorado log cabin-esque aesthetic. While the design culturally stuck out, the color palette complemented the surrounding forest. If it wasn't for the stripped land around the resort that led up the mountain for the ski routes, one would struggle to see the resort buildings and vacation homes hidden among the trees.

As they ascended the steps to the massive deck of the lodge, an icy blast from the east cut them to the bone.

"Thought it would be warmer today," Dags grumbled.

Sara tightened her jacket at the throat. Off to the right, toward the mountain, in the direction of where the elk would descend, the breeze intensified and ruffled her short black hair. Something large stood at the base of the mountain just at the outer edge of the closest ski slope. Sara raised a hand to her eyes and squinted into the wind, trying to get a better look at what was out there. "Do you see that?"

Dags didn't even look, just pushed past her up the stairs. Heat rose behind Sara's eyes as she glared at him before returning her attention to the ski slope. Whatever was out there had disappeared.

"Guess you were right . . . for once." Dags pulled on the heavy handle of the wooden door. It swung open, hinges creaking as they walked in. The lobby sat in the center of the two-story entryway, housing the registration desk. Off to the left, a massive stone fireplace served as a focal point to a lodge room with supple brown leather couches strategically placed about. To the right, a little coffee shop, and next to that, a grand staircase with a tree-inspired wrought iron railing wrapped partially around the lobby and up to the second floor.

They took the stairs, disregarding the Employees Only sign, to what seemed to be the administrative floor. Every door stood wide open. Curiosity enticed them to investigate each room and see if they could find anything that resembled AV equipment. At the end of the hallway, they discovered the security room with its door closed.

"Well, looky here," Dags said as he opened the door. One would expect the room to be humming with electricity and monitors displaying live video feeds of the resort's property, but the security room stood dead.

"At least we won't get caught," said Sara.

Dags shrugged. "Even if they had all this running, Eric would have handled it for us."

Eric was Dags's best friend and the area's game warden. He was the only person who knew they were at the resort. Eric had helped Dags plan this little excursion and then looked the other way. Sara didn't believe Eric held any power to aid them should they be caught trespassing, but she held her tongue as her eyes fell on another door to the left of the main security console, also closed. A green light shone on a keycard reader attached to the wall next to the doorframe, indicating its unlocked nature. Dags pulled the door open with ease, revealing the server room for the whole resort.

"Weird they left all this unlocked," Sara said.

"Who cares? There's the sound system." He pointed to a rack that held a massive stereo receiver full of knobs, buttons, and switches. In the entirety of the technology-filled room, the receiver was the only thing running. Not even the servers whirled. The panel went black when Dags pushed the blue power button at the top left of the receiver. "Let's go see if that took care of the damn music."

They walked into the hallway. Dags started toward the stairs, but curiosity pulled Sara's attention to closed doors at the other end of the hall.

"Wait. I want to see what's there."

"No, let's go. We need to get camp set up before dark."

"It's only noon. We have a few hours of daylight. This won't take long."

He followed her toward two wooden doors that stood tall from floor to ceiling.

"Wonder what they keep in there. Godzilla?" He laughed while Sara admired the hand-carved scene that adorned every inch of the doors, depicting the Colorado mountains with several elk herds wandering through the valleys.

Sara fingered an oddly carved symbol lightly etched on the side of a mountain. Three-pronged and curled, the symbol was reminiscent of a Celtic triskele. Compared to the craftmanship done on the rest of the panels, this looked like a toddler had carved asymmetrical, unclean lines.

"Here's another one." Dags pointed to one hiding underneath an elk. As they peered at the carving, they discovered more and more symbols.

Sara ran an index finger over another one, delicately tracing the symbol's design. "What does it mean?"

"Who cares?" Dags shrugged then pushed the doors open.

The darkness inside consumed them, and for a moment Sara thought she'd fallen into a pit. The atmosphere sat heavily on her shoulders as she proceeded blindly toward a thin crack of light emanating from the opposite wall. She waved her hands in front of herself at thigh height to ensure she didn't bump into any furniture.

As she threw open the curtains, dust motes littered the sharp beam of light that cut through the darkness of the office. Sara coughed as the overhead lights flicked on. Dags had found the switch.

The illuminated opulence of the office had a European vibe. Sara assumed the resort was established from old money brought over to America from across the pond and that the owner must've been of Nordic ancestry.

On the wall surrounding the fireplace, heads of various wildlife hung, their glass-eyed, vacant stares looking nowhere and everywhere. A shiver ran through Sara at the sheer number of stuffed carcasses that overwhelmed the room.

Full mounts of smaller animals sat in suspended animation on the fireplace hearth. Sara counted a bobcat, two pheasants, and a few weasels. In the corner next to her, a large black bear reared tall on its hind legs. The most peculiar mount, however, was the fat orange tabby cat on the resort owner's desk, which faced a large leather executive chair that Dags now occupied with his feet propped up on the desk. Hands behind his head, he sighed. "Pretty wicked in here. Can you see me ruling this place?"

"More like running it into the ground."

He laughed. "Oh, like you're so great. Can we go set up camp now?"

She rolled her eyes. "Yeah."

He stood and walked toward the exit. As Sara followed, she noticed behind one of the office doors the edge of a second doorframe.

"Hang on." She pulled the main door back to reveal a shorter one that stood just a bit taller than Dags. The door, painted black, had a larger carved symbol—the misshapen triskele—painted with gold sparkles.

"BDSM closet?" Dags laughed.

Sara glared at him then grabbed the brass doorknob. Locked. The only one locked in the whole place.

"Totally someone's sex dungeon," Dags said.

"Knock it off," Sara said as she pushed past him, leaving the office.

---

They set up camp on top of a small hill outside of the resort that had a clear view of the surrounding area. The sounds of nature without the beat of a certain 1970s rock song were music to Sara's ears.

"Prime location. Definitely bagging the one with the biggest rack." He loaded his rifle with a magazine cartridge and chambered a round.

"They aren't here yet." While Sara didn't necessarily hate guns, she sometimes didn't trust whoever operated the firearm. She especially didn't like having a loaded gun around when it didn't need to be.

"But I'll be ready when they come." He raised the scope to his eye, sighted into the resort, and hummed with satisfaction.

While he played sniper-atop-the-hill, Sara distracted herself by setting up camp and building a small firepit to cook dinner. She knew Dags wouldn't move from his spot until the food was ready, and even then, she'd probably have to bring it to him.

"I'm getting firewood," she said.

Dags didn't move to help or even acknowledge her.

———

Sara would have to make a few trips. First to gather kindling and then another trip to bring back a fallen tree or large branches that could be cut up with the ax.

The forest trees stood tall, dwarfing her against the foothill grasslands. A flora mix of aspen, beech, and evergreen trees—the perfect candle scent could be based on this exact location. As the sun began to set, the temperature dropped. Goosebumps electrified Sara's skin, elicited by a cold fear that raked through her body as she looked into the dark forest. She hesitated, not wanting to step foot beyond the tree line, yet at the same time an invisible thread tugged at her chest, as though the forest wanted to reel her in. A movement off to her right broke the trance.

Fifty yards away stood the biggest animal she'd ever seen. As a rather tall woman of nearly six feet, had she been standing next to the elk, her head would barely clear his shoulder. The elk's antlers were thick and gnarled like the branches of an old oak tree. They looked nearly impossible to hold up. Soft strings of sphagnum moss hung from the tines, giving him a gossamer appearance. He looked ancient, yet thick muscles and sinew rippled under his fur with each slight movement. However, for Sara, the most captivating trait of this beast took the form of a stark white streak that started at his coal-black nose and traced up between his eyes and antlers. The streak stood out in contrast to the ruddy color of the rest of the elk's body. She assumed that it continued down his neck and back but couldn't be sure of that from her vantage point. The streak stood out as parting an almost-glowing stripe through his tattered brown fur.

The elk snorted. The ground beneath Sara's feet seemed to tremble. She looked down to where his hooves met the grass and grimaced as fear quivered in her heart at the sight of them, nearly the same size as a Clydesdale horse's. If she provoked him in any way, she'd be trampled and killed instantly. Sara backed away in the direction of the camp, never taking her eyes off him.

The elk snorted once more and bobbed his head while stomping a hoof. Black eyes glinted with a mix of what looked like anger and curiosity. She continued to back away. He never moved but kept his eyes fixed on her. When Sara felt as though she'd put a sizeable distance between herself and the elk, she turned and sprinted back to camp. At one point she looked behind to be sure he still stood at the tree line, but he'd disappeared, as though the forest had absorbed him.

"Dags!" she called out as she ran into camp. "I just saw the biggest elk ever." Sara stretched her arms out as wide as possible with the tips of her fingers pointed to the sky. "The rack had to be at least this big."

"Give me a break. That's like over six feet. No elk has a rack that big."

"Dags, I'm serious! You need to look for him. The rack was thick, like a heavy tree branch. And old. And—"

"Enough! Did you get the firewood? I'm hungry."

"But—

"You embellish everything. You've never seen an elk, so how do you know how big they really are?"

Sara shut her mouth and turned away. Tears pricked at the corner of her eyes.

The sun descended behind the mountain ridge while they bickered. "I'm not going into the forest now that it's getting dark." She knew he'd never agree to go with her. "Guess we're having granola bars and PB&J sandwiches for dinner."

"Oh for fuck's sake, Sara!"

—  —

She shivered inside her sleeping bag. Dags hated having anything against him while he slept and wouldn't allow her to curl up next to him for warmth. Once again, Sara found herself wondering why she stayed with him. Her friends told her that he didn't bring any purpose to her life. In fact, being with him hindered her.

Sara wanted to achieve a level of success and greatness in her life that would make her father proud. She had wanted to move to the east coast to study astronomy and astrophysics at Villanova University. With that kind of education, she'd be able to make breakthrough discoveries that she could bring to the world, such as finding a new planet that humanity could inhabit.

Through the small plastic window on the roof of the tent, she stared at the night constellations, finding Taurus painted in the sky. Her father once joked as they lay on a blanket in the field next to her childhood home that stargazers must never look at the red eye of the bull—the star Aldebaran—as gazing upon it would drive a person mad.

"But, Dad, you always tell me I'm crazy with my head out in space." She laughed.

He splayed his fingers and grasped her face as he whispered, "We're all mad here."

"Dad!" Sara had pushed his hand away and smiled at the man she most admired in life. An accomplished NASA astrophysicist, he had left a prestigious job in Washington DC to move to Colorado, where he took on work as an astronomy professor for a community college. Sara never found out why her father made that move, but she believed it was for the clearer Colorado night skies.

"Your craziness will push you to take risks and discover new worlds. All scientists have a little madness in them." Those were some of the last words that he'd ever say to her. Two days later, he was a victim in a fatal car accident.

Her father was the only person who supported her dreams of space. When he died, her hope of achieving greatness died too. No one in her family understood her determination to be like her father. They thought her too fanciful and said she should focus on something more grounded, such as a business career that would make her money. Her family saw no value in looking at the stars.

Sara had felt lost until she met Dags when they were seventeen. At first, he fed into her fascination with the night sky, encouraging her to teach him the constellations and how to navigate by the stars. But once the newness of the relationship wore off, Dags turned his attention back to his own interests of hunting and working on his truck. Their late romantic nights in the field to stargaze and make love had ceased. Sara wanted to believe it was because the nights were turning cooler, but when summer rolled around, there was still no stargazing. And there hadn't been for the past four years.

But, Dags was stability. She knew what she was getting with him, knew her future. At times she yearned to pack up her life and try to get into the Villanova undergraduate program, despite graduating high school almost six years ago with average grades. She'd have to go it alone. Dags had no intention of leaving Colorado. Born and bred in these mountains, his whole lineage existed here on the land around Estes Park.

As she stared into the red eye of Taurus, Sara knew she'd never achieve anything beyond becoming Dags's wife. She'd chosen stability over risk. A man over her dreams. Her father was wrong. She wasn't a scientist. A scientist would be mad enough to gamble the risk of striking out on their own to achieve their life goals.

---

Dags woke Sara just before the sun peeked above the ridge. When he left the tent, Sara rolled over to absorb the body heat left behind in his sleeping bag. Once his warmth disappeared, she quickly changed her clothes and crawled out of the tent to find him already in his spot, observing the surrounding area through his rifle's scope.

"They're here," he whispered. Sara pulled his binoculars out of his pack, wrapped herself up in a blanket, and sat down next to him. She couldn't clearly see individual elk as the sun's morning rays hadn't fully surpassed the mountain ridge. For the moment, the migration looked like a black mass of movement undulating from the edge of the forest, down the fields, and into the valley surrounding the resort. A sea of bodies ebbed and flowed around the buildings.

"Can you see one?"

"There's like a thousand of them," Dags said. He took the binoculars from her. She opened her mouth to protest because he kept using his rifle scope to scout, but a glare from him indicated she would cross the line if she said anything. "This is going to be impossible to find the biggest."

"Maybe that old one will show up. I could help you look for him if I had those binos and you used your scope."

"Be quiet." He reached up and clamped a hand over her mouth, the binoculars steady in his other hand. Sara wrenched her head away, irritated that he'd grabbed her face, and returned her gaze to the distant herd in front of them.

---

They sat there for a few hours, eating granola bars and drinking water, looking out across the valley. The temperature warmed to where Sara spread the blanket on the ground, then lay upon it on her stomach to observe the area around the resort. For reasons she couldn't explain, she felt exposed on the hill as though something watched her from beyond the trees.

They hadn't spoken since he'd told her to stop talking. For someone who hated silence, he demanded it while hunting. Sara thought about counting the elk to see how many were in the herd, but there were many clusters so tightly packed that she struggled to differentiate individuals. Her attention drifted to a part of the herd that milled around the edge of the forest to the right of where they sat.

Those elk acted differently.

"Can I have the binoculars? I'd like to see something."

He ignored her.

"Dags," she said a little louder, knowing that would annoy him. He shushed her with a glare, then handed over the binoculars.

"Hold these while I go take a piss." He stood and wandered off behind the tent. Sara raised the binoculars to her eyes. The separate cluster by the trees looked agitated. Their heads bobbed, swaying their antlers in what seemed to be a defensive dance. From their noses, hot exhalations puffed small clouds.

Within an instant, they stilled and then backed away from the tree line. From out of the forest stepped the old elk Sara had encountered the previous evening.

"Dags, Dags!" she whispered as loudly as she could.

As Dags walked up next to her, he grumbled about making too much noise. He picked up his rifle and sat down. As he did, she shoved the binoculars back at him.

"There. Look there. It's him." She pointed and he raised the binoculars, looking in the direction she indicated.

"What the fuck is—"

"See, I told you!"

Dags gasped, "That's not an elk. There's no way."

"What would it be then?"

"Sara, it's huge! It's towering over all the other elk. The antlers are like a moose. Maybe it is like a moose-elk hybrid? He's rare."

"He's majestic."

"He's mine." Dags set down the binoculars.

"What? No!" She grabbed his arm as he raised the rifle. "You can't kill him. He's rare. You just said so."

"Are you kidding me?" He pulled his arm away. "Do you know how much money we could make off that rack?"

Sara sat up, grabbed the binoculars, and looked at the old elk, her heart heavy, knowing she'd damned him. She never should've told Dags, though Dags would have eventually spotted him. If only she had kept her mouth shut.

As the old elk walked down toward the resort, the herd parted, the others moving away as though he were plagued. He continued through the common center and exited their side of the resort, well within range for Dags.

Sara couldn't take her eyes off the old elk. He bent his head to the ground to nibble on grass and Sara clearly saw the stripe from his nose that continued over his head did in fact travel down his back, only to stop midway and twist into an odd pattern. Sara dropped the binoculars and rubbed her eyes. It couldn't be. She raised them once more to her eyes and registered a familiar symbol formed by the white of his fur.

The same symbol carved on the doors of the resort owner's office.

The elk lifted his head and looked right at her, chewing and swallowing a last bit of grass. His eyes beckoned her, and once more an invisible thread tugged at her chest, a feeling of being pulled toward him.

Sara jolted at the concussion from the rifle, but the binoculars never came away from her eyes. The bullet pierced through the old elk's neck. He staggered, his front knees buckling beneath him. The other elk backed farther away. He righted himself and stood tall, returning his intense gaze at Sara. A hot sensation of a sickening dread swelled in her chest. Killing this elk felt like a very bad idea.

Sara, numb to the sound of the second shot, watched as the bullet sought purchase right between those coal-black eyes. The old elk's head dropped. An odd-colored mucus splattered out of the back of his skull, and he collapsed to his right side. He didn't even twitch. An instant kill.

All the elk in the valley looked toward where the old elk fell and then dispersed, scattering in all different directions back into the surrounding mountain forests, away from Estes Park.

"Dags, I think we have a problem." The migration was running away. People would notice if this herd didn't begin to trickle into town later in the day and would come looking for them. Fear spread throughout Sara's body. All she wanted to do was tear down camp, pack up the truck, and drive away.

A fleeting feeling pulsed in her mind that those who would come looking for the lost herd would be the least of their worries. Dags seemed to have a similar idea, as he had already stood and was packing up his gear. She shook her head to clear the strange feeling, grabbed her blanket, quickly collected the camping items, and dismantled the tent. Every few moments, she looked toward where the old elk lay. The sensation of something bad looming made her hurry even more.

Carrying the camping and hunting gear, they trekked down the hill. Sara set her sights on the truck and kept her eyes locked on it as they descended. She didn't want to see the elk again. After several minutes of walking, she didn't feel Dags's presence. When she turned to look for him, she saw him at the elk's carcass. She should have known better. He needed his prize, and the risk of getting caught, or worse, was worth those antlers.

Her nerves rattled as she begrudgingly walked over to him. He had his hunting pack open on the ground with his hands inside, rooting around for something. As Sara neared the elk, his pungent scent caught on the breeze and smacked her in the face: gamey, woodsy, and decaying. The old elk was already dying before Dags had shot him. Dags just helped him along the journey to death.

"Dags, look." She pointed to the grass where a sickly, green-tinged yellow fluid haloed around the elk's head. There wasn't any blood, just the thick mucus-colored ooze.

Dags put down his bag and stood next to Sara, looking at the pattern of liquid that formed before them.

"That's . . . that's the same symbol as the ones on the office door." A tremble in his voice made Sara ponder if Dags was suddenly afraid.

"It's probably diseased." She stepped closer to the carcass, careful to not step in the liquid that spread across the dry grass. "And look, there on his back. The same pattern."

The greenish-yellow ooze continued to seep from both bullet holes. Dags reverted to his indifferent state, outwardly neutralizing any evidence of fear.

"Let's cut this rack and get out of here. That meat is diseased." Dags removed a Sawzall and skinning knife from his bag. He approached the elk and carefully stepped around the putrid ooze. With the Sawzall resting on the elk's shoulder, Dags took the tip of his skinning knife and nicked a hole in the scalp before hooking the skin with the sharp side. Sara looked away and focused on the resort. Her thoughts were drawn toward the registration building and the locked door inside the office. In distracting herself from what was going on behind her, she found that she couldn't get that locked door and its sparkly gold symbol out of her mind.

"Sara!"

She turned to see Dags with the skin of the scalp peeled apart, exposing the space on the antlers between the skull and the burr, his Sawzall blade already buried in that space. With one hand on the tool and the other above his head holding the antlers, he glared at her.

"Get over here and hold this," he seethed through his teeth. Anger flashed in his eyes, and Sara tamped down the thoughts of that door as she walked over to help hold the antler, careful not to step in any of the ooze.

A limp and thick purple tongue hung from the elk's mouth. His eyes were glassy and vacant, just like all those mounts in the resort owner's office. A wave of nausea hit her as she thought about the elk's head hanging on the wall above the shorter locked door. She breathed through her mouth as her hands grasped his bone-dry antler. She expected the antler to be gritty and dirty, but it was clean and smooth. Only the strings of moss that hung from the tines marred the perfection of the antlers.

Dags turned on the Sawzall again, and the intense motion of the cutting blade vibrated the antler in her hands. When he cut through the full length of space below the burr, the weight of the antler pitched her backward to the ground. She landed on her back, right in the elk's ooze. Her head was the last point to make contact. The antler crashed heavily upon her, a long sharp tine narrowly missing her abdomen.

She let out a wail. Wide-eyed, Dags dropped the Sawzall and helped lift the antler off her. Sara's entire body shook with adrenaline from the near impalement and being covered in the elk's diseased, sticky liquid.

"Please, I want to go home." Her voice quivered in concert with the tremble of her hands.

"Eh, sorry. We just need to get this other antler down." Dags set the fallen antler aside and moved toward the other one, not once checking to see if she was okay or bothering to help her up.

Sara felt hot as she lay on the ooze-covered grass, then the quaking of her body ceased. She went stone still.

"No." Her voice sounded distant, hollow, yet firm. The sensation of her back and hair coated in the sticky liquid doused all emotion within her. She felt nothing.

Dags ignored her and put the Sawzall to the second antler. "Hold this one while I cut it."

A fire sparked in Sara's belly, and a slow, burning rage flowed through her. "Take me home now and you can come back here and deal with this on your own."

Maybe it was the flat sound of her voice, or maybe the fire in her belly reached her eyes and he saw the inferno within her. Dags took a step back and set down the Sawzall.

Without a word, Sara turned and walked toward the truck. She heard nothing above the pounding of her heart in her ears. The rage had now fully engulfed her to where she thought about returning to Dags, taking his rifle, and shooting him. The thought passed when she arrived at the truck and saw that he had followed her with no gear or trophy in hand—he only carried his rifle, slung across his shoulders. His hands were jammed in his pockets, searching for the truck keys.

Sara patiently waited by the passenger side door for it to unlock. Nothing.

"Dags. Open the fucking door now." Her voice, still level, was full of venom.

"The fob's battery must be dead." His voice trembled.

*Good,* she thought. *He's scared because he knows I'm furious but remaining calm. He's probably thinking that I'm going to slit his throat in his sleep.*

The sound of the key sliding into the driver's side door, and seeing it open, brought her a slight relief until she saw his face through the passenger side window as he reached across to open her door. She climbed in and looked at the rifle that sat between them. Sara did her best to will the thought of "what if" away.

"I'll take you home and see if my uncle or Eric can help me get the rest of this stuff." With shaking hands, he put the key into the ignition and turned it. Sara calmly looked at him. She relished the thought that the elk's bodily liquid smeared all over the back of her clothes now stained his cloth seat. He'd just bought this truck six months ago.

The ignition just clicked. He turned the key again, again, and again.

"What's wrong?" Her anger teetered on the edge of explosion.

"The fucking truck won't start." He kept turning the key. "Did you leave the light on when you got the tent?"

Sara felt her mouth move but had no control over the words that passed her lips. She couldn't contain her anger any longer. "I'll kill you if you blame this all on me. Get me the fuck out of here."

Shock contorted Dags's face as he kept turning the key to no avail. "Um . . ." He ran his fingers through his shaggy brown hair. "Let's go to the lodge and see if we can find something to jump the truck."

Sara felt detached from her body as she swung open the passenger side door, got out, and walked toward the registration building. She heard Dags running behind her, breathing heavily.

*He's scared. Scared of me.* A giggle bubbled in her chest, but she wouldn't let it out. She wanted him to remain in terror.

They were nearly to the stairs when a voice called from behind them, "Dear friends, we are so grateful for your help."

Sara and Dags whirled around to find a group of about fifteen people dressed in black cloaks. The one who spoke stepped forward. A yellow stripe started at the throat of his cloak and traveled to the ground.

"Who the fuck are you?" Dags asked.

"We aren't from here, but with your assistance, friends, we were able to arrive here."

"Our assistance?" Sara felt back in her body again with the rage subsiding.

"Yes. You opened the doorway for us to come here. From our world in the Hyades, Carcosa." The man's smile grew unnaturally large, displaying a mouth full of crooked and jagged stained teeth. He bowed and pointed in the direction of the old elk's carcass. "My lady, we come to you from Carcosa through the doorway that he unlocked. We've come to revive our king. Please, come with us to help wake him. He would very much like to meet you."

"Dude, I don't know what kind of drugs you're on, and don't care about where you came from, but leave us alone." Dags stepped closer to Sara, but she moved toward the man. Just like the feeling with the elk and the forest yesterday, an invisible thread tugged at her chest. The group started to hum a tune she'd never heard before as the man drew a long sharp dagger from the sleeve of his cloak.

"Please, friend." He looked at Dags. "We need you to wake our king."

"How?" Sara asked.

The stranger raised his dagger and pointed the tip toward Dags. "He will."

Dags grabbed Sara's arm and pulled her up the stairs to the registration building. He crashed through the front doors, dragging her along. She didn't resist. Dags reached for the door as Sara turned to look at the strangers advancing up the stairs after them. All the strangers had the same crazy, unnatural smile plastered on their pale faces.

Dags slammed the door shut. He fumbled around the door handle, looking for a lock, but the lock required a key.

"Dags . . ." Sara said as he took her hand and pulled her up the stairs to the second floor. The disconnected feeling returned, but it felt right to have

Dags lead her down the hall to the resort owner's office. The large wooden doors still stood wide open, and he pushed her through, slamming them shut behind them. This time, there was a latch he was able to lock.

He jumped backward as she heard the front door downstairs crash open.

"We need to find a way out of here." He frantically looked around the room as Sara stood entranced by the small door that Dags had thought concealed a BDSM closet.

It sat wide open.

"In there!" Dags grabbed her hand and she followed with a light step, neither of them questioning why the door now stood open.

Archaic chanting echoed off the walls of the lobby as she heard Dags feeling the walls of the small chamber for a light switch. Sara stepped inside the room after him. The moment she crossed the threshold, the door slammed shut behind her.

"Sara!" Dags screamed. "Open the door."

She didn't move and welcomed the darkness. A loud crash signaled that the strangers had broken open the office door. The chanting's timbre increased as they neared the final door of separation.

With a popping sound, two large, hand-painted symbols began to glow on the walls, one on each side of them. The sickly yellow bioluminescent light from the symbols revealed what had been locked away.

Dags frantically looked around. "An altar. This room is a fucking altar."

Before them, on a short dais, stood a skeleton cloaked in a dark-yellow tattered robe, its skull bearing a large rack of antlers like the old elk's. Between the antlers sat a yellowing bone crown. The king. The open folds of the robe revealed the full skeleton. The most peculiar part of the king's body was his lower legs and feet. The tibia and fibula were thin, much thinner than a human's, and the bones ended in hooves like an elk's.

Dags pushed Sara away from the door, but before he could touch the knob, it sprang open, revealing the group of strangers. The chanting quieted as the man in the cloak with the yellow stripe stepped into the room. Dags took a step back, bumping into Sara who stood firm and immobile against him.

"Dear friends, once again we thank you for your help and generosity." The man took another step forward.

"Get out of my way." Dags seethed through his teeth.

"Hiisi's Elk made it quite difficult to find our king. The demon Hiisi hid the doorway between our worlds within his steed, for he knew that if the gate were to open, Carcosa and your dimension would merge, which threatened to usurp his power." The stranger ignored Dags and widened his grin, the corners of his lips now reaching his ears. "Quite ingenious, hiding the doorway in a sentient being that could evade capture. However, the beast's luck ran out today, with your efforts, and its death opened the doorway that led us here to our king. And our new queen." The man nodded toward Sara.

Dags turned and looked at her. She couldn't help the smile that stretched across her face. The elk's ooze still wet on her back and hair began to expand down her arms, legs, and then around front to her chest, enveloping her in a warm embrace. She became fully covered from her chin to her toes in a golden liquid that shimmered from the glow of the wall's symbols. The liquid tempered, becoming her new skin. Dags stepped away from her. The corner of the unnatural smile on her lips twitched in satisfaction. Sara could hear Dags's heart pounding. Pounding in absolute terror.

"I'm not going to tell you again, get out of my way," Dags said to the group of strangers.

"I cannot allow that. You are in the court of our king, and we need you for one last task. Please wake our Lord so he can bring Carcosa to this realm."

"Dags, we need your help. Wake our king." Sara, feeling an overwhelming sense that all was suddenly right in the world, grabbed his hand. Her smile expanded and a giggle erupted from her lips as she admired her sparkly gold hand holding his shaking one. Dags had given her a purpose in life after all.

He struggled against her pull, but he was helpless against her newfound strength. She dragged him to the altar and pushed him down onto his knees. Taking his face between her hands, she forced him to look at the king. Dags stopped resisting the moment his eyes met the skeleton's empty eye sockets.

"Thank you, Dags," Sara whispered, "for everything. You've helped me achieve greatness. I'm a queen." She tilted his face to look up at her. Only his red-rimmed eyes moved, meeting her intense gaze. Dags's dilated pupils signaled that the time had come. Someone touched her shoulder. She turned to find the man in the yellow striped cloak holding out his dagger. She took it.

"Sara, you are insane," Dags said, his voice hollow.

With one golden hand still holding his face, she drew the dagger across his throat with the other. His body crumpled to the floor, his blood splattering her king's robe. The jaw of the skeleton clacked as muscles bubbled out of bone and weaved around the skeletal structure.

She bowed to her king, then knelt by Dags's head. Placing a hand on his face one last time, she looked him in the eyes as his life force faded and transferred to her Lord.

Sara kissed his cheek. "Greatness and madness can share the same face."

With a love of scary stories and folklore, **Amanda Headlee** spent her entire life crafting works of dark fiction. By day, Amanda is a program manager; by night, she is a wandering wonderer. When not writing or working, find her logging insane miles on one of her many bikes or hiking the Appalachian Mountains. Amanda wrote of monsters and lore in her debut novel, *Till We Become Monsters*. Her macabre short stories appear in several anthologies, such as *Midnight from Beyond the Stars, CONSUMED: Tales Inspired by the Wendigo,* and *Somewhere in the Middle of Eternity.*

**Author Website:** www.amandaheadlee.com

**Social Media Handles:**
Twitter: @amandaheadlee
Instagram: @amandaheadlee

# LOCKS AND PROMISES

## N. M. BROWN

We went ice skating; our little girl, Hannah, skated in circles, gleefully laughing with snowflakes in her hair one minute, then in the next, a dark and foreboding jagged hole on the ice's surface marked the spot where we'd last seen her. My wife, Marjorie, fell to her knees over top of the hole, plunging her arms shoulder deep into the freezing water beneath the fracturing layers of ice. Her arms dipped downward, each time coming up holding nothing.

"Porter!" she screamed. "She's stuck under the ice! She's going to die if you don't get her out of there! HELP! PLEASE . . . SOMEONE HELP US!"

That was the last time anyone else ever saw our sweet girl. Her body was never recovered, not due to lack of trying. For the next five days afterward, nearly every fireman, EMT, police officer, and concerned citizen in town was on the perimeter of that pond searching as much as they could without causing the ice to break apart, which could have resulted in undoubtedly more tragedy. Still, despite all that effort, my wife and I honored an empty, child-sized casket at her funeral.

With all the trauma we'd been through, I thought it best to relocate. My wife didn't have the care or heart to argue. She seemed to be going through the motions. I wanted to move Marjorie and myself away from anything that had to do with our daughter. The agony of Hannah's death haunted us. The permanent dashes on our living room wall where we'd marked our child's growth, the window where she'd wait for me to come home from work every week, it was all too much. It didn't stop at home either. Her teachers would be at the grocery stores, their sympathetic eyes glazing over with tears as they regaled us with tales of how intelligent and sweet our dead daughter was.

We didn't want to forget her; it was the opposite of that, actually. Marjorie and I wanted to get to a place where we could remember her with love, without the tidal wave of suicidal sadness and grief.

We moved two towns over after viewing at least a dozen homes. My work was able to transfer me to a location there and, well, Marjorie never really went back to work after Hannah was born. In the end, I had to make the decision. I, along with a realtor, paraded Marjorie through home after home, and with a constant blank look in her eyes, she obliged. However, after the eleventh home viewing, I stopped bringing her on tour.

The realty agent made a comment about the spaciousness of the twelfth listing, with two bedrooms accompanying a large en-suite primary. My wife looked at him with tear-glazed eyes and muttered, "I don't care how many rooms it has . . . I just want to be with my daughter."

At that point, I was nearly done, until I came across a listing for a ranch-style home with barn-red shutters. Something about it seemed welcoming, even from the outside. For two weeks, I flirted with the thought of buying the house. It was the only listing that I'd come back to and taken multiple tours of, and it was only a breath's hair over our allotted budget. The deal on the house was closed and the paperwork signed in less than a half hour, and before I knew it, I was on my way back to our current home to tell Marjorie the good news and pack up for our new home.

————

I guided her gingerly through each room of the new house, doing my best to hide my excitement. It's not that I was happy we moved; our daughter graced my every thought and decision. But I wanted this house to represent more than her death; if her death was all that our life was going to amount to, we should have stayed at the old house. That wretched old house . . . those empty spaces were full of a luxury that I thought people like us were too poor to be afforded: potential. The new home provided the potential of a new life in a new place—the last straw of happiness that I had to grasp at and, God forgive me . . . I intended to hold on with both hands.

My footsteps stopped short in the hallway, causing Marjorie's body to crash into mine before bouncing away.

"Jesus, Porter." She winced as she rubbed the shoulder that had taken the brunt of the impact.

"I-I'm sorry honey," I muttered. "it's just that . . ."

The hallway was interrupted by a large wooden door on the left-hand side, one I didn't remember seeing the previous times I'd viewed the house. The orange paint that covered the wood, although faded, screamed against the cream-colored walls that surrounded the door.

Marjorie's voice broke my confused thoughts. "What's behind this one? Another bedroom? You said it only had two."

"Yeah . . . I'm not really sure. I don't remember this being before." My fingers traced the grooves in the Masonite panels that were decoratively placed in the middle of the door before I grasped the cold, brass doorknob. I twisted the knob to no avail. The door was properly locked. I ran to the kitchen, leaving a very confused Marjorie unattended in the hallway. The kitchen cupboards and drawers yielded no results as far as spare keys went, and while the key to the front door was meant solely for that entrance; nevertheless, I tried that key in the orange door's lock.

My wife suddenly became enraptured with this door and the possibilities it could reveal. Life burned in her, and the shell she had been hiding in since Hannah's death had cracked and faded. She'd broken two credit cards in half trying to unlock the door, a technique she used as a teenager when her drunken mother forgot to leave the house unlocked for her after work. Marjorie rushed past me as I returned with the front door key. She headed toward the kitchen, and from there, doors and drawers were opened and slammed closed. After a moment of silence, she returned with a butcher knife in hand.

"Was that left here?" I stood, confused, as the realtor had previously mentioned that the house was thoroughly cleaned shortly after we'd purchased it.

Marjorie ignored me and peered into the sliver of space between the deadlatch and strike of the doorknob before gently inserting the blade of the knife.

"What the hell are you doing Marj? You're gonna chip the paint!"

"Fuck the paint," she muttered, her face scrunched in exaggerated concentration.

"Whoa, you are bringing nighttime aggression to a daytime conversation," I joked. Her facial expression didn't change, and my heart sagged. That used to be one of her favorite lines.

"Seriously, Porter," she scolded me, bringing her gaze up to meet mine instead of remaining focused on where it needed to be. The handle of the knife slipped; as a result, the blade slashed through the soft flesh of her palm, peppering the door with dots of crimson.

"Goddamnit!" she shouted. The knife clattered to the floor at her feet, and she placed her injured hand against the door as if to steady herself.

A pert series of clicks reverberated throughout the hallway, and my eyes widened in astonishment. Marjorie's trembling hand, still dripping with blood, reached down and gripped the doorknob. The knob turned effortlessly. As she pushed the door open, Marjorie's body stiffened instantly.

"Hannah?" she called out, struggling to maintain proper balance as she removed her shoes one at a time. "I'm right here! Mommy's coming, baby!"

I reached out and grabbed Marjorie by the elbow just as she leaped for the doorway. I had come around the other side of the opened door and was finally able to see what she saw. My breath caught in my throat as I processed the sight before me.

The room wasn't a room. The space behind the door could easily have been as large as the universe. Behind the door was a sight as though we stood looking into an aquarium at the zoo—a vast, deep blue sea of water—and at the center, our daughter floated happily in the middle as she looked out at us expectantly. I put my hand inside the room, expecting to feel the ebb and flow of water. Instead, I became entangled in a pliant substance that acted almost as sort of a barrier, separating our worlds. Marjorie took a different approach and jerked her elbow out of my grasp before jumping inside. I attempted to follow but strained against the thick outer membrane that seemed to want to keep me out—yet I broke through.

Freezing cold consumed my every sense as I made an involuntary gasp. Water seeped into the corners of my mouth as I fought the urge to scream. Bubbles emerged from my wife's lips as she held our daughter to her chest. Hannah reached up and placed a hand over her mother's mouth before shaking her head back and forth in warning. The words "Don't try to breathe" floated through the burbled hydroponics of the aquatic atmosphere. My nasal passages began to burn with a yearning for a breath I could not take, as if on cue, and my eyes burned. I hitched an arm under my little girl and swam for the doorway, intending to use as much force as I could with the little breath I had left to push her through to the other side.

She stopped in awe just before the entrance, jerking her arm away from my grasp. She marveled in silence at the bright hallway on the other side. Her hand reached back for her mother while sadness shaded her features. At the last moment, Hannah placed her small hands on the back of our necks and shoved us through the doorway with an effort she would have never been capable of in life. An inhuman noise of despair rose from my wife's chest before we crashed back into our world and tumbled to the cold tiled floor of the hallway. The door slammed shut, unwilling to open again to my pull on the doorknob.

———

After that day, I had no desire to go into that room again. That room disturbed the natural order of life, and I was not prepared to bleed for it—even if it actually was my daughter, in there. I love my daughter but she's in a world that the living should leave well alone.

Our lives took on a sinister darkness ever since we entered the room. Marjorie had maxed out our credit cards by loading up on oxygen tanks and various scuba equipment, making our house heavily combustible now among other things. I'd come home to find trails of water-logged footprints leading in different areas of the house—the trails all originating from the room beyond the orange door.

Instead of being happy, I found my wife becoming moody and even more withdrawn, her every waking thought possessed by our daughter and opening that damned door. Marjorie rushed through meals and began to neglect the most basic tasks of self-care. Every moment spent in our realm, our reality, had seemed to become a waste of time to her, a performance for Marjorie to go through the motions of until she could return to her newfound aquatic heaven.

Arguments between us intensified and occurred more often. The dissolution of our marriage was becoming a tangible entity. I sank into my own "heaven" of alcohol to numb myself from the situation.

"Her body was never found, Porter!" The words exploded through my wife's mouth with an iron conviction.

"Anything could have happened to her body. That no longer matters. All that matters is that our daughter is in Heaven."

"No, she's here. She came here and is waiting for us, honey."

"Honey, that isn't our daughter—"

"You told me yourself. You said the moment you stepped inside this house you had an overwhelmingly good feeling that it was supposed to be our home. She brought us here, and as long as we aren't breathing, we can be a family again!"

Her words brewed a maelstrom of emotions within me: an overwhelming sadness mixed with the crippling fear that my wife's mental state was now broken beyond repair. I wasn't equipped to deal with this. I needed her. Hannah was my daughter, too . . . she had my eyes, for Christ's sake.

"Why can't I be a part of your heaven too?" I whispered as I longed for the luxury of also having Marjorie's disillusion. But I cannot bring myself to her reality. In my wife's mind, she and Hannah were very much together in a place where Hannah had not been lost.

———

It's been four days since Marjorie last entered the room beyond the orange door. That means it's been over ninety-six hours since she took her last breath of fresh air that wasn't from a tank. The final words at the end of our last fight echoed through my mind, becoming more waterlogged and unintelligible as the hours and days passed. *As long as we aren't breathing, we can be a family again* . . .

Slicing my hand, I pressed my bleeding palm against the door, praying it would open for me like it always had for Marjorie. The tumbler cylinder inside of the doorknob clicked. I grasped the knob, turning it and then pulling outward with a shaking hand. My lungs grabbed every spare centimeter of oxygen that they could contain as I pushed through the elastic membrane. White noise consumed the inside of my entire body, turning my blood and bones to static electricity as I plunged into the icy cold abyss that had now become my daughter's forever home.

It took me a moment to see my wife, and I swam to Marjorie, fighting buoyancy with every step. Motionless, she lay with the form of Hannah held in her arms. They were both cuddled on their sides atop a four-poster canopied bed. The sheets that partially shrouded their resting bodies billowed in tandem with the flow. My lungs began to twitch with impatience as I slipped an arm under Marjorie, careful not to disturb the entity that I was certain impersonated my dead daughter.

Marjorie's hair floated like an auburn halo around her face as I lifted her from the mattress. We had almost cleared the bed completely when her left foot became entangled in the pale pink canopy drapes. This small interruption was just enough to gather the entity's unwanted attention. A confused look shaded the amber eyes that resembled Hannah's, and it held up its arms, hands outstretched toward us as if wordlessly asking where Mommy was going.

I ignored the entity with a breaking heart. That wasn't my daughter.

My senses were becoming warped and fuzzy as my chest radiated with a white-hot heat. It was becoming harder and harder to hold my breath. The entity drifted toward us, arms still outstretched in a desperate longing. As we neared the door, I noticed the face that looked like Hannah's began to change. The once-rounded features were now pointed and angular, giving the face a malevolence that my daughter never could have possessed. The eyes became deep black pits of rage and snarled lips parted to expose jagged teeth that gnashed together as the head jutted forward to rip at Marjorie's clothes and flesh. As it missed Marjorie's leg by mere inches, the entity opened its mouth wide, unhinged its jaw, and emitted a roar that rippled torrents through the water, whipping currents about the room.

Once I was confident that I had closed enough distance between me and our way out, I swirled around, positioning myself feet-first toward the door.

My lower body wracked with convulsions as I found myself stuck between worlds. My bottom half had made it out successfully, while my top refused to let go of the only thing I had left: my wife. I pulled with everything that I had to get her through the other side to no avail. What's worse, the outer edges of the doorway had begun to shrink, making my exit into our world more difficult with each passing second. My muscles quaked, shuddering in agony as my strength waned. I had mere moments of time and oxygen left to get Marjorie through this doorway with me.

Most of the entrance had solidified, leaving a space only large enough for my hands to hold onto hers. The rest of my body had been violently spat through to the other side, but I had managed to keep hold of her hand. A jolt electrified me as I felt Marjorie's hand rip out of mine, our hands disconnecting for the last time in this lifetime.

By the time I rose to my feet, the cream-colored hallway walls ran continuously until they met the doorway to the kitchen. The orange door and its frame were gone, as though they had never existed.

**N. M. Brown** is a Florida native, wife, and mother of three who reads stories to her kids about chasing away monsters before writing them down to get them out of her head. She is also the Chief Operations Manager for the Chilling Tales for Dark Nights Network. Her written work appears in over forty horror anthologies, all of which are available on Amazon.

# SEAL OF SOLOMON

## FRED J. LAUVER

Ghosts. Demons. Haunted houses. I never believed in the supernatural. As a historian and archaeologist, it was all nonsense. I laughed at anyone who said a home could become a gateway to evil. Home can be hell for those widowed, but hell is not relevant to science.

Late last year, I lost my wife, Felicity, to cancer. Unbearable grief made it impossible to continue my professional work. I couldn't live in the home we shared with her memory in every corner. So, a year later, in 1935, I began house hunting. My real estate agent pointed me toward a fully furnished mansion at the edge of a small rural town in northern Pennsylvania. Thomas Sechrist, a wealthy timber and mining company owner, built the mansion more than fifty years earlier. Sechrist sold the company, but his son, Joseph, inherited the estate.

Abandoned and up for tax auction, the mansion had been filled by Joseph Sechrist with expensive imported furniture, and he'd made some noticeable improvements but left it all behind. He had disappeared without a trace, declaring no next of kin.

When I first visited the property, expectations were low, and I feared the mansion would be a rundown money pit. But, overall, the mansion's exterior looked to be in good shape and quite majestic, to say the least. As I stood in the yard on a cold, misty spring morning, I looked up at the large windows on the second floor and imagined my desk there, the view I'd have. The agent who had accompanied me on the train from Philadelphia unlocked the door and invited me to tour the interior.

Upon entering the massive home, I thought, if I wrote gothic novels, this would be an appropriate setting. The opulence of the architecture could not be subdued with high ribbed ceilings and arched windows. Inlaid parquet flooring ran through every room with what looked to have some makeup of ebony wood. While inspecting the house, I looked in every corner, crevice, and inglenook, turned all the sink faucets, and flushed all the toilets. In peeking under the white dust covers, I winced at the gaudy furniture; not to my taste, but at least my time would not be wasted selecting new furnishings.

The panorama outside the second-floor study struck me as spectacular—a bucolic landscape with a surrounding forest, and an elevated view of farm fields and the town below. The mansion would be the perfect retreat to write my book, culminating years of archaeological research.

I wanted to know more about the history of the mansion, but I had already fallen in love with the property. My only regret? Felicity and I would never share the new setting. After exiting, I turned for one more glimpse of that second-floor window. I stopped in my tracks. I thought I saw someone, or a shadow, move toward the window and then retreat. The face was indistinguishable, but I knew the realtor had already left. Perhaps, I thought, an illusion of light reflected off the window glass.

---

Joseph Sechrist's disappearance sparked my natural curiosity. At the town's library, I spent hours digging into stacks of the local newspaper back issues archived prior to 1936. Finally, I found an article published nearly ten years ago in which Sechrist announced an open invitation for a special séance.

Then I found an article published three years later and buried next to the classifieds. Sechrist put the mansion up for sale "to anyone foolhardy enough to take on the forces that inhabit the estate."

*Forces that inhabit the estate?*

Briefly, I had second thoughts about the purchase. I was more concerned about the mansion's reputation than about seances, but the bargain price made the property too good to pass up.

The county accepted my lone bid for the tax sale. The estate belonged to me to do as I please. Even if the property proved unsuitable as my new home, I was certain I had the option to resell it for a profit. I conducted one more inspection on my own to make sure I had not missed anything important. All the lights worked and the coal furnace seemed ready for the coming winter. The final walk-through completed, my outlook became optimistic about the start of a new life. As I exited the front door to inquire about telephone service, a local retired minister dropped by. He waved and introduced himself.

"Reverend James Hetrick," he said, shaking my hand and smiling.

"Cyril Walford. Nice to meet you. Would you like to step inside out of the cold air? I have tea in the kitchen."

"No, thank you. I can't stay long. I had to see for myself who would buy this house."

"Is there any reason I should have changed my mind?" I asked.

Hetrick kept looking up at the mansion as he spoke.

"Let's just say many people around here believe the house is haunted."

"Do you?" I asked.

He gave me a curt nod. "Yes, perhaps by evil forces."

My eyes narrowed at him. "I read the old newspaper article about Joseph Sechrist's séance. Did you attend this event?"

"Yes and no. On the night of the séance, I visited the Sechrists. As a man of God, I felt obliged to preach some sense into them, but Sechrist and his wife wouldn't listen to me. He invited me inside, and out of politeness, I stayed for a bit. But once the séance started, I left. I never went back."

"Ah. Well, I hold doctorates in history and Egyptology. Egyptian history may be steeped in the supernatural, but I've found no evidence of its reality. My former teaching colleagues at the University of Pennsylvania, as well as peers at the British Museum, agree when I say, mummies do not walk around after their tombs are opened. Neither do ghosts and other such nonsense."

"Hopefully, you have a belief in God," Hetrick said.

"I lost my wife last year to a brain tumor, so I have little faith in God."

He offered me a smile of pastoral sympathy. "I'm sorry for your loss."

"Thank you." I cleared my throat.

The minister looked up at the mansion once more and shuddered. "I must go, but perhaps we can discuss this in more detail another time."

I sensed his uneasiness and dropped the subject. We said goodbye, but our conversation left me wondering if he knew more about the house.

———

I settled into my new home, eager to resume work on my book. One of the mansion's best features included a substantial study and library. Dark walnut bookshelves built into paneled walls were perfect for my extensive collection of academic books. Annoyingly, it took extra time to remove hundreds of books left behind by Sechrist on such subjects as the supernatural, astrology, and alchemy, which I considered to be medieval gibberish. I stacked them in the greenhouse to burn when I had more time. I splurged on a large wooden desk and the most comfortable desk chair imaginable. I set both right by the large window, as I had envisioned during my first visit to the property.

With the mild scent of a warm fire crackling in the stone fireplace, surrounded by my books, I plopped into an oversized chair and sighed in contentment. I had always dreamed of owning such a study. At last, I'd find solace and consolation from my work.

Of course, I painfully missed Felicity, the love of my life and my research partner of twenty-five years. Whenever the grief stopped me from working, I'd pour myself a drink to ease the heartache. We were unable to have children, but that never diminished our relationship. I missed sharing the daily excitement of archaeological discoveries with her. I would have done anything to bring my wife back, if possible. At the very least, my next book would be dedicated to her memory.

I devoted mornings and evenings after dinner to writing about our discoveries in Egypt's Valley of the Kings. The hours flew by in deep concentration, as I ignored the telephone ringing in the kitchen and knocks on the front door. As a scholar, I prefer the isolation of a stone tower to socializing.

Old mansions are full of strange sounds, especially when the wind blows or the humidity takes a sudden turn. Creaking walls and floorboards, taps on the roof, pipes vibrating in the basement's coal room—nothing unusual. However, I noticed the noises becoming more frequent, even in calm weather.

One evening, an early December storm brought snow and gale-force winds. I went to bed early but woke several times when the wind-driven snow battered the windows. At one point, I thought I heard footsteps on the stairway. Fearing an intruder, I stepped into the hallway and cautiously peered down the stairway. When I turned on a hall light and descended the stairs, a sudden cold draft chilled me but then dissipated. The front door remained securely bolted, and the windows were still locked, so no one could have entered. I thought perhaps the wind had caused a tree branch to thrash against the house, but when I surveyed the outside perimeter the next morning, no trees or shrubbery were close enough to reach.

Fed up with restless nights, I fixed loose boards, secured rattling pipes, and insulated windows to the best of my ability. I uncovered the remaining furniture and cleaned years of dust from all eighteen rooms. To help with the upkeep, I toyed with the idea of establishing a boarding house and hiring someone to manage the operation. The largest local employer had closed its doors during the Depression, so I expected plenty of applicants. Strangely, even though I ran a classified ad in the local newspaper, no one applied.

That week, I stopped at the local minimarket to restock a few staples. As I reached for a can of coffee, part of a conversation between two men in the next aisle caught my attention.

"Sechrist mansion?"

"Are you going to apply for the job?"

I was about to introduce myself and interview the man on the spot, hopeful I had found a candidate. He quickly dashed my optimism.

"No way. I wouldn't step foot in that damned place. The mansion is haunted, I tell you—demons, maybe."

The ignorance of a backward town never failed to stun me.

Putting the guest house idea on hold, I moved on to clean the sixth and final bedroom, which I had saved specifically for last due to it having the least amount of furniture. The room held only a large empty armoire, and the open floor space gave me room to organize my remaining books and store stacks of moving boxes.

Two weeks later, I breathed a sigh of relief. I had almost finished bringing order to chaos. I had separate, neat piles of research papers, tax records, and photographs ready to prioritize and file.

Early the next morning, while shaving in the bathroom, a sudden, loud crash from that same bedroom startled me. My razor jerked and inflicted a nick on my neck. I rushed down the hallway, dabbing drips of blood with a tissue, and flung open the door.

"What the . . ."

My heart felt lodged in my throat. Scattered books and papers covered nearly every square foot of the wooden floor, as though someone had broken in and violently tossed things in all directions. Although I arrived at the room seconds after the noise, there were no vandals in sight. I thought a gust of wind might have blown the papers around, but, no, not to that extent. The bedroom windows were closed. An earthquake perhaps? But that was illogical. The entire mansion would have shaken. It didn't.

I then double-checked all the other windows and outside doors. They were all locked or bolted. I called the county sheriff, James Mc-Master, who, along with his deputy, investigated that afternoon. They checked every corner of the house and found nothing—no forced entry, no footprints outside, not one sign of anyone in the house, except the vandalized room.

"Maybe it was a ghost," the sheriff said when he completed his work.

My incredulous expression reflected back to me from a wall mirror. "What?"

"I'm just kidding," McMaster said. "I've been here before, investigating the disappearance of the Sechrists. I've heard all kinds of strange rumors, but nothing ever pans out."

"Mystery is simply a logical explanation hidden from view," I said.

"Keep your doors and windows locked," he advised. "Call us if anything else happens."

After they left, I didn't entirely dismiss this peculiarity, but I needed to clean up the mess and reorganize. Aggravation overtook my mood because local law enforcement offered little help and my important academic work had been senselessly delayed.

———

The first Christmas after Felicity died, I had no holiday spirit in our previous home. A year later in the mansion, however, I chuckled, imagining her scolding me for being a Scrooge. So, I cut down a small Norway spruce on the property and set up a Christmas tree in the reception parlor to the side of the fireplace. I was grateful I hadn't thrown out the box of Christmas decorations. My wife had lovingly collected the ornaments over our twenty years of marriage. Each keepsake represented a specific year of our marriage, an exotic place we visited, or simply our sentimental endearments of love.

With the tree finally decorated, I played seasonal music, poured myself a spiked eggnog, sat on the sofa, and stared at the tree's twinkling lights and ornaments, waiting for my Christmas spirit to return. Instead, flashbacks of embracing and kissing Felicity on Christmas Eve by the fireplace burned my heart. I raised my glass in a toast to the memory of that sweet woman.

I thought about throwing another log on the fire, but between the fumes from the fireplace and Guy Lombardo's "Winter Wonderland," her favorite holiday song playing on the Victrola Credenza, the moment triggered bitter reminders of the way she suffered at the end. Tears dripped from my eyes.

My grief still affected me more than I thought it would. I had not really gotten past the bitterness in my heart. I gripped my festive holiday drink and tossed it against the mantel. The glass shattered into a hundred pieces. I regretted my impulse instantly.

"I'm sorry, my love. It's just that I miss you so much."

My body stiffened, and I sobered my thoughts. Enough self-torture for one day, I thought. The fireplace burned itself out as I trudged upstairs to the study and buried myself in writing.

———

Later in the evening, after a few hours of uninterrupted writing about my discovery of a previously unknown pharaoh's tomb, a loud clamor jarred me. I rushed downstairs to the parlor and gasped in shock at the sight of the Christmas tree. It lay tipped over on the floor. My heart sank—many of Felicity's sentimental ornaments were smashed to pieces. Cursing between sadness and anger over the next hour, I swept all the broken memories into a dustpan.

I reset the tree, tightened the tree stand screws, and tested the tree for wobbliness. I rehung the surviving ornaments, and the sight of the restored holiday tree reclaimed my optimism, but I didn't want to trigger more depressing thoughts. At that late hour, I decided not to rekindle the cold fireplace and instead return to my study for some reading before bed.

A sudden blast of icy air made me shudder, and I detected the distinct odor of Felicity's favorite perfume, but instead of its sweet, alluring aroma, it smelled rancid. I pressed my nose to some of the cloth ornaments, thinking they had absorbed my wife's scent, but no; the origin remained unknown.

Behind me, what sounded like a voice whispered, "There is danger."

My skin prickled with goosebumps, and I spun around but saw nothing.

Exhaustion can cause sensory hallucinations. I had experienced them before after working long hours in Egyptian burial chambers. Perhaps I consumed too much brandy in the eggnog, combined with a gush of cold air pulled down the chimney—old-fashioned fireplaces are very inefficient. At least that's what I told myself. Tired and chilled, I closed the fireplace vent and went upstairs, ready for my warm bed.

A loud knock startled me from sleep and, for a moment, I wasn't sure if the knock happened in a dream. As I tried to clear my head, the sound of three slow, loud knocks occurred, followed by a pause, then three more knocks. In my drowsiness, I thought the knocks came from the front door, perhaps a lost stranger whose car had broken down on the nearby road.

My feet touched the cold wood floor, then found my slippers. As the grandfather clock in the hallway chimed three a.m., I hurried downstairs and flung open the front door but saw only a light snow dusting on the ground. The frosty cold left my breath visibly hanging in the bone-chilling air as I searched outside for footprints on the walkway leading to the portico steps. There were none.

Again, three loud knocks. Their origin redirected me inside and upstairs to the hallway, where I checked each room until I reached the sixth bedroom.

My hand hesitated on the doorknob before I slowly opened the door. Switching on the overhead light, the bulb flickered and buzzed for a moment before staying lit. No sign of anything unusual. I focused on the nine-foot-tall wooden wardrobe, large enough to hold a bear. Of course, there was no bear—a squirrel or raccoon, perhaps? I opened the armoire's double doors cautiously. Still empty. As I closed the doors, a scratching noise came from behind the armoire.

"Aha, there you are, you little bastard. Hiding behind there, are you?"

At first, I thought the huge armoire would be too heavy to move away from the wall on my own. I listened closely for another few minutes, and although the knocking didn't repeat itself, I couldn't go back to bed without investigating further.

I placed my hands behind one side of the heavy armoire and braced my body against the wall. Sliding from one side to the other, I inched the armoire forward, uncovering years of accumulated dust but no animals. My hand clamped over my mouth, and I gasped in shock. I stepped back, eyes blinking, trying to comprehend the unexpected.

A thick panel of sheet metal hung bolted to the wall. The metal stood about seven feet in height and four feet in width. Even more peculiar, Sechrist must have painted a large ancient symbol on the metal sheet in bright red—the Seal of Solomon, a hexagram symbol of protection that predates most religions. Ancient Egyptians and Greeks believed the seal held powerful magic against evil and demons.

Along the bottom of the metal, Sechrist had written in German, "Warnung! Entferne diesen Schutz nicht vor dem Bösen." It meant, "Warning! Do not remove this protection from evil."

I dismissed the hexagram as a superstitious attempt to scare off robbers, like the warnings carved into the stone around Egyptian tombs. To me, such a warning meant there must be something valuable behind there.

Eighteen fixed bolts protruded from inside the wall through holes drilled along all edges of the metal. Large nuts on each bolt secured the plate and could be removed only from my side of the wall. None of the hand wrenches I tried loosened the nuts. The sledgehammer from among my archaeological tools would be equally useless against quarter-inch-thick steel.

The sun was rising, and nothing more was to be done until I could contact someone for help. After a shower and a substantial breakfast to recover my stamina, I called the only locally advertised jack-of-all-trades.

"Frank Smith, contractor," answered the man at the other end, breathing like a chain smoker with damaged lungs.

"Hello, my name is Cyril Walford. I recently moved into my home just outside of town, and I need help with a minor job."

"How minor?" Smith asked.

"Someone bolted a steel plate to the wall, probably to cover up a hole. I want it removed and the hole patched."

"Steel plate? Where do you live?"

"It's the old Sechrist mansion a couple of miles from town. Are you familiar with—"

Smith's voice became shrill, and he stuttered. "S-Sechrist? I know about that place." His voice hitched. "Let me give you some advice. Just leave that alone. Don't touch it."

The phone line clicked.

"Hello?" I couldn't believe he hung up on me. "Does everyone in this town think this place is haunted?"

While rummaging in my garage and looking for other tools left behind by Sechrist, I discovered an electric impact wrench. This had to be the same tool used to tighten the nuts on the plate. When I tested it, it still worked perfectly and had a reverse switch to loosen rather than tighten nuts.

Although heavy to lift and my arms soon ached, the power wrench removed fourteen nuts, one by one. A stepladder allowed me to reach the nuts along the top of the plate.

"Damn it! Whoever installed this welded the four corner nuts."

I placed a chisel against the nut on the lower right corner and hammered it with maximum force. The weld finally gave after twenty minutes of labor, and the power wrench removed the nut. The lower left one took me more than an hour before the welding cracked. Though I was sweating, the room seemed to get colder. I thought there must be an opening behind the plate that leads outside the house.

My stomach rumbled, and the sun had set. *Damn*—the top two bolts had yet to be removed. Exhausted and hungry, I had no desire to cook dinner.

I cleaned up quickly and drove to the local tavern, hoping to get a hot meal. My exhaustion made me grateful for the small comfort of a warm ambiance. The tavern was empty, thankfully, except for a bartender in his thirties. I wasn't in the mood to chat with inquisitive locals, but I wondered if the bartender had overheard anything about the mansion.

"Can I still get dinner?" I must have sounded like a beggar.

"I can do that for you. Don't believe I've seen you around here before."

"I'm new in town. Cyril Walford."

"Call me Bernie. Where are you living, Mr. Walford?"

"Please, call me Cyril. I bought the old Sechrist mansion—at a bargain I couldn't refuse."

Bernie gave a whistle and raised his brows. "Sechrist mansion, you say? How are you getting along up there?"

"Fine. The house is in good shape, but it needs some minor work and updating."

"Lot of history there. Here's a menu. We're out of fried chicken and salmon, but you can order anything else on the menu."

"Just a hamburger, thanks, with all the trimmings. I'll take whatever beer you have on tap. Then maybe you can tell me what you know about Sechrist."

"You sure you want to hear about it?" Bernie asked.

"Absolutely. I'm very interested."

While I sipped a pint of beer, I pondered why Sechrist had painted that Solomon hexagram on the metal. What was he hiding? Removing the metal plate felt more like an archaeological dig. My muscles experienced the same exhaustion as after a day of excavating an Egyptian tomb. The difference is, in Egypt, the excitement kept my adrenaline going. I dreaded the remaining work at home, but I knew I must discover whatever waited behind that metal seal.

"Here's your burger," Bernie said, waking me from my thoughts.

"Thanks. Have a seat, Bernie, and join me. It's good to have company. Since my wife died of cancer last year, I've been a hermit."

"Sorry for your loss."

I took a ravenous bite of my burger. "Tell me about Sechrist," I said.

"I was young when Sechrist still lived there, but he wasn't friendly. Never saw him smile. And I heard stories."

"Like what?"

"Like debauchery. People coming and going all hours of the day and night. Some claim they witnessed everything from orgies to animal sacrifices. Sechrist collected all kinds of strange objects from around the world and used them in his seances."

"Imaginations can get away from people when they don't have the facts."

"Maybe, but too many levelheaded people I know insisted the stories are true. The scariest story? A friend told me that Sechrist's wife had some kind of sixth sense, but then a demon possessed her. It's pretty dangerous to mess around with evil like that, if you ask me. God didn't intend for us to tempt the devil."

I took a sip of beer. "Any witnesses I can talk to?"

"There's a retired minister living in town, Reverend Hetrick."

"I already met him. But he had little to say about the place."

"I think he knows a lot more," Bernie said.

"What happened to Sechrist?"

Bernie shook his head. "Nobody knows. He disappeared. The strange thing is, his wife disappeared about six months before he left town. She used to volunteer at the library and at church social events, but she stopped showing up. When the Reverend Hetrick inquired about the woman, Sechrist told him Mrs. Sechrist left on vacation to visit relatives. If you ask me, the guy killed his wife. There were rumors he physically abused her."

"Maybe they separated," I said. My hand shook as I wiped my mouth after finishing the last bite of food. I then downed the rest of my beer, grateful for the slight intoxication. The thought of murder in my house unnerved me.

Bernie shrugged then stood and collected my dirty dishes. "If that's everything, it's almost closing time. I must get home to the wife and kids."

My hunger satisfied and beer in my bloodstream, Bernie and I said our goodbyes. The tavern door locked behind me as I stared up at a full moon. Momentarily, I doubted my sanity for moving there. The distractions were far worse than they had been in Philadelphia. I shuddered in the night chill and returned home.

———

Sleep was out of the question, being so close to unveiling that seal. I strained and pushed the armoire farther away to give me more room to work. Using the stepladder, I climbed to reach the last two bolts on the plate. The moment I cracked the seal and removed the first bolt, the freed edge of the plate slipped off the bolt and swung down like Poe's pendulum. It gouged the wooden floor with a loud thud.

"Damn it!"

I moved the ladder to the other side, climbed up, and removed the final nut holding the plate. The heavy metal unexpectedly slipped off the end of the bolt, knocking the ladder out from under me. Within a split second, the plate crashed to the floor with a deafening sound, followed by the ladder, and me falling hard on top of the ladder and metal plate. My wrist and entire right side throbbed. I lay there and moaned until the pain subsided, hoping my ribs were not fractured.

Looking up from the floor, I expected to see a hole in the wall. To be honest, I would have been disappointed to find a simple hole after all that work. Instead, I saw an ordinary white door, but with a large Egyptian apotropaic symbol painted in green on it—the Eye of Horus—an additional warning.

My intense curiosity became the anesthetic to forget my painful fall. I stood and tried the doorknob, but it was locked. Disappointed, I grabbed a small chisel and hammered the top and bottom door hinge pins, which moved easily enough to be removed.

I tapped on the middle hinge several times. Without warning, the door literally exploded into pieces—as though an invisible force crashed through that door and slammed me against the back of the armoire. There was no booby trap or explosive device, but a powerful, unexplained force finally broke free.

I groaned from the additional pain and picked wooden door shards off my chest and legs. A trickle of blood ran from my nose, which I dabbed with my sleeve. My wrist hurt so badly that I must have suffered a sprain. As the air inside gushed from the opened doorway, my nostrils were assailed by foul odors reminiscent of rotting flesh and the raw sewage canals of Cambodia. My stomach churned in disgust, and I wondered if I had opened some kind of Pandora's box.

After regaining my full senses, I stood and peered into the darkness. Grabbing my portable work light, I cautiously stepped through the doorway, hoping for no more painful surprises. While the foul odor subsided, the air inside smelled as musty as an Egyptian burial chamber.

The work light illuminated a room nearly as large as the downstairs reception parlor. In the center of the room sat an artifact, like a museum display, on a marble table. I immediately recognized its shape—an Egyptian canopic jar. They were used during the embalming process to store vital organs of the deceased before mummification. Everything, admittedly, was bizarre, but the canopic jar stood as an incredibly strange sight on its own. Sechrist must have traveled to obtain this Egyptian artifact, and my only guess—he didn't want it found in his possession. Stolen artifacts often turn up in the estates of private owners, purchased on the black market or taken from the spoils of war.

Brushing off layers of dust with my hand, I studied the inscription and translated the hieroglyphs.

*Herein lies the heart and soul of Ra, ruler of Egypt, Usermaatre Setepenre, son of Seti. Cursed for eternity, may he never walk among us again.*

Son of Seti? The one the Greeks called Ozymandias? The most powerful and ruthless of all the pharaohs—Ramesses II? Many religious scholars claim Ramesses II oppressed the Israelites during the time of Moses.

During mummification, the livers, lungs, stomachs, and intestines of early pharaohs were placed in separate canopic jars. Embalmers left hearts in bodies because they believed the soul and mind resided in the heart and were needed in the afterlife. In all my years of study and research, never had I ever come across a canopic jar for a heart.

The top of the jar cap had the unique likeness of the Egyptian demoness Ammit, a goddess with the head of a crocodile. If Ammit judged the deceased in the afterlife as impure, she devoured the heart. However, the symbolism of Ramesses's heart in the jar suggested something cultlike—as though intended to deny Ammit's justice. The cap had been taped shut, so I removed the seal, set the lid aside, and peered into the dark interior.

Chaotic thoughts swirled in my head, but my eyes were drawn to the red brick walls, which were covered with painted hieroglyphs. Most were prayers to the gods of Egypt, invoking power and worship of Ramesses. Contemporary satanic symbols were also painted between hieroglyphs as though representing the battle of evil against the forces of protection. This had to be the séance room Sechrist hid from prying eyes.

In a back corner of the room, more recent masonry work looked to have bricked up a ventilation duct. Did Sechrist hide more stolen treasure?

I left the room, grabbed the sledgehammer, and quickly returned. After what I'd been through, an impulse surged in me to smash the canopic jar.

A soft feminine voice whispered, "Destroy it."

I held the hammer above the jar, but I could not bring myself to commit such an act of scientific sacrilege.

Gripping the handle firmly, my arms swung the heavy hammer into the brickwork, sending chips of stone flying. I ignored the pain in my wrist and swung the tool again as hard as I could. Five swings later, the bricks collapsed in a cloud of dust and noise. A new hellish horror occurred, much worse than imaginable.

A mummified body of a woman dropped out and fell on top of me, knocking me to the floor and filling my lungs with its deathly dust. I choked and yelled in terror as I pushed the corpse off me. Half expecting the cadaver to wake, I instinctively slid away. She didn't move. Someone had gone to a lot of trouble to hide the body with the expectation no one would find it for a very long time.

As I leaned in to inspect the body, from the corner of my eye, the movement of a shadow caught my attention. Terror can induce dizziness, causing a person to see black spots, but it wasn't a hallucination in my vision. An entity grew larger and larger from the area of the artifact. Its dark mass took shape—legs, arms, head, a formless face but with two glowing red-hot coals for eyes. Sliding back on the floor, I connected with the wall, a scream lodged, paralyzed in my throat—the path to escape blocked by an eight-foot-tall being.

All my beliefs about the supernatural were snuffed in that moment. Fear, not intellect, took control of my brain. All sounds drowned out by thunderous heartbeats in my ears. The entity turned its eyes and looked directly at me.

"You can't exist," I screamed but was no longer able to deny what I witnessed. Its mouth formed and bared jagged, terrible teeth able to rip flesh from me in an instant. Before I could react, the entity charged and passed straight through me. My lungs gasped for air, and I thought my life was being ripped from my body. In that moment, I stared into the abyss of eternity. Visions of the ancient Egyptian empire at the peak of glory flashed before me. At the same time, I glimpsed at pure evil, but it made me feel powerful, as though seeing through the eyes of a pharaoh.

I regained my physical senses, but the work light was off. I couldn't see the creature, so I bolted for the dim light of the open doorway. My foot tripped on the sledgehammer, and my head collided with the door frame. Everything went black.

How long I lay unconscious I had no idea, but as I woke, I felt a hand gently touch my cheek. Someone had found me. The smiling face of my dead wife looked down at me.

My eyes blinked in response to the stars that shimmered around her. I needed to see her clearer. But the moment my eyes reopened, she had disappeared. Felicity, my Felicity. Had she been here with me the whole time? I wanted to believe more than anything that those odd occurrences during my time in the mansion were her trying to warn me.

———

The body, according to the state police, was that of the missing Camila Sechrist. They found her husband, Joseph, however, very much alive and self-exiled to Brazil, where authorities agreed to arrest and extradite him to face murder charges.

Keeping the artifact risked my academic reputation, but I needed to confirm its antiquity. I contacted a colleague, a professor at the University of Pennsylvania, who discreetly agreed to examine the artifact. Not surprisingly, he authenticated the object. We agreed to send it to the Egyptian Museum of Cairo.

Although there were no further paranormal incidents noted, the Egyptians reacted strangely to the artifact. A curator friend in Cairo claimed the museum's director placed the jar under military guard; sealed it in a lead container; and moved it to a secret vault without notifying the press.

———

As Reverend Hetrick sat in my study drinking tea, I told him everything that happened. My admission loosened his grip on the rest of the story. He had known all along that Joseph Sechrist had purchased the artifact on the black market.

"When we last spoke, I implied I didn't stay long at the séance, but that's not true, and I apologize. I stayed because I believe evil must be confronted directly. The canopic jar of Ramesses II was central to their séance," he said. "The Sechrists believed it gave them the power to communicate with the dead. Camila consecrated a chalice with pagan spells and added something from inside the jar."

"If there had been the heart of a pharaoh in that jar, it would have turned to dust after thousands of years," I said.

"That's all she needed for her necromancy," Hetrick said. "She sprinkled a little of the dust into a glass of red wine and drank it. Whether or not you believe in spirits, all I know is what I witnessed." He had a painful expression, as though reliving the séance.

"What happened next?" I asked.

Hetrick took a deep breath. "Camila's eyes turned white and her voice changed to a deep, raspy, rumbling tone that was instantly bone-chilling. Then her eyes turned black, and the demonic voice became mocking, saying, 'Did you think you can stop evil, Reverend? Your god is nothing compared to my power.'"

"Perhaps the dust she ingested contained some toxin that caused her to sound crazy."

He looked at me skeptically and said, "Do you really believe that? After what you have witnessed in this house? I saw for myself. I know the difference between mental illness and a woman possessed by a demon. Camila was never the same after that."

"Did you know Sechrist murdered his wife?" I asked.

"Heavens no. I had no idea. I would have gone to the police. I will forever regret not going back. I could have tried harder to save Camila. After she disappeared, Joseph stopped talking to me."

"The coroner said she was still alive when Sechrist sealed her behind the bricks."

Hetrick shook his head. "How awful."

"I didn't know what to do with that steel plate. Workers dragged it into the hidden room and then walled off that doorway permanently."

"You're keeping the plate—with that symbol on it?"

"What else can I do? It's not something you can burn or set out for rubbish removal."

"I suppose," Hetrick replied. "I pray it never becomes a magnet for other spirits, but I'll leave that matter to you."

After the minister left, I sat at my desk, unlocked a desk drawer, and removed a few items to place atop my desk. A chalice found hidden behind the brick wall—the same chalice that Camila Sechrist used in her necromancy ritual. I also discovered her husband's detailed journal that revealed how the seances were conducted.

I picked up a small wooden art-carved box and slowly opened the lid. Wrapped in a small cloth were several grams of decomposition dust collected from inside the canopic jar.

My bitter loneliness had caught up to me. If only I could speak with my late wife. I poured a glass of red wine, took a sip, and stared at the ancient dust in the open cloth. One pinch sprinkled into the wine. With the artifact gone, what could be the harm?

**Fred J. Lauver** is the author of the sci-fi novella *Olympus* and the novel *Aziza and the Caves of Mars* (fall 2022). He is a former feature writer and assistant editor of the award-winning *Pennsylvania Heritage* magazine, co-author of *The Pennsylvania Trail of History Cookbook*, and writer and editor for several Pennsylvania history books. His short stories include, "Pink Roses," in *Miraculous Encounters* by Michele Livingston, and "Whispering Angel" in *Bitter Sweet*, an anthology from Sunbury Press, edited by Catherine Jordan. A Vietnam-era veteran, the US Air Force awarded him a medal for meritorious service. He has professional acting credits and enjoys studying family history and languages. Lauver resides in Pennsylvania and was married to writer, artist, and teacher Carol Lauver, who died in April 2022; their daughter Amy is also a novelist and professional artist. He has two other daughters, Rochelle and Eyvette, who reside in Colorado.

**Author Website:** https://fredjlauver.com/

**Social Media Handles:**
Facebook: @AuthorFredJLauver
Twitter: @FredLauver
TikTok: @writeroftomes3
Instagram: @authorfredjlauver/
YouTube: https://www.youtube.com/channel/UCDWChEvYbViydET-112UC7Q
Amazon Author Page (US): https://amzn.to/3anRusN

# FUNERAL PYRE

## CAROL A. LAUVER

Shanty feared two things in her young life: flood and fire.

When the Mississippi River overflowed, death and property damage followed. The flood left tree branches and belongings along the embankment, and the smell of rot wafted through town. Unexplained fires struck the houses in her neighborhood. The uncertainty of fire and flood made her anxious. Today's walk along the calm river reassured her. She was safe, for now.

But that was a false assurance. The horn bellowed an alarm from the local fire station. "No," she whispered, turned toward her house, then stumbled and fell facedown in a pile of rotting trash. "Crap!" she shouted, revolted by the stench. She brushed away the dirt from her face, spit on the ground, and fled up the hill, screaming in terror. "No, it can't be! You promised!" Flames danced and licked the roof of her one-story clapboard house. Shanty fought through the heat and ash and threw open the front door. "Mama! MeMaw! Get out! The house is on fire!"

Frantic, Shanty ran to the stand of trees at the back of the property. She pounded Mother Tree's trunk, bloodying her clenched fists. "You promised our safety. You vowed no harm would come to Mama and MeMaw and our house. You betrayed me. I hope the flames destroy you and your sisters. I hate you!"

Mother Tree knocked the lean bronze teenager to the ground with twisted branches, an attack Shanty believed to be a punishment for her insolence. The blow rendered her unconscious. Gnarly roots imprisoned her like a caged animal.

Mother Tree, in unison with her sister trees, sent an electrically charged message to Shanty's subconscious. "Learn the truth of our history and what we witnessed long ago. This will set you and your town free. Your mission is to tell the story. Do not fail."

On the edge of consciousness, she heard Mama and MeMaw coughing and crying. Black tears stained their cheeks. "Where are you, Shanty?"

They found her entangled body in the roots blanketed with moss. "There you are, our precious girl." She felt the earth move as they dug with their bare hands, both grunting as they frantically tore their nails to rip at the roots, their wrists and forearms bloodied with effort. They freed her from the grips of the tree and carried her unresponsive body to a lounge chair.

Mama raised Shanty's legs, grabbed a hand towel off the clothesline, and wet it with the outside spigot. She placed the wet cloth on Shanty's bruised and swollen forehead. "Wake up, Shanty dear. Please, God, we pray, restore our child."

Shanty's eyes fluttered, and a moan escaped her lips. "What happened?" She touched her throbbing head.

Tears flooded Mama's eyes. "You don't remember? We heard you calling for us to get out of the house. We found you out back." Mama turned to the smoldering home. Fire truck lights flashed as men gathered in the small driveway, gesturing and talking to each other. "The fire stopped and did little damage."

"Mama, don't believe for a second we're safe. Mother Tree broke her promise to keep us from harm. Maybe the destruction of our house would free us from Mother Tree forever. I see it in your eyes—you know I'm right!"

"Stop that Mother Tree talk right now. I'm sick of hearing that nonsense."

---

Shanty's headache persisted into the next day. Maybe it was from the remaining smoke smell, or maybe the inhalation. Maybe it was stress from her ordeal. Dreams of terror consumed her—pummeling fists, blood, knives, twisted ropes, screams. She couldn't purge the horror from her mind. Shanty placed a pillow over her ears to muffle the shrieking sound and sobbed.

Mama burst into Shanty's bedroom, a worried look on her face. She leaned over Shanty and put a cool hand on her forehead. "What's happening? Are you in pain?"

"Yes," Shanty said with a whine.

MeMaw entered behind Mama and then sat on the bed. She cradled Shanty's head in her lap.

Shanty wiped her nose with her sleeve. "I don't understand why nightmares replay in my head. I feel like I'm losing my mind." She told them about the haunting images. Mama and MeMaw hugged Shanty, as if to shield her from the past.

— · —

Shanty's fragile emotional state prevented her from returning to class on Monday. Mama called the school's guidance counselor, Mrs. Turner, who recommended Shanty meet with a therapist.

"Shanty," Mama said, "Dr. Parton can meet you this evening."

Shanty sighed, hopeful.

The knock on the door came right after dinner. Dr. Parton, a tall, thin, middle-aged man, greeted them with pleasantries. The setting sun bathed the kitchen in an orange glow. Collard greens and bacon still lent their fragrance to the air. Shanty chose her cushioned chair at the cleaned dinner table, across from Dr. Parton. MeMaw sat, then Mama. Mama put a hand on Shanty's bouncing knee, gripping her kneecap until she stopped.

Dr. Parton spoke first. "It's okay if you're feeling apprehensive. You'll be comfortable once we get started. Your mother filled me in on the details of your experience." Dr. Parton clicked his pen, ready to write.

Shanty licked her dry lips, took a sip of water, then nodded. "Go ahead, I'm ready."

"Do you recall when you first heard the cries of women and children?"

She answered in a whisper, "Yesterday."

Dr. Parton's pen scribbled on his tablet, probably writing Shanty's response. "What visions did you see?"

"I saw a grove of oak trees, hanging ropes, bare feet dangling, and unrecognizable faces of men, women, and children." Shanty held her head in her hands, eyes clouding with tears. "It's so painful to remember."

"I understand," said Parton. He placed a box of tissues on the table and handed her one. Then he went back to his writing. "Did someone ever harm or restrain you with ropes?"

Shanty blew her nose, then bit her lip and shook her head. "No"

"Do you fear for your life? Is someone threatening to do you bodily harm?"

Shanty blinked away tears and reached for another tissue. Rocking slightly, she whispered, "Mother Tree and her sisters."

His brow wrinkled. "You said Mother Tree and her sisters will harm you? Who are they?"

Shanty shifted in her seat. "Dr. Parton, look out the window. See the giant oak in the yard? The sister trees are on each side of Mother Tree."

He nodded in affirmation. "How can they harm you? Can you be more specific?"

She sighed. "Sometimes, the breeze blows gently and sweetly. Mother Tree hugs me with her low hanging-branches. When she's angry, the wind blows swiftly. I'm swatted and scratched by her branches. I know I must obey. And that time during the fire, she and her sisters wreaked such havoc they gave me a concussion. And nightmares. Their roots caged me like a prisoner." Shanty's lip curled as she glanced from her mama to her memaw. She looked the doctor in the eye. "Mama and MeMaw saved me from their cruel punishment."

Parton scratched his stubbly chin. "Anything else you fear?"

Shanty stiffened her back. Her body trembled as she covered her mouth with her hand. "Mother Tree and her sisters caused the fires on this side of town. There's no way to stop them. The fire department tried, but the trees are too powerful."

"When did your relationship with Mother Tree begin?"

Shanty blinked, thinking back, trying to remember. It had been a long time, that's for sure. But what did he mean by 'relationship'? As in, good or bad?

Shanty nodded with certainty. "Since I can remember."

Dr. Parton cocked his head. He didn't seem to like her answer.

"Did you tell your mama or memaw about Mother Tree?"

"Yes," Shanty said. "They know she and her sisters are powerful. Mother Tree commanded I do something, but I can't remember what. I worry that my punishment will be worse if I can't remember and follow her orders." Shanty pleaded, "Will you help me?"

The doctor pressed his lips together. "What do you know of hypnosis?" Mama and MeMaw both shook their heads.

He explained the unorthodox treatment to all three. "Hypnosis may be the remedy for releasing Shanty's subconscious and uncovering her lost memory. So, are you ready to begin? We can do this right now."

Mama cleared her throat. "Could Shanty get stuck in this hypnotic state? I don't want anything terrible to happen to her."

Dr. Parton shook his head. "Let me reassure you and Shanty—she will be safe." He turned to Shanty. "Relax and breathe slowly. Follow my eyes and listen to my voice." After repeating this several times, Shanty felt her head drop. It was like being half-awake and half-asleep. She heard the doctor, remained aware of her place at the kitchen table, but didn't feel the seat underneath her and felt all her inhibitions drain.

"Nod if you remember the day of the fire at your house," said the doctor. "You ran to Mother Tree, then what happened?"

Shanty nodded her heavy head. She suddenly screamed. "I hate you!" She beat the table with her fists, her body twisted, and she cried in a spasm of back-jerking pain. Moments later, her demeanor changed, and she relaxed her back and shoulders, her voice now composed. "Yes, I will learn what happened and tell your story. The truth will set us free and our neighborhood will be safe from fire."

Dr. Parton's calm voice brought her back to the present. "You will remember what Mother Tree and her sisters told you and follow their instructions."

Shanty nodded, "I will."

He snapped his fingers, and Shanty awoke.

———

The next day, Shanty returned to school and asked Mrs. Turner to help her set up a visit to the county's genealogical society for Saturday morning. Mrs. Turner first said no. "I'm skeptical, Shanty. And you've been through quite a trauma. I wouldn't want this experience to trigger any negative emotions from you."

Shanty insisted she could handle viewing the material. "I need to do this, Mrs. Turner. My doctor said it would be like therapy."

Saturday, the curator brought out historical photographs and documents from Mount Pyre during the Jim Crow Era.

Shanty gasped when she came to one particular photo. Her voice quivered. "Look, Mrs. Turner, this is my house. There's Mother Tree and her sisters. She's surrounded by a mob of men. A black man hangs by the neck from one of her branches. The caption . . . It explains that the trees were known as lynching trees. All these photos are similar and show bodies hanging, some set on fire. Now I understand why Mother Tree demanded I learn about the history of our town—dark and evil. The town is being punished for the sins of its past. Mother Tree chose me to tell the story."

That evening, rain pelted the windshield during the bus ride back home. The bus driver turned up his radio, and urgent radio voices warned about severe weather. Shanty silently prayed for a change in the forecast, and for guidance from Mother Tree.

During rainfalls, Shanty liked taking walks to the river to check the rising water, always fearful of another flood. Today was no exception. Waves slapped the banks of the waterway. Branches and trash swirled downstream. Her stomach churned in unison with the turbulent water. Shanty's imagination went wild with what-ifs. She feared her town would be leveled. Where would she live? How would her family survive without work? Would her school still be standing? What about her classmates and teachers?

When she returned home, Mama and MeMaw busied themselves moving sentimental possessions to the attic. Shanty removed her dripping raincoat, then ran up the narrow staircase to help.

"Is the river at flood stage?" MeMaw asked breathlessly.

"Getting close, MeMaw." Shanty reached for Bubble Wrap. "Let me help. You're doing too much. You are more important than these vases."

"Shanty." Mama's voice sounded on edge. "We're leaving. We have to evacuate."

"Oh," Shanty said, pausing. She squeezed the Bubble Wrap, popping the plastic. "I'm scared." Shanty's voice trembled.

Mama held her close. "Honey, we're together and safe for now. That's all that matters. This isn't the first time we've had to evacuate, and it won't be the last. You know that river can be unpredictable and violent."

"Mama, what if this time we don't make it out alive?" Crying and overwhelmed with uncertainty, Shanty ran back down the stairs and out the back door. She had to say goodbye to Mother Tree and her sisters before she left.

Dwarfed under the oak trees, their leaves dripping, Shanty said, "I know we're in for another flood. It looks bad. I'm not sure if I'll be back. I'll do everything in my power to tell the world your story." As she spoke, Shanty licked her salty tears mixed with rain.

She ran back to the house and helped her family pack up the rusted Dodge Charger. No matter how many times they evacuated, every time was traumatic.

"Goodbye, house. Please be here when we get back."

Shanty wept silently in the back seat while Mama drove to Mt. Pyre High School. Everyone from the town took refuge in the warm, crowded gymnasium. Babies cried and children ran around the cots playing tag. Parents, frazzled by the uncertainty of the situation, found a sense of community. The cooks from the cafeteria served fried chicken, corn, collard greens, and biscuits to the hungry crowd.

Mama's cell phone rang with an invitation to stay at Cousin Ruby's house. Mama said she'd think it over. "I'll let her know my decision in the morning."

The patched roof of the gym sunk beneath the deluge. It began to leak. A thunderous crack of what sounded like thunder exploded through the room as the roof opened, dumping water and debris; it could no longer hold back the steady downpour. Rain soaked everyone and everything. The water flooded the worn wooden floorboards and traveled along the hallways like a broken dam surging into the classrooms. Moans turned into cheers as school buses arrived in front of the double doors. Someone—she heard it had been the school principal—had quickly arranged bus transportation to move the evacuees to the next town.

Mama put a hand on Shanty's shoulder as she was about to step on the bus.

"Mama, why aren't we gettin' on?" Shanty looked at Mama and Me-Maw for an answer, her stomach knotting. "Don't you think we'll be safer on the bus than in your car?"

"Oh, hush now. I know what I'm doing," said Mama. "We can get to Cousin Ruby's faster than that old bus can get to wherever it's going."

MeMaw agreed. "Listen to your mama. She knows best."

Shanty bit her lip but couldn't hold back. "Mama, the roads are flooded and it's dark now. Please listen to me. The house, the trees— we've left it all behind and Mother might think I failed. I'm terrified something terrible will happen!"

"Child, nothin's gonna happen," said Mama. "Don't let your imagination run wild. We'll all be safe, I promise. I've just as much experience drivin' in floodwaters as that bus driver. Now get in the car and not another word."

Shanty obeyed reluctantly, not wanting to anger Mama.

Mama pulled out ahead of the bus. Once on the slick roads, she drove slowly for several miles, taking care as they splashed through water before crossing the rickety train tracks. The waterlogged roads and the heavy rain made it difficult to see debris strewn in their path. Mama turned to check on Shanty, who was writing in her diary. They hit a downed tree head-on, crumpling the car like a foil ball, killing everyone instantly.

———

Cousin Ruby's calls to Mama went unanswered. Before dawn, the Mississippi River overflowed its banks, scooping everything in its path downstream. Their vehicle, covered in muddy water, rocked furiously in the turbulent water. A rescue crew discovered their metallic coffin a week later.

The funeral director, overwhelmed by the number of dead, lagged weeks behind preparing the bodies of Shanty, Mama, and MeMaw. The funeral was held in their family church, close to where the accident took place. Mrs. Turner and Cousin Ruby chose personal items with special meaning for each of the deceased. They placed Shanty's pink journal, found among the wreckage, and her high school picture on a table next to her closed coffin. The journal was flipped open for everyone to see the last entry made about the lynching trees.

**Carol A. Lauver** was a writer, artist, and kindergarten teacher. Her previously published short stories include, "The Surprise Party" in *A Community of Writers*, and "Missing" in *Bitter Sweet*, both from Sunbury Press. She studied ballet at the Metropolitan Ballet Co., occasionally acted, and loved to cook. Carol attributed her love of the arts to living in New York City during her formative years. Lauver resided in Pennsylvania with her husband, Fred, an author and actor; daughter, Amy, also a novelist and professional artist; and their cat, CJ. Carol passed away on April 12, 2022.

# ROOM 333

## LORI M. MYERS

anuary's icy cold sent a chill through Jordy; the frozen air cut through him like a knife. His entire body trembled as he stared at the rickety building only a few yards in front of him, the schoolhouse—a place that appeared time and time again in his dreams—no, nightmares.

"You okay?" Pam asked.

Jordy scanned the dilapidated structure and looked up at the window where he remembered the nurse's office to be, its glass pane bubbled and jagged against the darkened interior.

"I'm good," he said.

"You can do this. You've worked so hard to get to this point."

Pam's reassuring voice, now padded with care and sympathy, brought him here and now. As he felt her arm thread through his, he realized that good times weren't strangers as much as they used to be. While he knew what Pam said to be true, he began to suddenly have doubts. Jordy thought he was ready, after weeks of emotional and intellectual pep talks to himself in the bathroom mirror. Confidence surged through him during the plane ride from the West Coast to the East, but the terror wasn't as real at 40,000 feet as it was now that Ligonia Village Elementary loomed in front of him.

His old grammar school stood amid chunks of brick and stone that lay on the ground alongside strewn garbage. Scraggly moss and ivy choked through and around the open crevices up to the roof. A broken seesaw lay on its side in the playground and a swing, dangling on one rusty chain, creaked in the breeze. The slide, which had always terrified

Jordy, was cracked and moldy. The decay was real after forty years of abandonment.

"Let's turn around and go back home." His breath hovered in the icy air like a ghost. Wrapping his arms around his chest, he squeezed tightly and begged his legs to run to escape.

Pam reached for Jordy's face and placed a hand on his cheek. He looked down at the snow on the ground, now a sheet of ice after weeks of lingering cold and no fresh cover. "Jordy, we're friends. I've been with you on this journey. You know that, right?"

He nodded, feeling like some sort of five-year-old who was admitting a wrong.

"What did the therapist tell you? Do you remember?"

"He said it's all about confronting my fears."

"And . . ."

"And that returning to my old school as a stronger person, as an adult, would prove those fears were unfounded."

"And . . ."

"And I need an answer to move on."

"You'll come out of that place, and we'll go grab a pizza. Of course, it'll be a miracle if there's a pizza joint in this ghost town much less any other breathing humans."

She turned him toward the building and gave him a gentle nudge. "Now go on in. I'm getting hungry. Room 333."

It was a needless reminder. This place and that room had haunted all his days. Jordy stepped forward and then turned around. "You'll be out here, right?"

"I'm not going anywhere. I won't move from this spot. Promise. Cross my heart and hope to die." She giggled, a staccato sort of laugh that began in the back of her throat and landed outward at a high pitch. Hearing it, Jordy took a step back as if by reflex. The sound filled him with dread. But it was Pam. Only Pam.

He had no choice but to pass through the playground to get to the entrance. The short distance of a few yards felt like ten miles. Memories, once distant, now too real, made his heart race. His body stiffened; every muscle ached as he balanced on the slick ice.

*C'mon, Jordy Pordy. Let's see ya crash down the slide!*

That voice. An emptiness gnawed at Jordy's stomach. He swore he just heard the childish voice of an old schoolmate call out to him. It sounded so close. Too close.

Jordy thought he had heard Simon, a kid whose flabs of baby fat and clusters of freckles all over his face had belied his demonic side. He had taken pleasure in taunting Jordy every single day because of his scrawny body and childhood anxieties; goading him to go down the side, he teased him to the point that there was no choice but to climb up the ladder despite Jordy's debilitating fear of heights. One time, his insides hurt so bad that he threw up his lunch and watched in horror as it slithered down the plastic surface. His teacher, Mrs. Van Nostrand, had to call the janitor, old Mr. Ferguson, to clean it up. Jordy never heard the end of that. He shuddered at the memory of the relentless bullying and name-calling, the snickers behind his back, the shoves, the bruises he came home with every afternoon and tried to cover up. But that was not the worst of it. He saw things inside that school, heard things, things that no one else saw or heard, things that followed him clear across the country and yearning for a fresh start.

At age forty, Jordy saw the inside of a therapist's office for the first time. For ten years, he sat on the same sofa, in front of the same Dr. Stenson, struggling to silence the voices from his past with his doctor's words. "It's just a building, Jordy," Dr. Stenson said. "Your tormentors are done. The nurse is gone. But you're here. You."

The building cast a grim shadow as he walked up the front steps. The wind almost knocked him off his feet, as if something unseen expected his return. A queasy pit in his stomach consumed him. He retched, tasting a mass of the oatmeal and berries he'd had that morning, which rose up the back of his throat and settled there. Several bits dripped out of his mouth and onto the concrete.

Jordy scanned the graffiti covering the front doors for a sign of warning, but in finding none, he placed his hands on the cold door handle and pulled. The moment he entered the building, it was as though the structure came alive like a threatening beast roused from a decades-long sleep, swallowing Jordy up as he shuffled deeper into the school's belly. To

Jordy, it seemed the narrow hallways groaned and swayed in an effort to crush him. Even the ceiling buckled above his head, threatening to crash down on top of him, trapping him forever inside.

He breathed in and nearly choked on the smell of the musty air that permeated the building. Bad memories once more stirred in his mind at the familiar scent of the school, which had become more intense over the years.

Jordy jumped at a skittering sound on his right, and he tried to convince himself that it was only a squirrel. He quickened his pace down the hallway, chased by the haunted sounds of the cold wind screaming through broken windowpanes and dripping water that endlessly echoed through the hallways.

Jordy glanced inside the classrooms as he walked by. Faded books, notebooks, and dried-up art supplies were all over the floors, and the desks—those old types connected to the seats—were overturned as if someone left in a hurry.

Faded sunlight trickled through the stairwell's picture window as Jordy climbed up to the second floor. Loose linoleum tiles slid beneath his steps as he ascended the stairs, and he kicked aside pieces of broken plaster littering his path. In the dimness, he could make out the tiny pawprints of rodents throughout the age-old dust that had settled on every surface like a magnet.

Jordy, out of breath, paused halfway up the stairs. He didn't know if he was out of breath from inhaling the grittiness and dust covering his shoes and clothing or from the panic that brewed in his chest.

"There is nothing to fear. There is nothing to fear," he told himself as he willed his legs to continue the ascent. For a moment, he believed there was nothing to fear until the sound of a soft whimper that seemed to descend from the floor above crescendoed to a yowl like that of an animal being attacked by a predator. Jordy's pulse thundered in his ears, and he thought of Pam. He reached the first landing and peeked out of a broken window to look for her.

Below, Pam walked in a circle in front of the black rental car, jacket bundled tightly and red scarf wrapped around her neck. Jordy nearly called out to her but held back as he didn't want to draw any unwanted attention to her from whatever or whoever screamed. Not knowing what made the sound and the thought of his friend waiting outside in near-freezing temperatures sparked his motivation to continue to the second floor.

A door hinge squealed as Jordy pushed the door to the second floor open, and the crescendoed scream came again, much closer this time.

"Hello? Are you all right?" He clamped a hand over his mouth. His anxiety shot up at the thought of someone else being in the building, possibly injured.

"Do you need help?"

*Yes. Help me.*

Jordy swallowed hard against the fresh tears coming to his eyes. The voice was closer now and so familiar. A voice that haunted his nightmares. The urgency of the pleas made his heart pound against his ribs.

Jordy stepped back into the stairwell and looked up to the next floor. "Where are you?"

*Up here. Help me. Room 333.*

The mention of the room paralyzed him. Of all the rooms that the child had to be in, it had to be *that* room.

*Please, I need you.*

"I'm coming."

Jordy tempered his fear and continued up the stairs with a focus on the door at the uppermost landing. Nearly to the top, debris tripped him to his knees. Jordy brushed off the dust and ignored the small rip on his pant leg and the trickle of blood forming on the scraped skin.

At the end of the dark hallway, a bright ceiling light beckoned him forward. Jordy walked toward the closed door underneath the light, knowing, even without seeing the familiar numbers painted on the wavy glass window of the door, that it was Room 333.

*Help me.*

A distorted shadow passed back and forth in front of the window on the other side of the door.

*Go in. Please. Now!*

Jordy hesitated in front of the door as the air around him thickened, suffocating him. The door opened and the air thinned as an invisible force from behind pushed him inside.

A freckled and flabby boy sat at a desk, facing him.

"C'mon, Jordy Pordy. You had too much fun on the playground today."

"Someone needed help." The words were out of Jordy's mouth without him realizing he said them, though saying 'someone' felt wrong.

"Yes, Jordy Pordy," the child said. "Someone does need help. That's why you're here."

"I must get back to class. I don't belong here," Jordy said.

"Ha. I love livin' inside that brain of yours. It's sooooooo interestin'.

"What . . . ?"

"It's time. The nurse will come out and see you now, Jordy. She's puttin' you at the front of the line."

Jordy looked around the reception area. There were a few folding chairs against the wall and little else.

He was the only one waiting. Simon disappeared.

Something clicked and creaked. The office door opened, and a woman wearing one of those white, old-timey nurse's uniform and cap came in. A hint of something red peeked from a pocket.

"It's cold," Jordy whispered as the temperature of the room dropped.

"Oh, you're here again, Jordy. Not a day goes by, does it? Not a day." She lifted a syringe filled with brown liquid then clicked her index finger against it. "That'll do it."

He ran to the window and pressed his face against the glass. Pounding on the windowpane, he screamed Pam's name, frantically searching for her bundled up in her coat and red scarf.

Not seeing her, he scanned the schoolyard. The area stood empty. Even the rental car that he and Pam arrived in had disappeared.

"She left me. She left me!" His breath frosted the window as he screamed.

"C'mere now, Jordy. It's just a pinch. You'll feel so much better."

*Help me. Please.*

That voice. The one he heard in the stairwell. The one beckoning him to Room 333.

"Help me. Please."

It was his own voice that called for help.

"I'd never leave you, Jordy." The nurse laughed, a giggle with a familiar staccato that began in the back of her throat and eventually landed
outward at a high pitch. "Got a bit chilly in here, huh?"

She removed a red scarf from her pocket, tightened it around her
neck, then stuck the needle in his head.

**Lori M. Myers** is an award-winning writer, Pushcart Prize nominee, and
Broadway World Award nominee of fiction, creative nonfiction, and plays.
Her work has appeared in *American Writers Review, The Dark Sire, Transcen-
dent, Night Terrors vol. 17, Bad Neighborhood, Dissections Journal,* and oth-
ers. Lori authored the dark fiction collection *Crawlspace* and is the Drama/
Nonfiction editor for *Masque & Spectacle* journal.

**Author Website:** www.lorimmyersauthor.com

**Social Media Handles:**
Facebook: https://www.facebook.com/LoriMMyersauthorplays
Twitter: @LoriMMyers
Instagram: @lorimyers316
Amazon Author Page: https://amzn.to/3NxTDjf

# ASHES TO ASHES

## DIANE SISMOUR

**M**om used to hurry me into the bottom cupboard to hide, knowing firsthand that a fist was harder to swing in a small place. A punch is coming, I'm certain. Alone in the confessional, I realize the basketweave walls only screen prying eyes, not the sins. The kneeler has indentations worn almost to the wood from those before me. My guess—this adds to the penance.

*The world is full of sinners.*

My knees can't manage any more praying. As a girl, when Mom bent to polish every bench and seatback after service, I'd switch on the pipe organ and press the pedals—the low notes that nobody could hear, just feel—and let the spirits speak in the tones. Hadn't been here for a year, but some habits are hard to kill.

The tubes soar three stories, reverberating deep within me as I push the pedals, lungs sighing and rising to the belfry's whistle in the ravaging storm. The old wooden church stands, creaking, and a crack of thunder quakes the foundation. Prayer candles flicker light through the darkness thick in the high ceiling to the wooden beams, the ribs of Saint Agnes, protecting the flock's faith, a guise that good vanquishes evil.

Moving to the pews, I sit in the middle of row six, where me and her sat each weekend until we drifted apart. The wood still glistens smooth from Mom polishing it over the years.

Before Dad tossed me into the street like yesterday's trash, I believed good and evil had sides. Mom on one and him on the other. The elbow to his gut was self-defense, but he hadn't seen it that way. The blistered flesh seared into my cheek tells me he's wrong. Mom didn't take me back either. The rift still burns a year later.

Reaching into my bag, I pull out the meds and shake the tiny white pills into my palm, pushing them around and counting. It's October fifth with sixteen left until the twenty-seventh. The merciless pharmacy won't refill the bottle until then. A nervous shudder runs through me. When the voice whispers, touching soft as a butterfly's kiss until a thrum fills my head, I pop one into my mouth.

*Fifteen left until the twenty-seventh.*

The candlelight illuminates the plum and cobalt and aqua and sapphire in the stained-glass window of Christ carrying the cross with spearheads guiding his way. Lightning flashes, crystalline against the window, reflecting a divergent image of Him rising above the masses, healed. Rain splatting the glass stops as abruptly as the front blew in. The wind continues to howl the cries of souls caught between.

*If an omission counts as a lie, then thousands had sat in that confessional before me and paved their paths to hell.*

The thought doesn't pass more than two breaths when Lydia Coscrove barges into the church, up the aisle, and plops her ass beside mine, stinking like a burned-out electric socket. Her pupils are black inkwells. *Crackhead.*

Bowing her gaze, refusing to return mine, she says, "It's time."

We hightail down the aisle and I flick the switch of the pipe organ before bounding through the doors. Outside, the ground drank the sparse drops faster than a thirsty alcoholic drains a bottle. Nary a puddle lays witness that it rained at all. Along the street, the red and orange and yellow piles raked this afternoon topple as the wind shoves us backward en route to her pickup truck. Driving through a towering pile, a myriad of dry leaves escapes the belly, and twirls in a dance, swooping to the cemetery.

When the oak and chestnut and maple hug against the gravestones, ominous chills race along my spine. "Drive faster."

The steeple diminishes in the distance from the rearview mirror. From the light of the headlamps, the naked trees claw the starless sky as we careen through Kutztown to Pennsylvanian suburbia. Lydia grinds the pickup to a stop one house from the intersection of Elm and Fourth.

Cars fill the driveway and spill onto the street. Recognizing all but one, I rummage through my sack purse and toss her a pack of cigarettes.

"Thanks for the ride, Lydia."

The weatherman's forecast of a fifty percent probability couldn't be truer. The rain hadn't hit this half of the town at all. A cold, sharp wind blows. The leaves blanketing the yard rattle across the uneven concrete walkway, swirling at the stoop. The sign on the door hits at eye level: No Smoking. Oxygen in Use.

*They don't want me here, but guess what . . . surprise.*

Flicking on a pilfered cigar torch and lighting a cigarette, I draw hard on the smoke to get the heady courage to walk into the house, blocking out everything except for the reason to step over the threshold.

The ash burns to the filter. The butt drops through the rubber mat. Without knocking, I grip the knob and shove open the door. Three generations of family with drinks in hand celebrating her departure fill the room with chatter sounding like geese honking at the park. The wind whipping in the doorway draws their attention to me.

Dad says, "Shit."

The hem of his sun-bleached T-shirt just covers the protruding gut. Does me good to watch as his hand moves low on his stomach to where my elbow had found his vulnerable target.

From the others—wide-eyed stares and slack jaws. Their yammering turns to silence.

Dad puffs a fat cigar. Mom's oxygen tank hides beneath the side table out of sight. She's always hated the stench of the smoke. A can of air freshener sits next to the water bottle beside her. I want to spray the citrus-fresh scent in his face but resist. This moment is between me and her, not him.

Mom's hiding cupboard stands behind him. The first time she hid me in there, I had cried quiet tears listening as bone hit flesh and Dad had knocked her out. Then he and my brothers found me. They handed me off, one to the next, ruining me, and I couldn't walk. Stealing my fingers across the burn scars running up beneath my arms, I recall deciding never to tell anyone. There is no telling. *Ever.*

I scowl at them. Dad, my three linebacker-sized brothers, and a man I don't know wearing a suit coat and collar stand between me and her. I plow through them to where Mom's thin, hunchbacked body lies silent on the makeshift hospital bed. Her nose crooked from running into too many doors. A bolt juts from her pinned wrist from the last time she fell down the stairs. Her fingers, arthritic claws.

*Beaten down and worked to death.*

No harsh rasps strangle her breaths. No white knuckles thinking each one will be her final. Nothing.

Unlooping the oxygen tube from her ears, I roll up the hose and turn off the tank. Leaning in, I whisper, "To think I had to learn you were breathing your last from Cousin Lydia. Had to give her a whole pack to hurry me over here."

I adjust her nightdress flat across her chest, kiss her slack cheek, closing my eyes to breathe in her scent—lemon and bleach—one last time, and whisper, "I forgive you." When I open them, she's shimmering white. Tears fall, smearing my ebony eyeliner done on the way over, but not caring a damn.

*She's going to Heaven.*

Turning to my brothers, blackness surrounds them. Dad, too. Hoagie dressing drips down his beard onto his shirt. Beer cans leaving condensation marks sit directly on the gleaming wooden table instead of on coasters. Mom would have scurried over to fix the mess.

My eyes draw to the kitchen counter of mostly empty sandwich platters. Ignoring the hollowness within, I will the growls to stop and wrist away the spent makeup. "You're all evil."

Everyone standing in the room backs away from me. They all return the hateful glare with grim faces, save for one. The stranger steps forward. *His aura isn't black; it's purple.*

In a defensive stance, I grab the can of air freshener and hold it at eye level like Mace. "Who the hell are you? You're not her spiritual director. Where's Father Abbott?"

He holds a Bible before him as though it were a shield, and jokes with a British accent, "I've been called worse. Father Abbot transferred yesterday to another parish. I'm Brett, Father Brett Law."

Glaring at my siblings, daring them to interfere, I throw back my shoulders and bring myself to full height, all of five-foot-one. "I'm Angel." Staring down Dad, I say in all sincerity, "But I've been called *far* worse."

He turns to them, gives the sign of the cross, and says, "I'm sorry for your loss. May the Lord be with you." Then he pivots to me and offers his hand. "Angel, you missed the last rites, but your mother is absolved of her sins."

"I know. She was glowing, ready for Heaven." I'm hoping he didn't catch my slip, but by the way his eyes widened, he's suspicious. *Going to have to be more careful around this one.*

Stashing the air freshener in my shoulder bag, from here I can see the family pictures hanging in the hallway. Not one includes me. Not anymore. A small plastic frame by her bedside has the only photo of me and her. The thrift store dress hung on my bony body the day she took me in. My smile missed a front tooth. *She looked tired even then.* I stuff that in the sack, too.

Giving one last glare at Dad and the darkness engulfing the room, I judge the distance between me and the table scraps, and me from freedom. Ignoring the priest's warm consoling clasp, I beeline out the door and just about make it to the sidewalk with a cigarette lit when from behind me, I hear, "Angel, I overheard you needed a ride to get here. Where can I drop you?"

Hell if I'll tell him. He wouldn't understand living day to day, couch surfing, and getting to the YMCA early for the free breakfast. He's in that fancy church on Main Street drinking out of gold cups and eating party wafers. Hate to tell him, but the wafer dish is empty, and the pews make for a hard bed.

"Back to the church. She'll be looking for me there."

He holds the Fiat's door open. Wedging the bag between my feet, I fill the front seat's floor with my belongings. When he opens his side, the wind screams of another storm brewing.

"Just a quick stop, then we'll get to Saint Agnes's." Pulling into Chrissie's Diner, he cuts the engine. "Do you mind joining me? The call for your mom pulled me from supper."

Kindness adds a layer of wall to my defenses. I'd rather walk to town, but the aroma of roasting meat wafting out through the kitchen fan into the parking lot has my mouth watering so hard an answer would sound as though I'm drowning. Nodding, I plod behind him.

A waitress veers to the coffee pot and sets a mug before each of us. She went to school with me. Stephanie Dea. Always thought with her looks she'd be the one to get out of this shit-for-brains town. The way her arm rests across her belly, I'm thinking she wrapped those long legs around one too many and is going to bring another brainless idiot into this world.

Without placing any menus, she stares at me dumping sugar into the cup until it's about to rim over. Expecting to hear an earful, instead, she asks, "The Special, Father?"

"Make it two," he answers and pockets his clerical collar.

Stirring the sludge into syrup, I can feel his eyes on me waiting to open the conversation. Even worse, the pills holding the universe in check call louder from the bag beside me filled with my world. I slurp half the coffee down, letting the sugar and caffeine strengthen my resolve to stay.

*Time enough to count them later.*

He's still fixing his brew, waiting, staring at me from over the cup, as the last of the sugar drips off the edge of mine. Still not a word. Stephanie clatters two plates, dinner rolls, and napkin-wrapped flatware in front of us.

The open-face pork sandwich on mashed potatoes laden with gravy sits inches from me. My insides quiver. He lowers his head to pray. Ten seconds later, thank God, I'm forkfulling boxed-mash and powder-made brown sauce. The meat needs no chewing.

When I'm sopping the plate clean with a dinner roll, he cuts to the point. "How do you know your mother is going to Heaven?"

Not meeting his eyes, I push the platter to the table's edge and say, "She just is. After slaving over my lazy-ass brothers every day and keeping a miserable existence with Dad, she has to go there." My gut cringes. I can tell he's not buying my stonewalling.

He's watching my every move and swiping that knife back and forth, back and forth, buttering a roll. He says, "I have a secret."

"Who cares? Everyone has secrets."

He thinks his silence will get me to ask. Of all the people, after hearing everyone's confessions, he should understand that secrets remain with the teller. I shrug and peer into the maw of my reality, hunting for the rubber change purse, and listening for the prescription rattling in the plastic bottle.

Pointing to the spot just past the last counter stool, he asks, "Do you see Marti Muhe's face there on the floor?"

"Someone's face is on the floor?" *And people think I'm crazy.*

There's nothing but speckles on the worn linoleum and a tracked path leading to the swinging kitchen doors. Grabbing the purse handles and inching off the bench seat, it hits me. I do remember an old woman named Marti. "You mean the bum from outside the barbershop? Why would her face be on the floor?"

Conspiratorially, he leans in and whispers, "She died right there," and nods in affirmation.

On a good day, the grizzly woman would toss a quarter to me and give a tooth-rotted grin. On a bad . . . I shudder from memories of more than a few deranged rants about my occupation. I'll just remember the positive.

Staring at the spot, I tilt my head one way for four heartbeats, then the other, squinting harder. "When did she die?"

"Two evenings ago, right there in front of me. Nothing could save her."

My eyes widen and my chin nearly smacks the table from leaning in so fast. "She went to Hell?"

Shaking his head, he says, "No. You can see the peace there on her face."

Closing my eyes so just a sliver of the floor shows. "I see it." *Sort of.*

Stephanie walks from behind the counter giving a wide deviation of the area in question with two plated slices of chocolate pudding pie and whipped cream piled high.

Mom always said, 'Nobody can own you if they can't buy you.' I may be selling my body, but I don't owe anybody for nothing.

Panicking to pay my way, I calculate the price on the Specials board with dessert and don't think there is enough. Squeezing the slotted rubber coin purse, change falls onto the Formica rolling in all directions. I'll need every cent to cover the meal. Doing what Uncle Roy showed me, I form a fist and BANG the table. The coins jump and fall flat.

Feeling the sweat bead at my hairline and drip down my forehead as I'm adding, my mouth parches. "I can't." And shove the coins at him.

In one swift motion, I'm out the door, the priest loses his supper partner, and I'm thumbing my way to town. A gust sends a garbage can rumbling across the parking lot. Trash flies in a funnel whipped up between two buildings.

Shouldering against the wind, I palm through the entirety of my bag and clasp the container of pills. Some fall as I finger one from the bottle and dry-swallow. In the black of night, I hunt for them on all fours in the gravel. *They are gone.* From searching so long, my knees hurt worse than if I gave the entire block free blowjobs.

A shudder quivers my core. I take another pill. By the time the diner is beyond smelling, peace takes over my racing thoughts, and my heart, that moments earlier nearly pounded out of my chest, calms.

The moon peeks through shrouding clouds long enough for me to recognize the old pickup truck heading my way in the southbound lane. Lydia stops on the other side of the road and lowers the window. "Swung by your place, but they said you left. Coroner showed, too." She shakes her head, hanging low. Her hair falls like tattered curtains across her face. "They took her, Angel."

I cross to the center line and lean on the driver's side door. Her aura isn't as pale a blue as when she found me earlier, and her pupils show enough iris to notice the brown in them again. *She lost her high.*

"It'll be okay. She'll find her way."

Headlights come from the northbound lane. Hurrying to the other side of the truck to avoid becoming roadkill, I climb into the cab. "Take me back to the church, but first stop by my corner."

The fifteen blocks there are quieter than midnight on a Sunday. The lamplight bulb dies a little more each night and flickers a dancing silhouette around my spot on the sidewalk. Almost a warning to the other whores to stay away, yet a beacon to draw whoever is needy.

No car hides in the darkness. Nobody lurks in the alley. No one is waiting on me. Pointing forward, we continue the four blocks to the church. I pluck a cigarette from my stash to thank her.

The entry painted red warns sinners to beware. I slip through the unlocked doors. The votive candles fail to reach the ambient evil darkening the corners where hours before light reached the rafters. The ornate carvings along the wooden beams cast shadows clawing at any goodness left inside.

While staring at the Virgin Mary's statue, the face shifts, the stiff cheeks droop, and the eyes sadden.

Relief sweeps through me. "Mom. I knew you'd be here."

Before she answers, Father Brett sweeps through the heavy curtain separating his chamber from the masses and marches from the pulpit straight at me. Unless ducking and scooting between the pews to the doorway is an option, I'm hog-tied.

He stands before me, places a white paper bag on the seat, and hands me a plastic fork. "Eat your pie, Angel. We need to talk."

A whiff of chocolate weakens my resolve, but I slide along the bench away from him. "What do you want to know, Father?"

"Do you see your mother here?" he asks, standing before me with his hands held high encompassing the room.

*He's worse than a mutt gnawing a bone.* With a shaking head and pursed lips, I mock, "Do YOU see her here? You're the one who sees dead people's faces."

"Who were you speaking with just now?" He sits on the pew beside me and slaps his hands hard against the seatback before him.

I don't flinch. *Does he think THAT will scare me into answering?* "Can't I speak to God? This is a church."

The verbal slap closes his gaping mouth and he leans forward in prayer with fingers aligned. "Of course."

A reprieve from his relentless questions, I lean off the seat with palms together, thinking of how the church had saved Mom from many a beating. *This place may have been a haven for her but it is far from Heaven.*

He waits until my back sits straight again before continuing the interrogation, his face an impassive mask. "While at your mom's side, you said, 'She's glowing, waiting for Heaven.' Did you see her glowing?"

Other than Mom, he's the first person to discover my gift. A gift she warned me to hide with my life after making a fool of myself in high school. Never did go back again.

His ire shimmers black on the edges of the purple haze surrounding him. "Tell me, Angel. Like me, you can see something most people can't." He opens the bag and withdraws the plated dessert, whipped cream to the top of the plastic cover, and displays the leftover container before me, wanting an answer.

If patience is a virtue, maybe *I'm* the virtuous one for withstanding that perfect slice of pie. *He's bribing me with food, Mom.* In my mind, she holds a finger to her lips.

I push away the bribe and shake my head. "No, sir. I can't say what I see."

"Angel, I know you're having a tough time with your mom's passing. I saw you speaking to the Virgin Mary. Let me leave you this opportunity. Some of my parishioners confess . . . sparsely. Either they don't know me as they did Father Abbott, or think God isn't hearing them, or they don't believe in their salvation without absolution. I just want to help them."

I'm edging away to the aisle.

He nudges the enticement across the pew even closer. "Just tell me this . . . can you see good from evil?"

*Mom, can I trust him? This man is supposed to be God's messenger.* Her image solidifies with Mary. The angry blackness around his purple doesn't change. It wavers on the edge like energy. The darker his aura, the more power he holds. I trust him like a rattlesnake. His warning sign is as clear to me as the shake of a snake's tail.

People might consider my ability a gift, but me, I'm sinning right along with them if I ignore his plea. Trusting him or not, I'm obligated as this man's disciple to help guide them to the right path.

Eyeballing him squarely, I say, "Yes," and snatch the pie.

Again, he waits.

The chocolate pudding has that skin that lingers thick on the tongue, as the sweet cream whipped light as air evaporates, and bite by bite, every savory morsel triggers happiness to override the situation. Handing him the spent container and fork, I grab my purse and head for the closest exit.

"Angel, you haven't answered me yet."

I stop, dreading to say the words to him, knowing others I've told have had their share of mocking me. The kind of names that make me cringe—psycho, weirdo, freak. This Man of God is supposed to have compassion. Maybe since he figured out my gift on his own, he might spare me.

I glance again at Mary's statue, and Mom has called it a night and melded with the Blessed Mother. I can't understand any of this at all. She just died but ended up in this church to guide me instead of going to Heaven. Until I sort through and figure out how to move her along, he's leaving me little choice. I'll need to keep returning until she ascends. And if my answer doesn't support the parishioners' learning right from wrong, what kind of person have I become?

"Fine, I'll help. What do you need me to do?" I say, regretting the words as soon as they leave my mouth.

His expression doesn't change, but the black outline pulses as he speaks. Dad's darkness had done the same just before he swung a fist. "When someone leaves the confessional, simply nod if they confessed all their sins or shake your head if they purposely omitted any."

I stand out of reach. "And what do I get out of this?"

"How does five dollars for each sound? You could buy food or a bus ticket out of here." He smiles and like magic the darkness vanishes.

*Has the day taken such a toll on me that I'm seeing evil in a priest?* The suddenness has me second-guess his suggestion to use my gift. Getting paid to just look at people's auras after hiding my knowledge for so long still leaves me unwilling to answer. But I could really use the cash. All the burn scars on my body aren't benefiting me in my line of work.

Willing Mom to return to the statue, I say, *You told me never to tell anyone about my secret.* Still nothing from her. *Dying must be exhausting.* Not certain if his shift in colors is a parlor trick or grief wearing me, I keep two steps away from him just in case the darkness returns as my thoughts gather.

"I may be a prostitute but I'm not stupid. Time here with you will take me away from working my corner. That British charm of yours could coax the panties off a nun. This church will fill three times a week and twice Sundays with every lonely woman in town. Your coffer will be full. Make it ten, and I'll think about it."

He mulls over my terms. I can see him debating to counter the offer as I stand and head for the door. There's no squabbling. If I say a price, that's what it is, whether it's a blowjob, a fuck, or cheating people in church. The doors slam behind me as I hurry to Lydia's to crash. It's been a night I don't want to continue. When alone, I count the pills and swallow one.

*Only seven left until the twenty-seventh.*

A quiver runs through me and stays deep in the pit of my stomach. Pondering about the day, my mind spirals. *Mom is dead. There's no reason to ever go back home.* I take one more pill and wait. The thoughts fade, but like an itch, are just below the surface waiting for me to claw them open. The butterfly's wings flap harder, the whisper is louder, then the screech buzzing in my ears calms and the haze washes away all feeling. Grief has a way of bending time. Mom is smiling at me like she did that first day—warm and happy she had another female around in a house full of testosterone.

*Six left until the twenty-seventh.*

Light spills in the window. Lydia left enough coffee for me. Dumping sugar and stirring to sludge, I gulp life into the day.

Sitting at the end of the sixth pew next to Mom, I get no comfort from the statue and slide to the middle when Father Brett does a blessing at the altar before going to the booth. He doesn't look at me, but I know he's seen me. The purple has more black veining through his aura. *Why is he angry with me? I have made it here, didn't I?* The butterfly wings fluttering in my head flap faster. The itch inside buries deeper. The whispers grow louder.

*Five left until the twenty-seventh.*

I'm sitting in the church nodding yes or no after each person confesses from eight in the morning until noon. We settle up before I leave. Scores are slow and the added income helps. I'm able to pitch in with

Lydia to buy food. The rustle of the bags of sour bears and gummy fish can't hide the rattle of the pills.

I wish Father Brett had never shown me his gift though. Now I can recognize the faces of the dead people I knew etched on the ground in the four blocks from Saint Agnes's to Lydia's house. They're in the alley, beside the dumpster, in the left-hand turn lane at the intersection of Main and First. A tire crushes through Uncle Roy's face where a car had plowed over him.

I pray to Heaven and back that when my turn strikes to walk into the light, my face won't bear the same. The terror stamped on them is enough for me to rethink confessing to him. He'd have to hear everything. The cigar burns on my body are a constant reminder to omit . . . *always*.

Pushing open the church's heavy oak door the next morning, in the gloomy light, only one head is visible. The hardwood floor echoes each footfall as I make my way to the middle of pew six, waiting to give a nod or a shake of the head to Father.

Mrs. McGinley is in my row. The woman passes my corner to go to every Mass. Her gray-streaked curls pin tight against her head. The pink lipstick, always too bright on her sallow skin. She turns my way and sniffs. She's muddy blue with a rosary in her hand counting beads for each Hail Mary.

Giving her a sickly-sweet smile, I say, "Well, hello to you, too."

She huffs.

*She's going to need another strand to count for those wicked thoughts. How can I make her see the error in her ways?*

The confessional door opens. A thirty-something mom carrying a diaper bag instead of a purse steps out and another woman enters the confessional. Nodding, I say to McGinley, "See that lady leaving?"

Mrs. McGinley glances over, and her lips move faster as her fingers slide along the rosary.

"That woman, she has a shiny sapphire shimmer around her. She told all her sins. Someone who lies will have a muddy cobalt haze."

Staring straight at Christ hanging on the cross, the old woman goes from lips moving to murmuring to hurry through her penance.

Tilting my head back, I count the church's ribs in the vaulted ceiling. "You know, Eve was formed from Adam's rib. And her hunger created Hell. Bitch, you lied to God. You're going to Hell . . ."

I'm about to say, "if you don't confess your sins," when she stands rod-straight and gasps. Her face twitches as her body convulses. The smack her head makes on the pew-back sounds like a solid strike on a cue ball. She face-plants into the aisle.

For an instant, I don't react. *Did I kill her?* Shit. I'm damned to eternity. I don't want to go to Hell.

My scream for help brings Father racing from the booth as I jump to her aid. A woman dashes out from the confessional door and taps her cell phone dialing the emergency dispatch.

"What happened?" he asks as we shift her onto her back. She appears at peace with a twisted grimace only pain can deliver. He alternates giving her chest compressions and mouth-to-mouth.

In a whisper, I say, "I think I killed her."

He stops. An expression of bewilderment crosses his face, and he shakes his head. "Then help save her."

Making money lying on my back doesn't offer much exercise. My heart races, ready to explode from the exertion of pumping her chest to the beat of *don't die, don't die, don't die.*

Father's face glows red from the effort of breathing for two. "Where in the bloody hell are the paramedics?" he shouts.

Suddenly, Mrs. McGinley sits bolt upright, grabs his vestments, and bellows a bloodcurdling scream, "Don't let the demons take me." Her eyes go wild as she glares at Father Brett and shoves him away. In a hoarse croak, she murmurs, "He's a demon," and just as quickly, passes out again. Her face muscles tighten, and her breathing is shallow, but she's alive. *Barely.*

With her shrieked accusation, his purple facade quashes, allowing deep black stains to show through much like curds separating in milk. I'm not certain what is happening before me. With a shake of my head, the royal color solidifies, but the black outline remains, pulsating.

Helping Father Brett sure does come with a price. Who can believe the rantings of that old bitch? But her revelation doesn't explain how his aura changed as it did. The way the purple blotched and the black bled through, he could be a wolf in sheep's clothing leading the flock into damnation. If his shine changes to dark again, I'll have to figure out what to do then.

Shit, if he is a demon, after making a pact with him, I'll get an express trip to Purgatory. I better not go to Hell because of her. I was just helping.

Moments later, the sounds of sirens ring in the air. EMTs and firefighters fill the building. The nosy neighbors step around me, as though I'm invisible, to crowd around the rescue and gawk at the dying woman.

When the rescue team stops their efforts and moves away from the corpse, I'm backing out the doors. The whispers in my head taunt me, *killer, Killer, KILLER.*

Digging in my bag, I tap two, then a third pill into my palm and swallow them, putting the bottle in my coat pocket. Torching a cigarette, I stash the lighter in the other one. The smell of singed polyester from the lining fills my nose.

Calm breaks through faster than a two-dollar hand job. Somehow, through the fog, I find the path back to Lydia's apartment and onto the couch. At some point that night, she tossed a blanket over me. I may think badly of her sometimes, but she's a decent person. She's still a crackhead though. She stole everything she could sell from my purse. Lightened my load considerably for two nights of hospitality.

Gossip travels fast. I'm forced to return to the church as Mom is still in limbo hiding in the Virgin Mary's statue. Upon arrival, the line of sinners waiting for confession is the longest I can remember since walking in for Bible study that first day with her. They stretch down the aisle, out the door, and onto the sidewalk.

No one wants to witness what Mrs. McGinley had seen on her return trip upon resuscitation. Her face etched into the hardwood reflects one of disbelief and fear. She expected a ride up the escalator, not down.

Hearing she went to Hell and back should loosen the tightest tongues. After today, I'm going to get a ticket out of this town to somewhere warm to stop shivering.

Mom is behind the statue. She still isn't talking to me, ashamed of what I've done.

*I killed someone.*

The whispers buzz, *You're going to Hell.*

*Because of that BITCH. I'll never get to be with Mom again. Fucking HELL.*

The last two pills call to me. I rummage through what's left of my world and am about to go kill Lydia for stealing my meds when the familiar rattle reaches my ears making me happier than the tinkling from the ice cream truck playing that endless tune on a summer day. Pulling the container from my pocket, with shaking hands I twist. The lid drops to the floor as I upend the bottle into my mouth.

The screams return to whispers, always buzzing, itching in my brain.

I see each person as they exit the booth but don't pay any attention when they enter. Father Brett is not paying me for that. Even with demons chasing souls, few confess all their sins.

The itch in my brain says, "They don't believe in him."

The pills, they're not working. The need to tell all that's wrong with their worlds gnaws. None have the kindness to give a condolence. They gape at me with pity on their faces.

I look at the statue of Mary. Mom's sad eyes stare back.

I rock on the seat, digging my fingers into my thighs, trying to bring focus. The screeching grows louder. Clapping hands to my ears to stop it, I cry, "I'm sorry, Mom. Tell me what to do. You don't belong here."

The confessional door opens.

*Dad.*

Blackness shimmers around him.

*Mine must be as black as his now. We're both going to Hell.* Grabbing my bag, I'm ready to bolt.

His cigar stench reaches me. Father Brett comes out of the booth and claps his back.

Dad pins me with a glare, puffs his chest, and says, "It's time for you to come home."

My reactions may be askew from the medication, but my ears are deceiving me. In disbelief, I ask, "You *want* me to come home?"

With a sneer, Dad says, "You can earn your keep. The house needs cleaning and dinner needs fixing, and you're a whore . . . the boys'll need fucking."

The whispers roar inside.

"The only good I am to you is by being your servant? A slave like Mom was for you to beat into submission?"

Father Brett grins as though he's just unloaded his biggest problem . . . *me*. His glow turns dark. As black as Dad's.

In disbelief, I say to him, "I believed in you."

Staring at the pulsing light surrounding him, reality strikes harder than a sledgehammer on a spike. The parish isn't telling him their sins because they don't trust him. By them omitting, he's gathering the true sinners for purgatory. The purple glow that had surrounded him means he's royalty; the blackness, evil. *The Prince of Darkness.* He IS the serpent in the tree bribing me to do his bidding as he did to Eve. *He IS the Devil.*

*And I'm the one to send him back to Hell.*

The pipe organ vibrates a low thrum and my body shakes. When the lock that keeps the mania contained within me shatters, the whispers tell me the way to salvation.

I march over to stand before them. Grabbing the air freshener from my purse, I do just as the directions say. To expel the unwanted odor, press the button and move the can in broad sweeps. Flammable. I draw the torch from my coat pocket. The mist lights at the nozzle.

I growl, "You're both getting an express trip to Hell."

The blue ignition expels a bright white flame to cleanse them of their sins. I spray Dad, the Devil, and the confessional. The basketweave catches to tinder the fire and engulfs the wooden beam above. An ethereal glow surrounds the stained-glass window of Christ hanging on the cross with the thieves.

People are hollering behind me as they stampede from the church, but theirs are a pittance compared to Dad's and the Devil's screams as their skin burns, turning as black as their souls. I continue to cleanse them as they flop on the floor like trout out of the stream for too long. Their hair fizzles and flesh bubbles, leaving their eyeballs seeing me for the first time.

The aroma of meat cooking doesn't drown my mouth, but it sure does quench my soul. As I step into the flaming confessional, I search for Mom. She's ascending past the smoke billowing at Adam's ribs.

**Diane Sismour** writes poetry, short fiction, and novels with a dry humor and fast-paced plots in Romantic Suspense, Psychological Thrillers/Horrors, and Crime Fiction, and takes pleasure in ghostwriting for others. Along the way, she won a few awards. She enjoys creating characters while shaded under the maple tree and greeting guests at her Leaser Lake B and B located in the foothills of the Pocono Mountains in Pennsylvania. Diane is a motivational speaker and a member of Romance Writers of America, Liberty States Fiction Writers, Sisters in Crime, the Bethlehem Writers Group, the Horror Writers Association, and the Hive Writers Group. Look for her at conferences or giving a workshop.

**Social Media Handles:**

Facebook: https://www.facebook.com/NetworkfortheArts/

Amazon Author Page: https://www.amazon.com/author/dianesismour

# DESPERATE IS THE LONELY HEART

## CATHERINE JORDAN

**Penobscot, Pennsylvania**
**1813**

The stone house had been built in a clearing in the woods to shelter Charles Wickesier and his wife from the world's increasing depravity, and he made sure to erect a fireplace large enough to keep his home warm in the coldest of winters.

But that first winter, his beloved Marianne had died giving birth to Lucia.

Charles loved his little Lucia too much. She looked just like her mother, God rest her soul.

Raising the girl came with ease. She was pure and humble, agreeable and obedient. When Lucia reached the tender age of five, Charles commissioned a portrait of father and daughter and hung it proudly and prominently over the hearth.

Lucia was six years old when his brother's daughter came to stay and help at her womanly age of ten and five. Wanton and lustful, she vied for the position of his wife. He sent the harlot back home to his brother. The thought of his Lucia growing up and turning into a woman, a victim of vice and immorality, made him shudder—Lucia's scruples and vulnerabilities were still fragile, that part of her brain not yet developed, and he especially hated the thought of her damning herself to the eternal abyss through corruption. For that would surely damn him, too, just as his immoral niece's actions damned her parents—his brother and sister-in-law. If accursed, Charles would never see his saintly, beloved wife again, and the two of them would be separated for eternity.

Therefore, after little Lucia's last reckless incident on her tricycle while in the company of a mischievous older boy, after she was safely found unharmed but her pantalettes torn and her explanation not forthcoming, Charles concluded it was his moral obligation as a father to steer her from the occasion of sin. Boys turn to men, and he could not fathom her becoming a victim of vice. He would rather she become a victim at *his* hands before the age of reason so he would worry no more over the status of her soul.

Even though he considered her death justified, he had committed the deadly sin of pride in thinking his decision to take her life was superior to her right to live it, regardless of any future choices she might make. Charles Wickesier had imparted upon his daughter a great injustice, and at his death, he was condemned to wander the empty house where he had strangled his only daughter, Lucia.

———  —

**Mountain Top, Pennsylvania**
**1979**

Lucy's station wagon tires crunched through the gravel and the car bobbed heavily upon the stones, past a grouping of fragrant overgrown pines and onto the unpaved driveway. Her windows were down, and earthy dampness and the fragrance of pine filled her car.

She never met the people who once lived in the old stone house one lot off the dead-end of Jamestown Road, just outside Walden Park's neighborhood. The abandoned home was set back in the woods upon an unpaved drive on a moss-covered hill. It wasn't listed in the neighborhood newsletter, and this off-road wasn't on the map. But Lucy had grown up in Walden Park, and as a kid, she often walked past the house, curious, hardly able to see much of it through the tall trees. She'd heard a ghost lived there.

*As if.*

Admittedly, the sky above the house was always darker and gloomier than the rest of the world, like a deluge might fall at any given moment. Like most people, she merely chalked the shadowy murk up to the dense woods and overgrown foliage surrounding the timeworn home.

When the 1972 Agnes Flood—the costliest hurricane to hit the United States at the time with a death toll of 128—drowned out a good part of lower Wilkes-Barre, people wanted to escape to a higher elevation away from the threat of the Susquehanna River. Most specifically asked to see homes for sale in this development.

Even though the stone house wasn't technically part of Walden Park, currently this was the only residence on the market big enough to house a family. The listing, going into its third week, had collected no interest. Not good. But her boss assured her that the foundation was solid, roomy, and it occupied over an acre of land—it just needed the right person.

Lucy looked over the big yard and up the long driveway. She remembered the little boy from 28 years ago. She used to ride tricycles with him, and they called each other boyfriend and girlfriend. Christopher. It had been a rainy day, foggy. He had been on his trike pedaling along, then paused and dropped over like a fallen statue, stiff as death, rigor mortis already in his muscles, flies circling his open mouth. The adults had investigated his strange death—no one found anything satisfactory. But when it comes to the death of a child, who does? Lucy was three at the time, barely old enough for memories, and couldn't remember what had gone through her mind, if anything, when he died. Yet, to this day, whenever she saw a red tricycle, his stone-white toddler face flashed in her mind.

Within Walden Park, she had yet to spot one of those trikes. Elsewhere, it seemed like one sat in every driveway.

Lucy pulled an errant thread from her brown jacket and adjusted her nametag. She discreetly spit her gum into a tissue and pocketed it, then took a deep breath, ready to open the front door. Being the only woman realtor in town, she told herself she'd do whatever it took to land the deal and would spend the better part of her day at the open house trying to sell the vacant property. Hell with her asshole boss and his remarks about how she should be home raising babies. Not like she had any luck with men, anyway. It was like a sign from above, how every guy she ever dated managed to fall off the face of the earth.

She walked past the breezeway to the south end of the wraparound porch. Even though it was February, this was the perfect spot to sip lemonade on a hot summer day—and it made for a good selling point. *Gotta remember to mention that,* she told herself. A stone chimney rose above the roof. The detached stable could easily be converted into a two-car garage. A gray stone gazebo covered in moss and ivy sat a few yards behind, right before the land sloped upward into the mountains.

She had expected it to be more run-down than it looked. According to tax records, the house had only one owner. That tidbit of info would normally be considered a plus, however, the house hadn't been lived in since the early 1800s, when Mountain Top went by another name—Penobscot. It hadn't changed hands, been sold, or been inhabited since.

"Long time," Lucy whispered while looking up at the structure, her hands on her waif-like hips. She gave a long sigh, wondering what she'd see inside.

Lucy rattled the door handle. She didn't have keys to the place, but her boss told her it'd be unlocked. It wasn't, damn it. Tall, wide, and solid, she swore she heard whispering behind the wooden door.

"Hel-looo?" she called out in a sing-song voice. "Anybody here?"

Lucy walked the porch and peeked in one of the windows. She had expected to be alone in selling this old property and was surprised to see that someone had furnished the house. Recently.

Open concept and spacious, the large fireplace with an ornately carved wooden mantle—maple, for sure with its tightly packed and strong grain—was almost big enough to crawl into, and the damp smell of ash emanated from its black-stained firebox. A woodpile sat on the grates as if waiting for a match. A lone portrait hung over the hearth—a gentleman in an old-fashioned suit standing behind a seated child.

She then noted the wood-frame windows—also maple, another excellent selling point—did not have screens, one slightly ajar. The damn thing wouldn't give—at first. With a heave and a bit of sweat, the frame finally opened enough for her to crawl through. Good thing she chose to wear pants this morning. After a couple of false starts, one final hoist, and a bit of wiggling, she finally made it through the opening, shutting the window tightly behind her.

Lucy brushed herself off then wrinkled her nose. Having been closed tight for years with little ventilation, high humidity, and darkness, the house held a musty smell. Still, not so bad for a place where no one had stepped foot in years.

So—who staged the rooms? Another realtor trying to steal her commission? Her boss? She'd make a few calls when she returned to the office, but for now . . .

She rummaged through her leather briefcase, manly and formal—that had been the message she wanted to send when she bought it—and re-read the contract. Yep, it clearly stated her realty group as the seller. Meaning no other salesperson should be here. No one from the competition, in other words.

After wandering the ground floor, she readied her paperwork and business cards on the rectangular oak kitchen table, set for two. Two gold-rimmed China plates—she turned one over and spied the brand name mark—Limoges. Polished silverware laid properly on white linen napkins. A water glass, wine glass, a tiny aperitif crystal glass, and an upside-down Limoges coffee cup covered its matching saucer. Quite cozy and intimate. Behind swinging doors was the kitchen, all in tune with the original structure.

Upstairs, four large bedrooms were furnished according to the period. In the primary, she dragged her palm down the fabric wallpaper. No tears, no visible edges. "Humph." She nodded appreciatively at the primary bedroom's high ceilings and wooden floors. Plenty big enough for an en suite bathroom—a costly addition, but doable. If only the room had proper lighting.

She shivered and hugged herself. "It's cold in here." Hopefully the electrical had been updated.

A murmur of voices suddenly came from downstairs. "People are here already?" she whispered, wrinkling her brow. Crap. She hadn't finished prepping. A neighbor probably saw her car with her realtor magnet on the side and walked in. Homeowners loved to meander through neighboring houses to see the potential, how it's decorated, and compare the asking price.

According to her watch, she still had a half hour before showtime. She had intended to light a candle—sugar cookie scent—flush all the toilets, and run the faucets.

But she remembered the front door had been locked. No one had crawled in the window—she would have heard *that*.

"Hello?"

No answer. A cold shiver tickled her forearms.

She sniffed heavy and loud. *Is that smoke? Or just the damp fireplace?* Definitely smoke, along with the crackling of fire. "Crap! No, no fire. Hey, who's here?" Thinking her sexist boss showed up to check on her, she got pissed and considered leaving despite her original intentions.

Clattering out of the primary bedroom to head downstairs—damn heels, should've worn the comfy flats—she half stumbled, caught herself, then ran into the great room.

The fireplace was alive with the clean burn of hard wood. She put her hands on her hips and surveyed the room. "Hey!" she shouted, expecting her boss to answer.

Her eyes went back to the portrait on the wall, its frame gently rattling. A breeze from the open window? No, she had closed it. Hesitantly, she stepped closer to the portrait, then it stilled. "Weird?" She put a hand to her chest, brow furrowed. "Nah, that's not weird," she said, assuring herself that old houses continued settling even after many years.

Wait . . . Hadn't there been a man in this picture? An assumed father with his hand on the back of his daughter's chair? The young girl with golden ringlets and the bluest eyes sat alone in the picture. Lucy, mouth agape, reached up toward the wooden frame. Confused and not quite ready to look past what her eyes had seen, she told herself that it must have been another old house and another old picture—a popular mass production back in the day.

But this girl—there was something odd about her picture. The image seemed lifelike, and familiar. Maybe this was the original, the one every other had been based upon? And maybe the girl resembled herself as a child.

Watch hands ticked away as Lucy, mesmerized, stared into the girl's eyes.

A long-ago memory struck—*Father watching with pride while the artist painted her image. She squirmed and Father pursed his lips and shook his head at her.*

Hold on—how could she know that? She didn't, of course. By looking in the eyes she only figured those thoughts had been on the little girl's mind, and surely her parents would have been there in the foreground, watching.

Heavy footsteps—she heard but saw no one—clopped upon the wooden floor toward the dining room table. She tilted her head and looked into the open room. Both chairs had been pulled out.

Her body went cold with paralyzing dread. *I'm so scared I can't move.*

Before she realized it, tears welled in her eyes, her stomach turned, and she started to cry. "I'm leaving," she said. "Right now."

"Stay," a mystery voice said.

"What?" She whipped around, seeing no one but feeling a presence.

That voice didn't sound like her boss. It didn't sound like anyone she knew. Her gooseflesh rose painfully on her arms like pinpricks, and she crossed her arms, hands rubbing them for warmth even though the fire burned strong.

She picked up her bag, gathered her business cards, and dug for her car keys.

"Stay with me," again from a disembodied masculine voice.

She ran to the front door, pulled and kicked and slapped at the wood, her hair sticking to her sweaty brow. But the door would not open.

Back at the window, fog had rolled in and covered the landscape. She gasped, the dense fog thick as milk. She could not see her car through the fog, and the weather might as well have been a blizzard—she feared she'd get lost if she dared to step outside, even if she could open that damned door.

The fog snaked toward the window. She swallowed hard and dropped her bag when a pointed tendril reached out to her like a finger, beckoning her beyond the glass.

She shuffled backward, squealing.

Then heard another whisper from behind. "Stay."

"Who are you?" she asked, her voice quivering, her nerves hot with fear.

A firm hand gripped her shoulder. She screamed, slapping at the phantom hand, backing away from it.

Disoriented, Lucy didn't recognize where she stood, the fog billowing in the house through hidden cracks and crevices, too thick to see anything. With arms outstretched, she felt her way like a blind woman, shuffling away from the strange voice calling out to her.

When squeaky wheels rolled by, she followed the sound, tiptoeing her way through a door and into a mystery room. The fog dissipated, and a red tricycle sat in the room's center. Christopher's. Other mementos filled the room from almost every boy and man she'd ever known. An empty brown leather wallet covered with stupid childish stickers—her first suitor from high school, John. Trey's Phillies baseball hat—he was an obnoxious fan. Mike's Eagles jersey? There was more, much more, and she couldn't fathom the implications behind what she saw.

She thought she heard thumping but realized it was only her heart in her throat.

"Stay with me," this time in a clear voice, behind her.

She turned around and, in a blink, saw a man in an old-fashioned suit. Or did she? If she had, and she was pretty sure she had, he had disappeared into the ether like the fog. Even though he had come and gone quickly, she knew he was the man from the portrait.

"Stay with me," he called, this time from the dining room. A chair scraped against the dining room floor.

Panicked and flustered, she backtracked toward the room, in the direction of the front door and the window—the only way she knew to escape.

A chair had been pulled out for her, the man's hand on the back of her chair. The same man who had vanished from the portrait, no longer within its frame, but here.

He gestured with a wave of his hand for her to sit.

She could not move.

"I'm so lonely," said the ghost, as if loneliness was all the reason he needed for her to dare and venture closer to him.

She swallowed hard, wondering if it was okay to engage a ghost. Was there a rule book for dealing with apparitions, like a Ouija board? Not that she'd ever played one more than once.

"Why?" She had to know why, and what it all meant.

He looked her in the eye and sighed, his breath a cold shot of air that ruffled her hair and even fanned the fireplace fumes. "I didn't like the way they looked at you. Stay with me, Lucia."

"But I'm not—"

"You've come back to me." He reached out and circled his cold hard hands around her neck. "We'll never be separated again."

Raised in the Pocono Mountains, **Catherine Jordan** is inspired by come-uppance and Flannery O'Connor. Catherine has been featured in a variety of anthologies. HarperCollins published her recent short story "Hachis-hakusama" in *Don't Turn Out the Lights: A Tribute to Alvin Schwartz's Scary Stories to Tell in the Dark.* She is the review coordinator for horrortree.com, the email announcement manager for HWA (active member), and edits at Fortress Publishing. Ms. Jordan is an award judge and writing mentor and facilitates creative writing courses and critique groups.

**Author Website:** https://catherinejordan.com/

**Social Media Handle:**
Amazon Author Page: https://www.amazon.com/Catherine-Jordan/e/B00A3BVMEO

# THE LAST KISS

ALYSON FAYE

t was the singing, the low, sweet notes, that drew Jake toward and then into the derelict warehouse, the one he walked past on his way home from work every day. His brain told him to keep on walking, but the song tugged at his memory and something else, deeper, in his very DNA.

It was a chilly winter's evening, the air already nipping at his cheeks; his stomach and energy levels were both running on empty. It had been a long day at the virtual coalface of his computer. But, as he paused to listen, curiosity and the taunting familiarity of the tune grabbed his attention as the first snowflakes drifted down. There was no one around to see Jake duck under the vandalized 'Keep Out' signs, nor to see the shadows at the empty windows shift and surge in welcome.

Memories pulled Jake onward, over the glass-splattered threshold and inside the guts of the decaying building. His dad had worked here, over thirty years ago. Back then, the warehouse had been booming and bustling. Most days after school, Jake would sit doing his homework in the foreman's sweaty glass box of an office high up on the decking, waiting for his dad to clock off. This building held the ghosts of so many memories. Jake didn't dwell on the notion of who or what other ghosts might be nestling under the leaking roof. He didn't believe in ghosts anyway. Years ago he had gotten away with murder, and he'd not been haunted since, not once, not even for a few minutes.

Ghosts were a sign of weak minds, he believed. Or so he'd told himself after a few whiskeys in the small gray hours.

The song wavered. Tracy Chapman's "Fast Car," Jake suddenly remembered the title, one of their faves—back when they'd been dating and in love, making plans. He shivered and pulled up his collar. The temperature had to be closing in on zero, and wavering ribbons of snow were drifting through the holes in the roof. He really didn't want to hang around here much longer. Perhaps he shouldn't be here at all.

"Hello?" he called out. "Anyone about?"

The song died. Jake eyed the debris lying abandoned on the warehouse floor. The wreckage of the machinery, the many black coils of wiring snaking across the floor, the piles of hardened bird poop, a nest of rags in the corner that was . . . moving?

Rats? He thought. I hate rats. Please don't be rats.

The air around him crackled as though a charge had gone through it. Impossible, Jake thought, the electric was switched off. Years ago. This place is dead. A shell.

He checked his iPhone. 'No service' flickered at him. He waved the phone around his head. Another charge fizzed through the air and the hairs on his arms and legs stood erect. He felt . . . vulnerable—a new and unpleasant feeling. Jake liked to always be in charge, of himself, his life, his job, his relationships. There had just been that one 'unfortunate episode,' and that had been years ago. All in the past now.

"Hiya, Jakey," a voice whispered through the air, leaving only dust in its echo.

Jake jerked around and looked up toward his dad's former office.

"I've been waiting for you." It was an odd voice, which he didn't recognize, yet also sounded a little familiar. "Come up."

Jake glimpsed a shadow in the office, dancing and twirling as though spinning in the foreman's swivel chair.

Like she used to do.

Long buried memories stirred. "Jakey, c'mon up. I love you. Jakey . . ."

No one else had ever called him Jakey, not even his now-deceased parents, and especially not his dad. Mr. Formal himself.

The voice began to sing the words to their song—"Fast Car"—with its promise of a shared shiny future, of the flight of young lovers to new places.

"Who are you?" Jake called, but his voice shook. Snow settled thicker now on his expensive coat and haircut. "Whoever you are, you should go home. It's freezing cold in here."

A trickle of laughter. "I am home, Jakey. You'll see that when you come and find me."

Jake didn't want to go up the rickety stairs; he wanted to go home to his SmartTV, his wall-to-wall sofa, underfloor heating, where he could listen to hours of calming jazz. But chilled as he was, something burned inside him, a hope, a question—could it be . . . her?

At the top of the stairs, the office door hung half off its hinges, and the smell of mold was overwhelming. The dancing shadow had vanished; there were only the remnants of forgotten furniture, a scattering of dog-eared paperbacks, and his dad's old swivel chair with its ripped seat, vomiting foam.

Jake picked up one of the paperbacks. He was gut-punched to see it was *I Capture the Castle* by Dodie Smith. Not one of his dad's, nor one of his, so—she must have left it; had, in fact, been reading it on that last evening. He closed his eyes and heard her low voice talking about it with such enthusiasm. Music, books, art—she had opened his eyes to them. Before her, he'd been all about sports, drinking, and scoring. He stroked the cover of the battered book, remembering . . .

Nina—with the long red hair, the braces on her teeth, and the freckles, who at seventeen had blossomed and caught his eye, and more than that, his heart. Nina, who loved Pollock, Chapman, and poetry.

'Who? Who and who?' He'd asked her as she'd dragged him to the gallery, the cinema, and the library, opening doors in his mind and head that had stayed open forever, helping to make him into the man he now was.

He shivered again. Damn, it was getting colder, and below him, the floor of the warehouse was covered in a patchwork quilt of snow mixed with gray concrete. In the farthest corner, he glimpsed a shadow flitting and weaving between the machine carcasses.

"Nina?" he called, then felt idiotic. How could it be? She'd been gone for years. A lost person. Her mom dead, her dad had skipped out on them years before. Her friends had moved on and away. But Jake had stayed in Bradfield, stayed near home, got his degree, but never moved away. He didn't have the heart for it. He'd never married either, never committed to any other woman, committed to nothing except his job, which had bought him the high-end apartment in the former mill town, Saltaire, right by the weir.

The weir. The waters ran deep there and held its secrets. His and others.

"I've been waiting for you, Jakey, waiting for so long." The shadow twirled and danced across the floor, leaving no footprints in the snow but stirring the air. A coil of wiring lifted and floated toward him, as though an unseen figure was carrying it as a lasso.

"Nina, is it really you?" He gripped the window frame so hard shards of glass cut into his palm, and he saw his blood speckle the wood.

The shadow flowed faster toward him, as though lured by the droplets of blood. The cold in the air bit harder and Jake felt his heart slow, his flesh flourish into goosebumps, and the tips of his fingers turn numb.

For the first time that evening, he felt anxiety—not just that, but gut-wrenching terror. He was not safe, he was not in control, and he did not know who or what this shadow or ghost—OK, at last, he'd said the word to himself—what the ghost of his ex-girlfriend, his one true love, could or would do to him.

"I loved you, Nina," Jake said to the shadows pooling below him. He saw an arm reach up, saw fingers, with the nails painted her signature silver glitter as she reached, impossibly, a whole floor up toward him. He felt her touch, after more than three decades, but he remembered it so well. Her fingers stroked his cheek and then his lips. A familiar gesture.

"Jakey, my love, my only love," she said, this ghost girl from his past.

Jake gasped at the iciness of her touch, his cheek burned, and his lips began to bleed. He licked them and tasted salt mixed with copper.

"What have you done to me?" he whispered and wiped his hand over his cheek. To his shock, a thin layer of skin rubbed off, like dried Copydex.

"I loved you." He knew it was Nina's voice. It was stronger now, closer, right by his ear, worming inside his head. Her hand, taking form and flesh to the bones, stroked his hair and then across his eyes.

"Do you see me now, Jakey?" she asked.

He closed his eyes, and opening them, jerked backward, his spine pressing against the shattered window frame.

"This is what's left of me. After you killed me. Remember that night?"

And he did—in that moment he remembered everything. The years of sleeping pills and alcohol had not completely smothered the memory of that last stolen night spent camping in the warehouse, snuggling under blankets, eating a picnic, drinking beer, laughing, singing "Fast Car," making plans to get married at eighteen, running away because Mr. Formal would never approve. Getting drunker, smoking weed, and feeling the paranoia chip away at the buzz.

Then he'd heard the noise of keys jangling, saw a torchlight flashing in the downstairs windows, heard the heavy, oh-so-familiar footsteps. Panic bubbled up inside him. They'd be found out. He knew it. Then his world would fall in, implode.

"It's Dad, he's coming to check."

Nina soothed him. "No, it's not. It's the night watchman, and he won't come up here to the office. Keep quiet."

Jake was losing it, and Nina laughing, laughing—at him, because she was stoned, high, happy, and so in love. His hand on her mouth, his heart in his mouth. She hardly put up a struggle, she went down and under so quiet it was as though she were toppling into a bed of snow. It had been snowing that night, too, he remembered now.

"I'm sorry, Nina. It was a mistake." Jake's lips could hardly move, his eyelashes wore an icy crusting, his skin burned with the cold.

"Love you," his ex-girlfriend whispered with her chill, chill breath. "This way we can be together forever, Jakey. Like we always wanted."

Jake tried to push her blue face with her vacant glassy eyes and rotting skin away from him. The stink of her, the decay coming off her, it was overwhelming. She was not his Nina, yet she was his Nina, looking like the last time he'd seen her but a thousand times worse. This was how she had come to him in his nightmares. Before he'd carried her to the weir and let the river take her away.

His own eyes were blurring, all he could see was a snowstorm and all he could feel was the cold, eating at him, as Nina bent down to give him one last kiss.

**Alyson Faye** lives in the UK, she works as an editor/tutor; her dark fiction has appeared on the Horror Tree site, in many *Sirens Call* magazines, and recently in *Don't Break the Oath* from Kandisha Press, and *Night Frights 2*. She is often on the moor with her Labrador, Roxy.

**Author Website:** https://blackangelpressblog.wordpress.com/

**Social Media Handle:**
Amazon Author Page: author.to/AlysonFayeAmazonAuthor

# MEETING THE MONSTER

## JOHN KUJAWSKI

The knock on the door made me think of my childhood fears.

No doubt, answering the door always caused me anxiety, something I never liked while growing up. I thought, if opened the door I'd see a monster waiting for me—or maybe a horrible maniac wearing a mask—that would slice me to pieces as soon as he laid eyes on me. But this night was a special evening. Halloween, and I was prepared. Still, I despised the sound of that knock on the door.

The trick-or-treaters had been running around collecting candy. I was alone in my apartment as usual. As a bachelor, I didn't have anyone to distract me from my creative ideas. I thought of ways to deal with my phobias, and I wanted to put one of them to use on this wonderful holiday night.

Even as the kids' small feet ran toward my place, I still thought they could be zombie kids or vampires. All they wanted was a treat, but I was prepared to give them something else.

I always felt that when someone feared a monster, they often became one. I wanted to be a monster this Halloween. It was I who wanted to cause the nightmares this time, so I knew what I needed to do.

I went to my freezer and got out the one thing I needed—a human arm. Now, there was no question that only some type of terrible, animalistic human would keep that in the freezer, but it had not been there long. I found it one night in the park, and I froze the thing. Before that, the arm was horrible to even think about, but when I saw it in the wooded area by the walking path, I had to have it. I ran to the car, got a towel, and managed to get that body into the trunk with no one watching. I had no intention of getting rid of it. I just needed to use it once so I could truly be a menace and play my little trick on the world.

Anyway, I had that arm in my hand as quickly as I could get a hold of it, and I put on a clown mask. The arm might have left a frozen feeling in my hand, so pale and lifeless that it was truly sick. The mask, a silly plastic piece of junk I picked up at some discount store, was far more amusing. It wasn't made by any genius of an artist. It looked like something a kid could have drawn. I suppose I got what I had paid for, but I figured it would do. I walked over to the apartment entrance to greet those trick-or-treaters.

When I opened the door, clearly, the four costumed guests didn't get what they expected. I remember the screaming and the sound of the running feet and heavy breathing that seemed to echo into the wind of the night.

Three of them went running when they saw what I held as I smiled under my mask. I stood there with the arm in my hand thinking, *I just played the ultimate trick and became the true vision of evil that everyone in the neighborhood feared.*

But, the fourth child. This one didn't scream. This one didn't run. He stood there in his Spider-Man costume with the cheap plastic mask that reminded me of the one I wore. He simply didn't move. He seemed calm, he remained quiet, and I suspected he was staring straight at me, but thankfully, I couldn't see his eyes. Next, I heard the sound I'll never forget—laughter, an evil laugh with a hint of enjoyment and pleasure, almost inhuman.

Part of me felt terrified. After all, this kid, indeed, was some type of monster.

**John Kujawski**'s interests range from guitars to the Incredible Hulk. He was born and raised in St. Louis, Missouri, and still lives there to this day.

# DOORS OF DEATH

## THOMAS M. MALAFARINA

*In the universe, there are things that are known, and things that are unknown, and in between, there are doors.*

—WILLIAM BLAKE

The man and the woman sat on the cold, filthy concrete floor among the reeking stench of urine, vomit, feces, death, and decay. The man stared silently at the woman, whose gaze was distant and unfocused. Something would happen soon. Something had to happen. And when it did, one of them would probably die, and one might have a chance to live.

Their number had initially been five. Three men and two women. Five strangers, thrown together with one common goal; survival. Now, only these two remained. Byron wondered how long he could hold out before he was forced to make an impossible decision.

Under other circumstances, he might have been attracted to the woman, but not now. Because now she was a wretched shadow of what she once was. Her hair was greasy and unwashed. She stank from vomit and from soiling herself on many occasions. This was not to suggest that Byron was much better himself since he was every bit the stinking, filthy wretch the woman was.

Byron was an engineer by profession and believed any problem could be solved by logic and scientific reasoning. He felt, if he could just last a bit longer, the woman might give in and take her chance. If so, Byron might yet make it out of this mess alive.

He couldn't recall the circumstances by which he had ended up in this situation. He wasn't even from this part of the country. Byron had been on a business trip, having flown east several days earlier. Then he realized his original estimation of time was likely no longer valid. If he was accurate, he had arrived several days before his abduction. He had no idea how long ago that had been. However, since he was dehydrated and starving, he suspected it had been at least two or three days.

He knew people could survive a long time without food, but what about going without water? He didn't know, but he suspected not much longer. He had not yet gotten to the stage where he was willing to drink his urine. Then again, he couldn't recall the last time he needed to relieve himself. No input, no output, he assumed.

As far as how he had ended up here, the last thing Byron remembered was stopping by a local restaurant and ordering dinner. Since breakfast, he hadn't had time to eat, so he ordered the most significant steak dinner on the menu. He had started with a drink and an appetizer. The server had also brought out a small basket of hot, fresh bread.

Byron recalled the alcohol in his drink had been strong, and now that he thought about it, the beverage did have a slightly different taste. At the time, he assumed the whiskey had come from a local distillery, which often could account for a somewhat unusual flavor.

After taking only a few healthy swallows while enjoying his bread, he was surprised that he had already started feeling drunk. It typically took several strong drinks to do him in, even on an empty stomach. But how could only one drink take him down? Byron decided he had most definitely been drugged. But for what purpose? The amusement of some psycho?

He wished now that he would have been able to eat the meal he had ordered. To the best of his recollection, he had only had time to nibble on that single piece of bread, and then it was lights out. When he awoke, he was in this horrible place with four other equally confused strangers. Byron was hungrier and thirstier than he had ever been. How long had he been out? Hours? Days? As famished as he felt, it could have been days.

The room in which he awoke was a giant hexagonal structure more than thirty feet across. It was painted black from floor to ceiling and illuminated by small, dimly lighted candle-style bulbs positioned in sconces, one on each of the six adjacent walls. Also on each wall was a door. The doors had numbers from one to six scrolled on them with dripping red paint. Byron suspected the color was to project the illusion of blood to screw with their heads.

The message was painted in large fluorescent yellow letters above the doors, lit by a series of blacklights. It wrapped entirely around the room. The statement read, "Welcome to Doors of Death. One door leads to freedom. The others lead to death."

"What . . . what the Hell . . . is this all about? And who . . . who are you people?" one of the strangers mumbled in his sleepy confusion as he stood staring up at the glowing words.

Byron had been the first to respond, although doing so in his still foggy mental state was difficult, "I . . . I don't know. I don't understand. One minute . . . I was eating dinner . . . and the next, I woke up here. I have no idea why we're here or who you people are. But apparently, we've been here for a while. I'm Byron, by the way. Byron Addison." The man who had initially spoken didn't respond. Instead, he strolled around the room, examining the walls and doors.

A slim, confused-looking middle-aged woman extended her trembling hand and said, "I'm Sarah Jenkins, and I don't mind saying I'm quite terrified."

Byron gently shook her hand and replied, "As am I, Sarah. As am I. This is a strange place, and unfortunately, I think we all have good reason to be scared."

The other woman in the group came forward and introduced herself. "I'm Janice Parker. I have no idea what going on here, but I don't like it. This is highly irregular."

"Wow, that's profound," the young man said as he walked from door to door. "Such an incredible overstating of the obvious."

"There's no need to be like that, buddy," a well-built man appearing to be in his early sixties said. "None of us wants to be here and have no idea how or why we are. This has to be some sort of misunderstanding. Incidentally, I'm David Slater." The man shook hands with the others except for the young man, who was still examining the six doors.

"Well, aren't we all just one big happy freaking family?" the cocky young man said with more anger than seemed warranted. "I'd tell you all to call me Chuck if I was going to hang around long enough to get all buddy-buddy with you, but I'm not. I have places to go and people to see. This isn't one of them, and you folks aren't either."

Byron had no idea why this Chuck fellow was so hostile and rude, but he suspected the young man was just as frightened as the rest of them. This abrasive false bravado was apparently how Chuck dealt with his fear.

Now, many days later, as Byron sat on the cold floor, the image of that young man's face was as present in his mind as it had been on that first encounter. Byron suspected that look, Chuck's name, and what eventually happened to the man would remain ingrained in his memory for as long as he lived, however long that might be.

Byron had instinctively known this Chuck fellow would be the first to try a door. The man was young, strong, impatient, and likely believed he was immortal, as all foolish young people did. If there was one thing Byron had learned in his fifty-eight years on Earth, it was to take his time before making a decision. What was that old saying? Fools rush in where angels fear to tread? Yeah, that was it. Byron had little doubt that Chucky boy would be the first. However, it had happened even more quickly than Byron expected.

Chuck had looked around at the four strangers and said, "You can't take any of this crap seriously. Can't you see we're being punked? This is some idiot's idea of a joke, a prank, a gag. Don't you get that?"

"Someone drugged us and brought us here for some purpose," Byron tried to reason with the man. "I think that's rather extreme for a practical joke, don't you?"

"I agree with Byron. Something nefarious is happening here," David added.

"Nefarious? Did you actually just say nefarious? What are you, like a hundred years old or something? Jesus!" Chuck complained.

"Easy, Chuck," Sarah said. "There's no need to be like that. We're all frightened here, but we're all in this together. We have to figure a way out of here."

"We? We? What's this 'we' crap? Do you have a mouse in your pocket or something? Wee wee wee! There ain't no we, babe. There's me, and there's you bunch of losers. And I ain't no part of your little band of bozos. As far as I'm concerned, you morons can stand around looking like lost sheep until the cows come home, but I'm outta here." With that, Chuck made a beeline for the door with the number three painted on it. Before anyone had a chance to stop him, his hand was turning the knob, and the door swung open.

What happened next was something Byron could not explain with either his beloved science or logic, although later, despite his distress, he couldn't help but wonder about the mechanics behind it.

From the darkness behind the door came what sounded like the whir-ring of a dozen circular saw blades. In the few seconds that followed, the young man turned briefly to look back at his companions. The finality in that accepting look on his face spoke volumes in its simple comprehen-sion. In his silence, it said, "I'm a dead man."

That was when his head was separated from his body in a spray of blood and buzzing saw blades. Simultaneously, the rest of him exploded into fragments as dozens of rotating razor-toothed circles of steel tore him to bloody bits. A few of them passed right through him, ricocheted off the remaining doors, and flew into the group of strangers.

Sarah was slightly wounded as one of the blades skimmed across her forearm. David only marginally missed getting neutered by a whirring blade that passed between his legs. Everyone was screaming and diving for cover.

When the chaos was over, Sarah was grabbing her arm through blood-soaked fingers and crying hysterically. What remained of Chuck was scattered in pieces all over the room. The concrete floor was awash with his blood and gore. The stench of his death filled the room, as well as the reek of vomit when several of the group threw up upon themselves and on the floor. That was when Byron suddenly realized there was no toilet in the room and no sink or source of water whatsoever.

Byron keeled down and examined the wound on Sarah's arm. It wasn't deep, and it wouldn't need a tourniquet. However, it would leave a nasty scar, and if untreated in this unsanitary environment, it would most definitely become infected. Then again, Byron suspected fear of infection was the least of their immediate problems. He had managed to stop the bleeding with a bandage he made by removing and ripping his outer shirt. Afterward, he wished he had found another way to make a bandage. The room was quite chilly when all he had to wear was a sleeve-less undershirt.

When things calmed down, the strangers sat huddled in the middle of the room as far away from the splattered remains of Chuck as possible. They were all stippled with crimson castoff from Chuck's bloody demise. Sarah had stopped sobbing and had collapsed into a mentally exhausted sleep.

"Oh my God, did you see that?" Janice whimpered. "That Chuck guy . . . he was . . . Oh, Jesus!"

David put his arm around the young woman and said, "It's OK, Janice. Let it out. There, there."

Byron watched David console Janice as Sarah slept nearby. His thoughts began to blur as he felt the effects of adrenaline crash overtaking him, and soon he, too, collapsed onto the floor asleep.

He was startled awake by the sound of an explosion. He had no idea if he had been asleep for a few minutes or hours. All he knew was he was hungry and thirsty. As his eyes regained focus, Byron saw another of the doors standing open. It was the door labeled number five. He walked on trembling legs to see what had happened.

In front of the door lay the bloodied remains of what was once that woman, Janice. Her torso was separated from the lower half of her body by what appeared to be a shotgun blast. One of her hands still twitched in what Byron hoped was only a nervous reaction. The idea of her still being alive and in agony was more than he could imagine. He felt his stomach turn, and then he vomited what little remained in his stomach onto the bloody floor. Byron felt weak and dizzy. How much time had passed? He returned to the center of the room and lay down on the cold concrete floor, unsure if his wobbly legs would support him.

"Why are we here?" Sarah cried. "Why is this happening to us, Byron?"

Byron didn't answer. He lay silently in the fetal position on the floor, trying futilely to make sense of everything that was happening. He could smell the sharp scent of urine and realized some of his companions had been soiling themselves rather than exposing themselves to the others. It was quite dark in the room, dark enough to hide any wet stains but too light for complete privacy. As he lay, Byron listened to his two remaining companions discussing their plight.

"I think it's the government. You know, some sort of scientific mind game. It's probably the military," David suggested.

Sarah said, "I agree. I read a lot, and in my books, the government is always screwing with people. You know, using us in their weird experiments."

David said, "Mind games, I tell you. They're killing us one at a time to see how we react. They're making us wallow in our own filth and the rotting remains of these poor dead souls."

Then David stood on his weakened legs, raised his fists to the ceiling, and screamed, "What the Hell do you people want from us? If you want us dead, then kill us now. Don't drag this out any longer. Either let us go or kill us."

David's tirade was met with silence. Sarah began weeping, which echoed pathetically in the tomb-like quiet of their prison.

Byron said quietly from his prone position, "You might as well blame space aliens while you're at it." Then he sat up and chastised them, "It's obvious, Sarah, that you read a lot of fiction. But you must understand something. That crap in books is all made up. That's why it's called fiction. Nerdy writers put these stories together, sitting at their computers typing and lying their collective butts off. That's what they do."

David said, "But even fiction has elements of truth in it. So this actually could be a government thing."

"It most certainly could be," Sarah agreed.

"I don't know what government you two are talking about. Any government I know about in this country couldn't successfully conduct a one-car funeral. I don't understand what's going on here any more than you both do," Byron continued. "I can't pretend to know who is doing this or why. And to be honest, neither of those things matter anyway as they won't change our situation."

"Meaning what?" David asked. "Are we just supposed to give up? Do you want us to bend over, spread our cheeks, and tell them to have at it?"

Byron waited for a beat before speaking, then said, "We're helpless here. Four doors remain, and there are only three of us. Sooner or later, we're each going to have to open a door and either die or find the way out of here. I assume once the door to freedom is found, then all of us still living would be free to go. But sitting around trying to figure out who's responsible won't help us one little bit. To be honest, at this point, I don't know what will help us. So, for now, why don't you both please keep the volume down, relax, and try to rest and save what little strength you have left. Lord knows I need to get some sleep."

With that, Byron lay his head back onto his arms, and before he realized it, he was fast asleep. Sometime later, he awoke to a blood-curdling scream. As his eyes focused, Byron saw it was Sarah wailing like a banshee. Before he could ask her what had happened, he saw David in the distance. It took a few seconds for Byron's mind to comprehend what he was witnessing.

The door numbered six was standing wide open. David was standing in front of the open door with his waving arms outstretched as if trying to maintain his balance while simultaneously appearing to be having trouble comprehending what had just happened to him. All the while, Sarah screamed like her last piece of sanity had just shattered. Perhaps it had. After seeing David, Byron wondered how long he could hope to keep his mind from splintering into a million insane pieces.

David stood with an eight-foot-long, six-inches-around shaft penetrating his abdomen. It not only had entered through his stomach and now extended a foot out of his back, but after skewering David like a human shish kebab, the front of the massive spear had opened up like an umbrella. But this umbrella was made of eight razor-sharp blades. The edge of each blade arched back toward David, and in the few seconds remaining, Byron understood what was coming next.

An unseen force, the same one that had sent the projectile outward, now retracted the weapon at unimaginable speed, pulling the impaled David with it into the darkness beyond the door. The horror was all over in seconds.

Sarah had mercifully stopped screaming. She had also stopped sobbing. Then Byron realized the young woman had become like a clock whose spring had been overwound to the point of breaking. Sarah had shut down, falling into some self-preserving catatonic state. She sat silently on the floor, staring at nothing.

That was when Byron saw the small stream of urine seeping out from under the woman. It wasn't much; they were both too dehydrated for that. Nor was it the first time she had soiled herself. Hell, they all had. In addition, they were weak, thirsty, and starving. So, when they deemed it necessary, they went in their clothes. Sarah sat in her most recent filth, not moving or reacting to what she had done.

Now, God only knew how much later, Byron sat on the floor across from Sarah, waiting to see if she would eventually rejoin him in the land of the barely living. So far, she was showing no signs whatsoever of recuperating from her silent state.

"Sarah? Can you hear me in there? I need you to come back. I can't do this on my own. Look, Sarah, we're both starving and dying of thirst. I don't know how much longer we can go on like this. I'm not ashamed to say that I'm terrified. I don't want to die like this, but I can't find the courage to open one of those doors either.

"I'm going to lie down and sleep. If I'm lucky, I won't wake up. There are worse ways to die, as you've seen firsthand. If I don't wake up again, I just want to say how sorry I am. Not only for not being more helpful to you but also for leaving you behind. I don't want to give these sick bastards whatever it is they seem to want from us. I only want it all to end. So I suppose this is goodbye, Sarah. Stay strong."

Byron lay down once again on the cold, chilled concrete floor of their prison among the stench of the rotting, tattered remains of his fallen comrades. He wanted nothing better than to die in his sleep and hoped his final wish would come true. He closed his eyes and let the darkness of sleep envelop him.

His wish was not granted, however. Byron awoke sometime later. He had no idea how long he had slept, but judging by how weak he felt, he knew it had to have been a significant amount of time. His stomach was cramped with hunger. His mouth and tongue were desert dry and his lips cracked and bleeding. It took a while for his dry and pasted eyes to gain focus. That was when he saw Sarah was gone.

He looked over and saw the door marked with a number two standing open. There was no sign of Sarah, so Byron hoped against hope that perhaps Sarah had found the door to freedom, even if it was pure chance.

He stumbled over to the open door and stopped dead in his tracks. There was a trail of blood leading from just outside the door into the blackness within.

This was no safe exit, no door to freedom. It was another death trap, set by whoever was orchestrating this bizarre experiment. Byron heard the sound that resembled the noise made by a ball rolling. It was coming from inside the blackness of whatever world lay beyond the threshold. Seconds later, he saw Sarah's severed head roll out into the main room. A scream caught in his throat as his stomach clenched. Her hair had all been shaved off to give it a more spherical, ball-like appearance. This violation only served to make the scene more repulsive.

Byron had had enough. He knew he had to end this no matter what. He was near death, and his mind was on the verge of shattering if it hadn't already done so. He stumbled toward the door marked with a bloody number one. He had a random thought about a bumper sticker he had seen on the back of a truck hauling portable toilets that read, "We're #1 in the #2 business."

He chuckled insanely to himself as he grabbed for the handle, and without taking another moment to consider the consequences, he yanked open the door. Byron was not prepared for what awaited him on the other side. He assumed he would be blown to bits by some explosive device or sliced into a dozen pieces as his companions had been, but that was not the case.

This door opened to a hallway about three feet wide and thirty feet long. Byron thought he must be imagining things, but the hallway seemed to lead outside. At the far end of the hall, Byron could see a most beautiful afternoon complete with sunshine, grass, trees, and even a stream.

He had done it. He had picked the right door. He found it ironic that the door to freedom would be the first of the six they had to choose. Perhaps whoever was orchestrating this twisted experiment had understood that it would be human nature to try any door but the most obvious. Had Byron been reasoning more coherently and taken the time to think about it, he might have chosen the other remaining door rather than one. Had he done so, then instead of heading to freedom, he would be dead by now.

Byron used what little strength he had remaining to trudge slowly down the hall. He already knew the first thing he would do. He would head right for that stream and take an enormous cleansing drink. Then he would crawl into the water and wash the filth of his captivity off of him. Byron didn't know if there would be any fruit trees or vegetables nearby, but he didn't care. He was going to be free. He would find food somewhere or find a road that would lead him back to civilization.

As he approached the outer end of the hallway, Byron hesitated for a moment as he looked at the scene of the beautiful day awaiting him. Something wasn't right with the image he was seeing. Upon closer examination, Byron noticed that a small fold appeared in the upper left-hand corner of the scene. He realized what he was looking at was a picture or painting, but not the real outdoors. He reached out and touched what he thought was a stream and felt the hardness of a wall behind the scenery.

He heard a noise like a door opening behind him and, at first, was unable to gather the courage to turn to see what it was. Then he heard a deep guttural growl of an animal coming from the darkness. As he forced his back helplessly against the outdoor scene now blocking any hope of an exit, he stared at the two glowing eyes as the creature made its way toward its dinner.

**Thomas M. Malafarina** has published seven horror novels, as well as six collections of horror short stories. He has also published a book of often strange single-panel cartoons titled *Yes I Smelled It Too*, as well as a Microsoft-based technical manual, "Link-Tuit." He has written and published more than 200 short stories. All of his horror books have been published through Hellbender Books, an imprint of Sunbury Press (www.Sunbury press.com).

**Author Website:** www.ThomasMMalafarina.com

**Social Media Handle:**
Amazon Author Page: https://amzn.to/3QYXKru

# CHILDREN OF THE GOAT MAN

## DOUGLAS FORD

Charlie heard nothing from Elsa in years, but he promised to drop everything and come over when she called him.

She provided no explanation. "Just come over," she said. "There's someone here you need to see."

"Someone I know?" Charlie said, feeling the weight of years and the ache of a decade's absence. He started counting when no immediate response came, making it to thirteen before she said anything else.

"That's hard to answer. I can't really say one way or another."

Charlie didn't know what that meant, but he verified that she still lived with her father, though she declined to call what her father did "living." More like waiting out the effects of smoking four packs a day since forever, she explained. His chief reward for a diligent habit: congestive heart failure and a slipping hold on reality. Elsa stuck around and helped him pay whatever bills he couldn't cover with his police pension.

Charlie said, "This person I'm coming to see—is it your dad? Because I doubt he wants to see me."

"Just come over," she said, hanging up before he could reply.

On the way, Charlie recognized the neighborhood, though it looked a little worse than he remembered, with more than a few cars on blocks and plenty of listless people sitting on doorsteps, taking a break from doing nothing.

He found Elsa waiting outside for him, taking quick puffs from a cigarette that looked all filter. He didn't know if he should hug her after not seeing her for so long. They did a lot more than hug in the old days. She crossed her arms after throwing away the cigarette, so he just gave her a little wave.

No greeting in return. Instead, she led him up a walkway overgrown with weeds, toward a side garage door. She paused with her hand on the door and looked at him. "You remember Cole?"

"No," Charlie said.

"Me neither." She opened the door and gestured for him to follow.

The person called Cole sat in a chair in the middle of the garage, surrounded by tools and broken machinery. At first, Charlie misread the scene of the skinny man sitting so straight and rigid, thinking that ropes held him bound to the chair. But he stood up when he saw Charlie and beamed like a million dollars just walked in.

"I can't believe it's you, really you. Jesus Christ. I never thought I'd ever see either of you ever again," the man said. Charlie took in the height of the stranger—well over six feet even with hunched shoulders. Impossibly thin, too, like he never ate, with a chest so hollowed out a bird could nest inside it.

Charlie looked at Cole, then Elsa, then back to Cole again. "Do I know you?"

"Yes, you fucking know me, and she knows me, too. You left me in the fucking woods, in that fucking place, but I finally got out. And the part that sucks is we need to go back, and I mean right away."

———

Cole meant the woods behind the high school, a refuge for scrub jays and empty beer bottles and weather-torn porno mags. With the Internet, nobody bought porno mags anymore, but somehow, they kept finding their way to the woods for teenagers to discover, because only teenagers went into those woods, looking for a reprieve from adults and of course to find trouble.

Cole said they had a gang back then, and on occasion, they liked to explore those woods together. On a cool October day, they cut school early just to see how far back the trees went and how long it would take before they ran into any sign of civilization.

This led to them finding the hospital.

It sat there, nestled among the trees with broken windows and wild vines nearly covering it entirely. None of them expected to find it, nor did they know it even existed. Except for Elsa. She recalled her dad talking about some abandoned hospital off the beaten path, but she didn't remember him saying anything about it existing so close to where they lived or how it could sit back here in the woods without them even knowing it. There wasn't even a road leading to it. Or maybe the hospital went so far back, perhaps all the way to the 1920s, that over time, nature just reclaimed everything. That suggestion seemed to jar more memories for Elsa, and she remembered her dad saying something about it having served as a convalescence home for people with TB, later becoming an orphanage or mental hospital—she couldn't say which—but she also remembered her father warning her not to follow any of her dipshit friends into it.

"This is the one," Cole had said.

"How many abandoned hospitals are there?" asked Elsa. "I'm not just being sarcastic. How many are there really?"

Cole started to say, "Probably a lot," but the words didn't have time to come out because he saw the first goat. A large white one, with magnificent horns, grazing, just at the far corner of the building. This discovery at first delighted them, but they soon began to feel uneasy. To find some farm animal grazing out here in what otherwise seemed unoccupied land made them feel vulnerable, watched. Then Max pointed in another direction toward another goat, this one partially obscured by a tree, but grazing just like the other one.

("Wait," said Elsa. "Who's Max?")

("You don't remember him either, I guess, but he was part of our gang. An important part. You forgot all about us.")

Soon enough, two more goats appeared, then two more after that, and they began to realize that a whole herd of goats occupied the area, many of them camouflaged by the surrounding woods but gradually becoming visible as they stood quietly, stricken by what Cole described as a feeling of both awe and terror.

Those feelings only increased when they saw the largest goat of them all—the apparent lord and master of the rest, one that stood out because of its pure whiteness, though that alone couldn't explain how magnificent and large he seemed, with horns that dwarfed all the rest, standing long and rounded to intimidating points. This one stood before an empty doorway, and unlike the other goats, he regarded the teenagers with intelligent curiosity. Perhaps to show his lack of fear, this goat sniffed the air contemptuously and turned around to disappear through the open doorway, as if daring the teenagers to follow him inside.

No one spoke. Cole searched each of their faces for clues to their thoughts. All of them seemed to feel the same magical rush, a sense of having stumbled upon something forbidden. However, something buried within Cole's consciousness began sending him a warning signal. A thought struggling to form.

Before he could pinpoint it exactly, Max took a step toward the entrance where the goat had vanished. "Well, who's coming with me?" he said, looking over his shoulder.

No one else moved, and though Cole couldn't say for sure what went through everyone else's minds, he found himself approaching a stubborn, resisting thought, a memory really, and before anyone could take another breath, it finally broke through completely, a phrase forming in his consciousness.

The Goat Man.

There it was. He spoke it, and Max halted his movement and turned.

Yeah, all he knew about the Goat Man came from crazy Uncle Larry, a guy who liked to drink beer, ride motorbikes, and shoot the shit. He told Cole the story—how he went camping in the Everglades one night during one of his many treks to find the Lost City, where Al Capone allegedly hid a bunch of money, though Larry never did find any such thing. It happened that Uncle Larry pitched his tent and settled in with a good fire going, eventually nodding off after enjoying a few cans of beer. A full moon lit up the surrounding area pretty well, so when he awoke and saw what he saw, he saw it pretty clearly. The Goat Man. Sitting on his haunches on the other side of the fire. Just looking at him. *He was the devil, kid, I swear it*, Larry said. *Pure evil, through and through.*

When Cole related this story to his friends, they laughed and reminded him that every single one of them had an Uncle Larry—a delusional drunken relative. Max told him to calm down and follow that goat into the building. "Stay close and keep me safe if you're so worried," Max said.

But Cole remained rooted to his spot, unnerved by what seemed like an unnatural determination to follow the goat into that building. No discernible purpose in that. Nobody ever took Cole to church, but he grew up with what he considered a healthy fear of the invisible world—he had a grandmother who made sure of that, believing that only a lingering fear of eternal damnation would keep him from the kind of life his dear uncle lived. That strategy didn't work out as well as she would have liked, but it did make Cole think that only evil machinations could explain Max's determination to follow a goat into an abandoned building.

But what did Elsa decide to do? She suddenly ran off in a different direction, apparently transfixed by the appearance of a baby goat. Charlie ran after her—as usual, he only had one thing on his mind, and Cole could hear him making all sorts of promises about how he'll catch one of those babies for her. Cole realized then that none of his friends took anything he said seriously, and none of them respected the obvious *gravity* of their situation. Not even Max, his best friend in the world, who smiled at him just before disappearing into the empty doorway.

What else could Cole do? Their doubt in him proved contagious, and he didn't want to stand there alone in front of that creepy building. No other choice but to follow Max. Which he did.

———

Charlie forced himself to laugh at the end of all this. But nothing in the story struck him as funny. Something felt wrong.

"Look, I'm sorry. I just don't know you. I've never met you, and I don't know anybody named Max. I've never even heard of an old orphanage in the woods."

"It was a hospital," said Cole.

"Whatever. Right, Elsa?"

Elsa said nothing. She watched Cole, searching for something.

"We've got to go back," said Cole. "Max is still there."

"Still where?"

Cole looked at Charlie as if he had just discovered the dumbest person alive. "*The hospital*. He and I were kept there. As slaves."

"Slaves to the Goat Man? The Devil?" Charlie looked at Elsa just to verify that she heard all this. But she continued to regard Cole with a blank expression.

"Does your Goat Man want something?" she said, as if she sensed something. "In exchange for Max?" She avoided Charlie's questioning gaze.

"Yeah. He does. He wants his offspring back. The one you stole."

———

Elsa loved animals. Charlie remembered that. He remembered any number of cats that varied with indoor or outdoor status, at least two dogs, and at one point, a rabbit and a parakeet at the same time. In the backyard, she also kept a goat.

Leaving Cole in the garage, Elsa led him to the backyard, where they stood quietly side by side watching the goat graze on grass long overdue for cutting. Around the goat's neck hung a bell—a quaint touch without any practical purpose. Elsa just thought a goat should have a bell.

"You remember where I got Farnum?" Elsa said.

Charlie didn't even remember the name of the goat until she mentioned it. "A fair?"

She shook her head and chewed on her pinky. "Maybe. I'm struggling to remember. I can tell you the complete biography of every animal I've ever owned—but Farnum here, I can't rightly recall. I feel like I'm waking up from a spell. Like I've been clobbered over the head."

That last comment made Charlie look away. He understood that Elsa knew what clobbering felt like. Charlie had promised to pick her up that time her father got drunk and laid into her with his fists, calling her a whore. He should have met her at the corner like he promised, and then they'd have both escaped this miserable town. He struggled to remember his excuse. Cold feet? Nervous about their prospects for finding jobs and living on their own? When Charlie didn't show, she took her bags and went inside, where she'd stayed for the remainder of those years.

But maybe that miserable excuse of a father could finally serve a purpose.

"Your dad remembers, I bet," said Charlie.

She snorted without humor. "You won't like what he does remember."

———

Elsa's father wore a dress shirt with boxer shorts, along with a hose of oxygen going up his nose. According to Elsa, she preferred he wear boxers because he liked to squirrel things away in his pockets. She especially had to make sure he didn't get ahold of his car keys—he'd likely kill himself and anyone unlucky enough to get in his way if he ever took the wheel of a car again.

That subject apparently weighed heavily on the old man's mind when Elsa reintroduced Charlie to him. Her father sat at the kitchen table with his legs spread, a tuft of hair showing through the fly of his boxers. "Saw a report on the news," he said, "there's a new law—you got to wear a helmet while you're driving any sort of vehicle. I'd love to be a cop now. Know how many people I'd pull over for not wearing a helmet?"

Charlie looked at Elsa for help. Her expression told him to just roll with it. The dementia.

"Zero?" said Charlie.

"Zero! That's fucking right. What'd you say your name was?"

"Charlie Panchuk. We've met before."

"You fucking my daughter? It's OK if you are, I just don't want to know so I don't come barging in her room and see nothing."

"We're not fucking anymore, Dad," Elsa said.

"That's probably a good thing. All sorts of new diseases these days. Got to know who you're fucking. Who was that boy you were with before?"

"That was Charlie, Dad. He's right here." Elsa signaled to Charlie with her eyes. Over by the kitchen entrance stood Cole, out of her father's sight. "Dad? I'm going to leave you for a while. I'm going to take a hike with Charlie here, and we're going to bring someone else along. Someone you might know."

She gestured for Cole to come closer. Looking hesitant, he complied.

"Hey there, Mr. Campbell," said Cole.

"Why, how you doing, Cole?" said Elsa's father.

———

The three of them stood just behind the high school on the forest's edge, regarding the path that Cole insisted would lead them to the abandoned hospital. Elsa carried a satchel and held a rope that led to the neck of Farnum the goat.

At first, Elsa resisted taking Farnum, but Cole insisted, explaining that without Farnum, they'd have nothing to bargain with, and thanks to them, Max would find himself abandoned to a living hell for the rest of his life.

"What exactly is this living hell you're talking about?" Charlie had asked before they left.

Cole said, "He likes to do things to us. Make us do things to each other."

"What 'things'?" said Elsa.

Cole answered by pulling up his shirt and turning around. Charlie and Elsa gasped when they saw the scars crisscrossing his back. "I could show you more, but I'd have to take off my pants. I'll spare you that, Elsa. You never liked me that way. And you'll never have to worry about me."

"Did I have to worry about you before?"

"Not really," said Cole. He glanced quickly at Charlie. Charlie noticed it, but he couldn't tell if Elsa did. He looked closely at the marks on Cole's back, and they did look real. He noticed that they constituted more than random patterns—that some of them consisted of what looked like deliberate shapes and designs. "They're called sigils," said Cole, as if reading his thoughts. "He carved them into me. They're why everyone has forgotten me."

"Not everyone," said Charlie, thinking of Elsa's dad.

"There's these, too." Cole sat down and showed him the dirty bottoms of his feet, where cross-shaped scars appeared. "I can never step into a church now. I'll burst into flame."

"You could've done these yourself," said Elsa.

"I couldn't have done the ones on my back though."

"Let me talk to Charlie alone for a second. You can go wait with my dad. Give us just a minute."

She led Charlie to her bedroom and closed the door. It had changed a lot since Charlie had been there. Fewer posters, no stuffed animals. She didn't seem stuck in the past at all, not like Charlie felt. He waited for her to say something, but she began rooting through her closet until she found what she wanted. She presented it to him: a high school yearbook. "Look him up," she said. "If he's in there, I'll bring Farnum. But only if he's in there."

Charlie flipped through the pages meant to commemorate their senior year together, both of them having just turned eighteen at the time. Had he written her something, even though they'd both gone separate ways by the end of that year? He couldn't remember, and the book contained few markings or notations. Elsa didn't have many friends then—at least so he remembered—and probably didn't now.

"Here he is. I think." He showed her the image of a skinnier, less-grubby version of the person now sitting in the other room. *Mark Cole*, read the name.

So, Elsa found a bit of rope in the garage, and Farnum the goat joined them as they pushed their way through vine-covered pines and wild-growing sable palms, Cole leading without any objection from Charlie or Elsa. Thunder rumbled from someplace distant, and the air felt wet and heavy.

"What's this Goat Man—this Devil—look like?" said Elsa when a black snake crossed her path.

"You've seen him," said Cole, not looking back.

"Excuse me?"

"You saw him. That day. You stood outside and called for me and Max to come out. He showed up in the doorway, and one look made you run away." He looked back and nodded toward Farnum. "You ran away with him in your arms."

Charlie exchanged a quick glance with Elsa. "If you were inside, how would you know what we saw and did?"

"I watched from a window. I thought you'd come back for me, but you never did. You forgot it all—everything—just like he promised."

———

The sky itself seemed to change as they came upon the hospital ruins. The air already felt hot and sticky, but the presence of the building seemed to infect its surroundings with an ugly yellow smear. Its ivy-covered intrusion made Charlie feel ill. He thought he'd have remembered such a sight, with its graffiti-covered siding and shattered windows.

"I don't see any goats," said Elsa. Attached to the rope she held, Farnum the goat began feasting on the shrubs near her feet.

"He's hidden them. He doesn't want you stealing them."

"This is just an old hospital," Elsa said. Something in her voice told Charlie that she didn't really believe that. "Tell your friend to come out and stop playing games."

"Games? I thought you believed me. We have to get Max out of there."

"I don't believe anyone's held prisoner in there," said Elsa. "I don't remember this place at all. I admit it, I might've known you way back, but you obviously made zero impression on me. And just so you know, in case you thought that this would be a good way to rape and murder me, I brought this." From her satchel, she withdrew what looked like her father's old service gun. "I don't like it when people show up at my house, acting like they know me." She pointed the gun at Cole but then paused as if to reconsider something. "Here, Charlie, you take the gun. I need to hold Farnum."

"Your dad knew him," said Charlie, not taking the gun.

"My dad's a retired cop. Cole probably got arrested for doing something stupid or for being an asshole. What'd you do, Cole? Diddle little girls? Take the gun, Charlie."

When Charlie still wouldn't take the gun, she turned her head and saw him leaning over, his hands on his knees. He began to dry-heave. "Now what the fuck is wrong?"

She didn't see Cole lunge at her. Even if she had seen him, he did so with a speed she couldn't have expected from someone who looked so malnourished. Even Charlie stopped being sick so he could marvel at how supernaturally fast Cole moved.

Not to mention how strong he proved. He held off Elsa's blows as he twisted her wrist and wrenched the gun away. Then he threw it as far as he could into the forest.

Elsa swore at him and rubbed her wrist. Farnum barely moved during the struggle, just kept on chewing.

"I'm sorry, I'm sorry," Cole said. "You never liked me much, but I always liked you, and I never lied to you or let you down." Shooting Charlie a dark look, he added, "Not like some people."

That made Charlie's heart skip a beat, but then the dry heaves returned. Something about this place made him feel sick.

"Know who else never let you down? Max. He'd have done anything for you, and you ran off with this lying motherfucker, leaving me and him trapped in this place for a whole fucking decade. All for a god-damned goat. Charlie grabbed a baby goat, and you both ran off with it. You took it, and you paid with your memory, and I'm guessing, a whole bunch of bad luck. 'Just leave them,' he said, and that's what you did."

The dizziness and nausea finally began to abate, and Charlie found himself able to focus. He saw Elsa staring at him. A look of memory and regret. He remembered that look.

"He needs his child—the animal—back. I served him for a decade, earning his trust. Those carvings on my back allowed me to hide in shadows, to sneak into places when we needed food or supplies. Sometimes he needed blood to spill, and I did that for him, too. At first, he told me he used to be a doctor in the hospital. Then he told me he was really a magician who transformed himself through a spell. Finally, he revealed the truth—that he was the Devil, and I mustn't ever disobey him, even if he told me to spill *your* blood. But I pleaded with him and begged him. Please, please, not you, not someone close to me. 'But she abandoned you and took my offspring,' he said. 'She needs to pay,' he said. And I begged and begged, and he whipped me for being insolent, and he carved more of his spells on me. Once, he made it so I couldn't eat, and I lived on goat's milk for a week, but still, I refused to hurt you. Finally, he told me if I could get you to come here of your own accord and bring his offspring, he would let me go. 'What about Max?' I asked. He thought about it. He has no love for Max. Max refused to bow before him. So he made Max eat his own eyes."

He paused to let that sink in.

"Max is blind and suffering. He'll probably die soon. I asked again, '*What about Max?*' and he finally said that he would let both of us go—if we brought someone in return."

He gestured toward Charlie, and Charlie felt the heaviness of Elsa's gaze. The time had come to speak up, to say that they needed to turn around and go back, leave this forgotten ruin to decay into nothingness, to get away before the path vanished in the darkness. There arose a rustling sound, and in an empty doorway appeared a massive white goat. He stood still and regarded the three of them. A memory fought its way to Charlie's consciousness, and he fought it back. He didn't want memories.

"I suppose that's the Goat Man," said Charlie, though he knew it wasn't. They all knew because they all remembered now.

"It's the emissary," Cole said. "He wants to know what word to bring."

Charlie wished he had the gun now. He and Elsa looked at each other. He pleaded with his eyes, but her expression remained unmoved.

"Let me see Max," said Elsa.

"You won't recognize him," said Charlie. "He could be anyone. Anyone working with this lying cocksucker."

"He has dark shoulder-length hair," said Elsa. "Olive skin. Brown eyes."

"That's all correct, except the eyes. He doesn't have eyes anymore," Cole said.

"That could be anyone," Charlie repeated, though he knew the description would prove correct. He remembered, too.

A clattering from inside the building. The white goat stood motionless and alert.

"You need to drop the rope," said Cole. "Let it go. He'll follow the other one inside."

Elsa held the rope, her turn to look resistant.

"He's yours," said Charlie, "don't do it. Don't let go." As if to punish him, another wave of nausea struck him. He thought, *I'll say anything I want to say, you fucker*, and a voice deep inside replied, *Not if you're going to lie.*

The sky grew a shade darker, and a single horn of half-moon appeared over the husk of the building.

"He'll reward you with better things. Your freedom. My freedom." Elsa allowed Cole to approach her. He touched her wrist. "It has to be your choice."

Elsa dropped the rope. Then she began to weep.

The white goat turned and walked back into the building, expecting the other one to follow.

But Farnum continued to chew grass, untroubled by the commotion.

"He doesn't want to leave," said Elsa, her voice filled with hope.

"He has to," Cole said.

"He has a choice," she said.

Farnum remained in his spot.

"He's been spoiled," said Cole. "Corrupted." He reached behind his waistband and drew forth a knife that no one knew he had. "I'm sorry. There's no other way. You have to do it."

Elsa tried to reply but produced only a choking sound. She wouldn't take the knife.

"Take it," said Charlie, nearly standing erect now. "Or I'll take it."

Ignoring Charlie, Cole whispered, "I can't do it for you. It has to be you."

"Take it and kill him," Charlie said. He meant Cole.

Elsa ignored him, too. Everyone watched Farnum in silence.

Finally, acting quickly, Elsa snatched the knife. She cut quickly and deeply into Farnum's neck. The goat bleated in surprise and tried to run, but the blood ran thick and quick, and before he could go far, he slowed and fell, bleating in betrayal. From a distance, they watched him die.

A sound from the building drew their attention. The white goat re-appeared, leading out a stumbling figure, a man with matted hair, olive skin, and empty pits that once held brown eyes.

"Cole?" the figure said.

"It's OK, Max. Everything is going to be OK again. Elsa did it. She's saving us."

Cole looked at Elsa. Her eyes shone brightly.

"There's just one thing left to do. Before we can go." She nodded her understanding and with the knife approached Charlie.

"We don't know who the fuck that is, Elsa," Charlie said. She didn't reply. Instead, the voice inside his head answered. *Yes, you do.* More pain wracked his insides, and he doubled over.

Behind Elsa, Cole said, "Not the neck this time. Just make sure he can't run."

The pain made it so Charlie couldn't fight, but Cole held him anyway as Elsa cut both of his Achilles tendons.

He collapsed onto the ground and screamed. He screamed so loud he couldn't hear Max saying he would need help navigating the path and Cole assuring him that he would never make him do it alone.

Charlie screamed after them. He begged them to come back for him. He screamed until both horns of the half-moon appeared above the roof of the building and filled the clearing with glorious light.

When he finally fell silent, Charlie could hear clattering from within the abandoned building. Then he saw it, tall and cloaked, standing just outside the empty doorway—a doctor, a magician, the Devil; he wasn't sure. Maybe all of them at once.

He saw its horns, long and curved, with tips as sharp as knife blades. As it reached for his eyes, he knew it was the Devil.

**Douglas Ford** is the author of *The Beasts of Vissaria County*, a novel released in 2021 by D&T Publishing, as well as *Little Lugosi (A Love Story)* and *Ape in the Ring and Other Stories of the Macabre and Uncanny*, both published by Madness Heart Press. His fiction has appeared in *Dark Moon Digest*, *Diabolical Plots*, and *Tales to Terrify*, along with several other small press publications. Upcoming publications include *The Trick*, a novella from Madness Heart Press, and *The Infection Party (and Other Stories of Dis-Ease)* from D&T Publishing. He lives on the west coast of Florida, just off an exit made famous by a Jack Ketchum story.

**Social Media Handles:**
Instagram: https://www.instagram.com/author_douglas_ford/
Facebook: https://www.facebook.com/profile.php?id=100064149938106
Amazon Author Page: https://www.amazon.com/~/e/B01NBEJIMC

# THAT SHADE NEXT TO YOU

SERGIO "ENTE PER ENTE" PALUMBO
EDITED BY MICHELE DUTCHER

A shade sat next to the almost bald blue-eyed man of about 75, at the table eating lunch inside the Old City Merchant restaurant. About this, the woman was certain. At first, the unearthly shadow had appeared to Lecia like a sort of smudge in the restaurant's background, but its form became clearer and clearer as time went by. It never looked like a precise figure, however, because in the end, it still stood out as a dark shade though endowed with human traits and childlike features. It seemed to be a boy, *the soul of a dead boy*, and even if the woman who knew what it was tried her best to avert her eyes, she simply couldn't stop seeing what that shadow was doing, as it was a very strange and characteristic posture: the pale, almost transparent right hand pointed to the old Welsh man at the table.

Lecia knew the gesture had to mean something, though she didn't want to interfere or step up and talk to that man right away. Graying, with two deep chestnut eyes, and still very slender despite her age, she wasn't interested in throwing herself into these situations. Although she knew she had the power to see the souls of the deceased and that the dead themselves tried at times to tell her things, the woman didn't want to get involved. She always kept a low profile, which was much better for her personally, staying safely away from complications, preferring not to eke out a living by becoming a professional medium.

But the spirit wouldn't go away. This happened infrequently, when a soul would appear next to someone—whether it was a beloved, an adversary, or an acquaintance—only for a short time before reappearing again a second or third time. When this reappearance happened it obviously

meant *something*, which at the same time made her think that she had to
do something sooner or later, though she tried to force herself to turn her
mind to other thoughts at present.

But it wasn't easy, surely not easy at all.

Old City Merchant was not far from beautiful Cardiff Castle. In
particular, the eatery was near one of the many nineteenth-century ad-
ditions to the medieval structure that had been built much later than
the first heart of the place itself. The dining room was not full, but there
were customers here and there, and one of those was that aged man,
accompanied by that dead boy's soul. The venue was stylishly retro, but
informal and very comfortable, serving tasty Welsh food.

In a way, the restaurant was the same as the city of Cardiff, which
was being transformed by urban programs into a much more modern
town. The castle situated outside the window seemed to have really un-
dergone modifications and deep changes over the course of the centuries.
This restaurant hadn't escaped a sort of similar process as it mixed new
renovations with the much older wings of the building itself. But she was
unable to remove that presence from her mind, unable to forget about
that unusual posture and the real reason why that shadow, the dead boy,
was pointing to that man now.

The dead boy was dressed in worn-out reddish clothes and had long
water-soaked hair. Though the figure had two eyes of no color in particular—or perhaps they were dark chestnut, it was difficult to be certain
about that—on an empty face that caused a sensation of discomfort and
anxiety, there was no way she could be afraid of the ghost. Its boyish
look and its overall semblance didn't make her fear that something bad
was going to happen to anyone in the restaurant, or even to her in the
end. So, what was it all about? Why was that soul of a dead human being
standing there, unable to move away?

Since she had been a child, the woman had known she had the power
to see things, strange things, or shades, and that had made her doubt
her mental health on many occasions, as a matter of fact. Eventually, she
had survived her visions of childhood and had learned how to deal with
that unusual ability of hers. A friend of her mother's, who knew about
such things, had greatly helped her to come to terms with such an unwanted ability. However, she had never been interested in the practice of

mediating communication between the dead and living human beings. Still, her capability hadn't disappeared with the passing of the years, and now that Lecia was nearing sixty, she thought she would have to bear it for the rest of her life. Willingly, or unwillingly.

When the older man in the jacket finished his lunch, he stood, went to the bathroom, and then headed back to his table where he took his bag and then stepped outside. The shadow followed him, and it was at that point that Lecia knew she had to stop eating, pay her bill, and exit to follow the two. Not that she wanted to, but she had to; she felt it was the right move.

The woman happened to pass through one of the main points of Cardiff itself, the city center, laid out with beautiful Victorian and Edwardian streets and gardens, and the covered market, before entering the south of the center itself, where docklands were being transformed into the second main point of attraction: the creation of a freshwater lake and waterfront.

As she caught a glimpse of them in the open, she kept walking, following at a distance.

It was when they were almost there, near the Arts Council of Wales, that the man changed his course and seemed to head for a modern building, probably where he had his home. As the woman kept looking at the shade and paid attention to the unusual way the soul's eyes looked at the back of the man—with a sort of surprise, sadness, and anger mixed together—she thought she had to do something. Lecia didn't know if the ghost was ready to act against the man once the two got inside, whatever the reason for his hatred might be, or if he just wanted to make resentment clear. This indecision left the woman doubtful for a while. But in the end, Lecia approached the man.

"Good morning, mister," the woman addressed him in a pleasant tone. "I believe I need some information from you."

The man heard her speaking and turned to her as if he had noticed the woman for the first time. He didn't seem to remember seeing her at the restaurant, or maybe she hadn't attracted his interest. This might be why he replied in a calm tone, "Hi, madam. How can I be of help?"

As Lecia readied herself to ask him a question, another gesture from the ghost stopped her. She observed the strange position of the dead figure's boyish mouth—it appeared to be opened in a sort of cry, that finger now raised to point to the aged man's face. *What did it mean?* She had to say something and do something! Otherwise, why did she stop eating and leave the restaurant to follow this person and the shade next to him?

"Actually . . ." Lecia started, "I saw you eating at the Old City Merchant and wondered if you enjoyed your meal there."

"The Old City Merchant, you say?" The elder stared at her for a moment. "Yes, I go there from time to time. What do you want to know about? The service? Or do you need a recommendation for somewhere else to eat?"

"Well . . ." the woman continued in a low tone, but her tentative and difficult speech was cut short as she noticed that the mouth of the boyish ghost appeared to open more, as if he were yelling, or calling for Lecia's full attention. "That's not the real reason I'm talking with you." In the end, Lecia knew she couldn't escape that strange matter anymore, now that she had brought it all to the other's attention anyway.

"So, what do you want?" he inquired of her, with an addled look on his old face.

"Actually, I was thinking. Did you have a nephew, or a son perhaps? A young boy, I mean?"

"What? I'm 75 now and I've never had a child. Of course, my memory deceives me at times. It's not as good as it was years ago." The man scratched at his face and admitted in a low voice.

The woman looked at him. "So, maybe you had a son, and you don't remember?" If his memory was really this bad, it would make everything more complicated.

"Are you asking for a recommendation for a place to eat, or did you want to talk to me about something else?"

"Well, there are other reasons, but this is not easy for me," Lecia added, saddened. It would not be easy under such very unusual circumstances. "I was wondering if you ever had a son or a nephew who liked wearing reddish clothes and had long chestnut hair."

"Why would that be of interest to you?" the other asked the woman.

"Actually . . ." she started speaking again. This might prove the most difficult part of all. "I must tell you something unusual, and you're probably not going to believe me. This is hard for me, too. Not that I'm a medium, but . . . well, I followed you here because I noticed a sort of shadow next to you."

"A shadow? What kind of shadow are you talking about?"

"A ghost, to be more precise. The shade of a dead boy. That is why I asked you about possibly having a son, or perhaps a nephew. Maybe you lost a child who was close to you in the past?"

"That's a stupid thing to say!" the aged man said. "What senseless questions you're asking me! I don't believe in mediums and all that. As I already told you, I never had a son or a nephew." There was a pause as if the elder were slowly struggling to come to terms with something in his mind. "At least, from what I can remember."

At that point, a worried Lecia considered that, possibly, the strange behavior of the boyish ghost, and his yelling, might indicate a display of anger against his killer, his hatred against someone who had put an end to his life. Was this dead boy pointing at the man who had assaulted him? Was the soul of the child trying to testify against the culprit in a kidnapping, a man who had hidden a corpse in his past? At times ghosts did that, the woman knew very well, and this made her scared, leaving her speechless for a few moments.

She never wanted her power; she didn't like being able to see ghosts. The only thing the woman wanted was to be a common individual; a shopkeeper—as she had become after college—was enough for her. That fulfilled all the woman's needs. But she kept having visions, those un-earthly sightings when customers came into her shop, or when she was simply walking down the street. She ordinarily knew how to hold out against them, and how to behave.

But, in this case, she felt very strong sensations and didn't know what to do. And the woman had never felt an intense aloneness like the ghost child portrayed today.

She was almost to the point of explaining again when the ghost elon-gated his arm and reached for hers. And once his pale fingers touched her, a shaken Lecia had other visions, and images of past occurrences flashed through her mind.

Lecia saw a glimpse of that boy, looking much younger than he did now—about four or five, though appearing like a ghost—and his feet stood next to a grave. The scene was a cemetery, the day of a funeral. Both his parents had died, and he remained alone. Then, her visions portrayed another figure next to him. It was that man, the elder, who looked at least ten years younger in her vision. She also heard, or sensed, a name in her head—Uncle Euan. The man was the boy's only next of kin, and the authorities believed no one else could care for the youngster better than his uncle could, of course.

But then the images changed. Other events replaced a moment of calmness. The boy—Peter was his name!—had settled in his uncle's home, and he was now around ten years old. He was taking a bath and appeared happy, despite everything he had already gone through during his short life. He dressed himself after drying and put on reddish clothes.

*Reddish clothes?* The same ones he wore now that he was the ghost. A moment later, a seizure seemed to have caught the boy unexpectedly, a sort of neurological disorder with uncertain characteristics. He fell to the floor, his head and his upper body stuck in the tub that was full of water as muscle contractions continued, making it impossible for him to get out of the tub. His need for air grew stronger, but time was going by, and life ebbed away from the poor boy.

Then, her vision transferred to the sitting room where his Uncle Euan sat alone that day. He didn't seem worried or concerned about why his nephew took so long in the bathroom behind the closed door. It was getting late, so why wasn't he worried? *What was he thinking about?*

The man's eyes appeared lost, in a way, and his mind asleep. But he wasn't asleep; he just wasn't paying attention to what went on at home. It was exactly as if something else took the better of him at present.

So, the boy could have been saved! Why didn't the man intervene? Did he want him to die that day? Was it all on purpose? Or not?

A downstairs neighbor rang the bell to warn the man about the leaking water. The two forced their way into the bathroom and found the dead body of the boy.

At last, the woman finally figured out the truth: Uncle Euan wasn't worried or angry because he didn't remember his nephew lived with him. A very saddened Lecia understood: the man was affected by dementia. He had possibly started experiencing symptoms gradually enough to go unnoticed since he was healthy and agile when he had accepted custody of his nephew.

He probably never thought he might have such an illness at that time, and once he detected the first symptoms, or considered the possibility of oncoming dementia, he turned to denial. The man thought he still had time and that he didn't need immediate help.

This was why the boy had drenched hair as a ghost, the same as the day of his untimely death. This was also why his finger pointed to his uncle, as if still asking for help, accusing him of his demise.

This also explained the unusual way she had previously noticed the soul's eyes looking at the back of the man—with a sort of surprise, sadness, and anger mixed together. The same emotions the boy must have felt when he understood that no help was coming.

The boy named Peter was surely angered, and sad, but he also seemed to comprehend in his heart that it hadn't been his uncle who had neglected him that day, because the man would have never wanted to hurt him but simply couldn't take care of him properly. And so, things happened as they happened.

Then, as suddenly as he had done before, the arm of the boyish ghost moved away from the woman and her eyes returned to reality, once again seeing the reality of the world around her.

"I had a nephew. I remember . . ." There was a pause, again, and Lecia took the chance to make her speech.

"Yes. And he understands now. He does not blame you. He wants you to know that."

The elder man smiled, and a peace settled over him, a look she had not detected or seen on him. "I never meant to worry you," the woman said in a reassuring tone.

"Ah, now, what kind of restaurant were you looking for? That's what you were asking me about, right? Or was it about a direction, or a street?"

"Well, actually, I wondered if you could tell me how to get to the restaurant called the Old City Merchant."

"Yes, yes." The elderly man nodded. "It should be easy to walk. Just get to the city center, follow that street, and . . . You'd better ask some passers-by. I, too, get lost occasionally while walking around."

"I think it can happen to anyone." The woman lowered her gaze. "So, thanks for your recommendations." And with that being said, Lecia moved away from the aged man and the ghost that had once been a boy named Peter.

As the woman slowly walked back to the city center, she thought that the town was a perfect place for pedestrians, which was a good thing as she felt now a bit sad, and absent-minded, simply putting one foot ahead of another. And summer—the present season—was by far the best time to visit the area, which had large festivals and dining and drinking. She needed a good stiff drink just now.

She hoped her strange visions would keep well away from her, at least for the rest of the day. She wanted no part of other unearthly things or shades. Because she had had enough of them, at least for the moment, anyway.

**Sergio Palumbo** is an Italian public servant who graduated from law school and works in the public real estate branch. He published the fantasy role-playing illustrated manual, "War Blades." His short stories appeared in *Aphelion Webzine*, *Weird Year*, *Quantum Muse*, *Antipodean SF*, *Schlock! Webzine*, and *SQ Magazine*, with numerous works published in horror, science fiction, fantasy, steampunk, and urban fantasy anthologies in the United States, Britain, Canada, Australia, and India. He is a co-editor of the *Steam-powered Dream Engines*, *Fantastical Savannahs and Jungles*, *Xeno-biology – Stranger Creatures*, and the *Bleakest Towers* anthologies published by Rogue Planet Press, an imprint of British Horrified Press.

**Author Website:** www.lacenturia.it

**Social Media Handle:**
Amazon Author Page: https://amzn.to/3bzWfQd

# A FACE TO DIE FOR

AMIE DESTEFANO

nside, I'm dead; there's no more spark. I wouldn't have given this or any other building a second glance as nothing held any meaning to me, but as we approached the doorway, it pulsed to life. The edges and corners blurred, and the doorway melted into the alley as if a portal to another world had opened. Just as abruptly as the aberration happened, the entire thing snapped back into shape.

Bringing my arms up came reflexively; with my heart flip-flopping, I leaned away, stepping back into my sister.

She grabbed my shoulders and steadied me. "Ouch, Lettie. You're on my foot." Her breath puffed in small clouds on the cold winter night.

"DeDe?" My teeth were chattering. "Did you see that?"

She looked at me.

Maybe taking me out tonight wasn't the best idea.

"See what?" she asked.

I stared at the tattered and beaten vintage door frame in the decrepit concrete building that stood in the same sad state, pitted and crumbling. *Just as irreparable as my face.* The metal grid protecting the small, antique bubble glass window had more of a "do not disturb" vibe, much like the defensive wall I erected against everyone.

Worried that the deteriorating concrete could collapse on my sister, I tugged DeDe's coat sleeve and pulled her toward the center of the alley. Patches of ice filled the potholes, and light snow fell. The streetlight at the far end of the alley was like a star in the sky, illuminating where the alley met the street. The darkness between the distant streetlamps suited me.

"DeDe are you sure this is the right address? Maybe we should turn around." I shook my head. "I just want to go home, be left alone." *To die.*

DeDe sighed heavily, ignoring my typical negativity. "This is where she said it would be," Dede said.

A sign above the doorway sparked on with an electrical zap. I read the name, the words spilling over what was left of my lips, "Mother Moon."

Directly in front of us, amber light poured out of the opened door into the alley, eclipsing the night. A lit hallway silhouetted a woman in the doorway. The light caught her hair, braided and twisted into a pile on her head. Her neck long and slender. *A ghost? Must be a figment of my imagination, like the doorway morphing into the alley.* Besides, real or fake, I could not care less.

Something deep in the dark alleyway shifted. Chills sprouted along my neck and down my arms. Suddenly, my right cheek—my good cheek—tingled. Light touches from icy fingers traveled down from my forehead as if someone carefully dragged and jerked sharp fingernails down my face. I shook my head, the pain and pressure intensified, and I batted away the violation, careful not to touch my face. *I* never touched my face, not anymore. The invisible contact froze me in place, unable to move. It took every bit of self-control to not touch and feel my bubbled scars—and then finally, the scratching sensation faded.

"Lettie? You're still as a statue, what's going—"

"Nothing," I said before she could finish her question, and I took a cleansing breath. *I'm losing my mind.*

The woman's head lifted and she smelled the air, inhaling like an animal sniffing for predators. Her nose wrinkled and flared. "I wouldn't stand out here too long if I were you." She studied the alley to her left and right, and as she pivoted, her long, flowing black dress swayed around her curvaceous body. Her focus stopped on me. "Many unwanted visitors darken my doorstep. Hurry now, come in."

DeDe snatched at my arm, but I jerked away and moved deeper into darkness as she walked toward the light. Her puffy black jacket sleeves swished against her as she walked, as though scratching at the night.

When she realized I hadn't followed, she turned and gave me an all-too-familiar look of disappointment. "Come on. I booked both of us with the psychic. Thought it would cheer you up. She's going to charge me for you, too, whether you stand out here or come in with me."

"I really didn't want to come with you today, because . . . because . . ." I couldn't fight it anymore. I took a deep sigh, wanting to retreat. My fists clenched as I ground out the words, "DeDe, listen to me. I want to die, to be alone. To die. To Be Alone. To Die. TO DIE!" I paused, breathless, and took a deep breath I wished was unnecessary. "I don't need a psychic to tell me that."

DeDe faced me. "Lettie, you can't mean that. You can't give up."

*Always the optimist, but she doesn't have to live with . . . this.* I adjusted my eye patch out of habit. "I've got nothing left to believe in." I finger-combed my hair, stroking it forward, obsessively, trying to hide the left side of my face, knowing the ugly side of me would take more than hair to camouflage my scars.

DeDe doubled back my way and looked me over carefully, head to toe, inspecting me as if I were a piece of chipped fine China.

*She needn't look so hard; all I am is cracked and imperfect.*

She reached out to me. "You don't even believe in me?" she asked.

I turned my back on her. I wanted to throw something, to scream all the ugliness and torture that I felt. *She will never understand. After all, she has a perfect face.*

She always looked at me like I should be able to drag myself out of bed on my own, go back to teaching, and live some kind of life. Right now, the darkness in this alley wasn't enough to hide my features.

*She is too perfect. Everybody's face is too perfect. Their smooth, soft, un-marked skin reminds me of what I pine for.*

I turned back toward DeDe, her lips parted, fingers interlaced at her heart, snowflakes salting her dark hair. Anger and love entangled my voice. "Sometimes you're not enough, and sometimes you're all I have."

She sighed. "Lettie, I have to talk to you about something." She paused and took a deep breath before continuing. "I know what you do. I've seen you . . . standing in front of the mirror."

I cringed inwardly and turned away from her as if I could still hide my secret from her. *How could DeDe spy on me, how could she do it? The one thing I had control over, and now it's ruined, tainted.* DeDe was very good at ruining things.

My face felt hot despite the cold. *True, I do stand in front of the mirror until my feet hurt and my back is stiff.* I knew exactly how to approach my reflection, tilting my face just so as my image slid into view across the mirror, slowly, so only my good side remained visible. The right side reflected the good half of my face; smooth, olive-toned, with freckles. Freckles I'd once hated but now ached to match on the left side of my face once again.

I'd been so careful with my wishful secret, but now it was exposed and ugly; peeled back and vulnerable, igniting a rage within me.

I paced the alley's width, leaving footprints in the powdery snow, and yelled, "I'm dead! That other person . . . the one I was before . . . she's gone." But as I stared at her pleading face, I felt like I had to give her hope, even false hope. Maybe we both needed that. "I'm trying to bring her back."

DeDe shot back, "You . . . are . . . *not* dead!"

"I might as well be because if this"—I pointed to the left side of my face—"is what I have to look forward to, then death is the only option." *The only solution.*

About time she understood there was no bringing me back to the living.

Pity never entered my sister's expression. Her empathy always sounded true as she tried to pull me from the pit I'd fallen into.

"You're not healthy," DeDe said, pleading with her eyes. "Your face has become an obsession."

Standing toe to toe with her, I swept my hair aside from the disfigurement to remind her of what I saw every day. "Do I look healthy?"

My sister did not look away, never winced. "You look like my sister, and you need help."

"*Like* your sister?" I said, ready to snap at her again, kicking up bits of dead leaves. "Is that how you'd describe me to someone?" My temples pounded. "Wouldn't it be better to say I look like something out of a horror movie mixed with a pirate?" I scoffed. "I don't look anything like your sister anymore."

"Please, I want you to move forward."

"I'm tired of bargaining with the mirror, hoping if I stare long enough at the healthy, freckled side of me—of what remains of the woman before

the fire—I could change back, complete and whole." I wavered in place
and sank into a squat with no fight left in my voice. "It's a joke and a
letdown every time."

My skin, at one time soft, was now mangled as if raked by claws of
fire, partially exposing what should never see the light of day. The deepest
fatty layer of skin bore white-yellow pustules. Bright blood-red scar tissue
had recently turned brown, streaking from my forehead to chin.

Lumpy burns raised beyond exaggeration on my cheek. The fire
had eaten my upper lip away to nothing, deeply pitted my temple, and
burned a chunk of cartilage off my nose, exposing my inner nostril. My
left eye—dead and useless—remained hidden behind an eye patch.

The psychic's commanding voice pulled me from my miserable con-
templation. "This is not the time for quarrels. The spirits of the night are
nearer than you understand."

My sister ran for the door. The psychic positioned DeDe protectively
behind her, then called to me, "Come in now—I won't be able to temper
them much longer." Her voice wavered slightly, yet she stood tall, palms
facing outward. "Unless you'd rather stay out here with them."

I snorted and said, "Yeah, I'll stay out here. I have nothing to lose."

I headed back toward the alley's entry. Five steps into my retreat, a
sweet and intensely floral scent assaulted my sinuses. I gagged, and it
triggered a long-ago childhood memory—flowers, so many flowers in
the trunk of a long black funeral car, and me attached to my momma's
legs. *My father's funeral.*

She and I stood against the open trunk, the funeral home staff pulling flowers out so fast that the buds and stems slapped my face. Powdery
pollen in my eyes and nose. I couldn't see, and I was choking, barely
breathing. I was stuck against my mother and the trunk, unable to free
myself as more and more flowers descended upon me, overwhelming
me with the thought that I would cough and choke until I died. No one
helped me; death surrounded me.

There in the alley, the flowery smell—synonymous with death—
drove me into a coughing fit. I heaved till I was bent over, my lungs not
doing what they should. My body wouldn't defend against the attack.
*Death is here for me again.* And I thought, *Didn't I want this?*

Deep in my heart, I knew, yes, I wanted to give in to death.

So, I released my struggle; I let go and invited the end, then slipped away.

My head filled with fog until a warmness enveloped me. My sister— I knew she was there, tucking me to her side, leading me back to the door—where I didn't want to go—toward the amber light. My body shook violently against her, our jackets rustling and crinkling.

A wind picked up, the snow blew harder and mixed with the leaves, twirling them together in a violent cyclone, round and round, spinning until they incinerated into nothing.

As we neared the open doorway, my breathing eased, and my coughing vanished. Safely inside the entrance, I looked out into the pitch black, and my body stilled. DeDe slammed the door, shutting the darkness outside.

*You can't close the door on darkness. Death is sneaky, transparent, slipping through the cracks, hiding and waiting. It would always find me one way or another.*

We stood in the long hallway directly under the red light, the psychic nowhere in sight.

I moved down the hall away from the brightness and settled for a dim spot next to a coat rack fixed to the wall. I presented my good side to my sister, sliding my coat on the hook.

"Why did you do that?" I hissed under my breath. *Why bring me here and steal me from death, all I want and need?*

She rubbed her temples. "Because I thought you needed help."

"I don't want any more of your help." I had to fight the notion to stomp in a tantrum.

My sister looked away and spoke with a choked voice. "If I can't help my sister, who can I help?"

*Anyone but me, everyone but me.*

"Wouldn't you do the same for me?" she asked.

"You've done *enough*." I ground out the words and let the last one linger. My ears pounded as my blood pressure rose, heat rushed up into my hairline, and an electric jolt filled my body. "Do you know how many times I relive the night of the fire?" Retelling what happened that night would hurt DeDe, but I couldn't help myself. "If you hadn't left the candle burning that night. If I had checked the house before bed. If you hadn't been staying with me." My voice rose and strained around a tightness in my throat. "If, if, if, till I'm crazy and my biggest wish every day is to go back in time."

DeDe cleared her throat and stared at the floor. "I'm so sorry," she said, earnestly. She looked smaller at that moment, inferior. "I've tried to make up for that night ever since it happened. The candle was a stupid mistake." Her voice broke, and she looked up slowly. Tears spilled down her cheeks. "But when I replay that night, I save you every time no matter if you want me to or not." She slid her jacket on the hook beside mine, wiped at her tears, and hugged her arms around herself.

My shoulders slouched inward, and I had trouble looking at her, both of us alone in our own torment. I wanted to tell her, you save me every time, but I wish it was you wearing the face I have now. Guilt pulled me back and instead, I said, "You should have let me die."

The psychic appeared before us and I jumped, taken off guard. "Welcome. I'm Mother Moon." She was tall, at least a foot taller than me, with glowing hazelnut skin and deep brown eyes, beautiful and dark. Braids twisted high on her head like a nest of snakes entwined.

I'm a monster compared to her.

She drew in a breath and continued. "Death isn't always at my doorstep. But tonight . . ." She paused and looked down the hall toward the door where DeDe and I entered. The wind thumped the door so hard it moved slightly against its frame. "Tonight, it still lingers.

"You should be grateful your sister was there; instead, you are spiteful."

I adjusted my eye patch and kept my good eye on the floor, listening to my heart beat fast within my chest. Her stare—I felt it scorch me like a sunburn. I forced myself to look up and spite her for gawking at my scars. Her eyes were directed on mine, but with no horrid expression, nothing but deep interest as if my insides told her all she needed to know. Except for DeDe, no one ever looked *at* me, only through me, or away.

I was torn between shrinking back again or holding my head up high.

"How do you know she's my sister?" I asked, shoving my chin forward, not willing to give in to her chiding tone.

She smiled. "Well . . . I am a psychic. Plus, DeDe told me she was bringing her sister when setting up the appointment." She chuckled.

I inwardly rolled my right eye, wishing for a quick reading.

Gracefully, her fingers parted the sheer golden curtain separating the hallway from a small room. As we entered, I zeroed in on a small table donned with a silver tablecloth and a tarnished ornate platter filled with obviously fake fruit. The table left just enough room for the three of us. A gold chandelier hung above. I imagined the chandelier crashing down on us and coughed to hide my sneer.

From where I stood, I noted a bay window straight ahead. One closed white painted door was to the right, as if the room had a side note of attraction. An oval mirror hung beside the doorframe.

The psychic cocked her head to the side, wisps of loose hair flowing hypnotically. "I have much to tell you. Sit."

I looked down and away from the mirror, taking a seat with my back to the door.

DeDe and I sat beside each other with her across from us. "You must say that to everyone," I said sarcastically.

"Only to the non-believers." The psychic winked.

"I'm not a believer in anything," I said, leaning back in my chair, arms crossed, vinegar in my veins.

"Just give it a try, please," my sister said.

I shook my head and looked at the psychic with as much apathy as I could muster.

"I'll read you both together," Mother Moon said, plowing ahead, determined, seemingly unconcerned whether or not I'd enjoy it. She offered her hands to us. Her long warm fingers sent heat up my arm, filling me with interest in her power, and suspicion.

Mother Moon closed her eyes and paused, then hung her head forward so her chin sat on her chest. Looking like an oversized rag doll, her braids slithered as the loose updo flopped forward. She stayed this way, her mouth forming words devoid of sound.

Mother Moon pulled on my sister's hand, yanking DeDe forward. "You are alive with much regret. And your pain wafts like sickly-sweet perfume."

The woman tugged on my hand harshly, and my chest bumped against the table's hard edge. "You stink of the other side, like an old putrid, decaying wound; barely alive."

"You've got to be kidding me," I said to the psychic. She was putting on quite a show. "All you did is read what you've seen between us."

"Shh," DeDe said, kicking me under the table. "We could learn something."

The psychic carried on without reply, mouth moving without sound, her head still tilted forward, the nest of hair snakes where her face should be.

I suddenly heard music. It definitely hadn't been there before. A piano—it played behind the door, muffled and serene, soft touches on the keys, one note at a time.

Mother Moon exhaled deeply, tugging on my arm where the warmth crept further through my body toward my heart. Her voice dragged over each word. "Death is coming for you . . . one way or another. This is a seriousness that you must fully understand. You have a huge decision ahead of you."

"Okay. Where are the fortune cookies you memorized for this?" I eyed her from across the table.

"Fine. I will show you. It's always the same with you non-believers." She exhaled, looking almost comical with her head on her chest. "You won't understand my warning unless it's painted upon your face."

"My face, huh? Nice word choice," I said, not backing down.

She lifted her head and stretched her neck in a circle, her hair wobbling under the weight. The psychic's mouth curled into a big toothy smile. And there, in her wide grin, I noticed a chipped front tooth. *She wasn't perfect after all.*

Mother Moon rose quickly, pulling on our arms, forcing us to stand or be subjected to a shoulder injury. "Join hands with each other." Her smile was gone. DeDe grabbed my hand, and begrudgingly I took hers. The psychic led us around the table.

The piano music grew louder, fiercer, darker, keys conquered with skill, the tune overtaking my body. My eye closed and opened, closed and opened until we found ourselves sitting once more, the music almost absent yet again.

Mother Moon went in and out of focus, fuzzy then clear. My tongue was loose and ready to speak, but not in my control. My will faded.

*Mother Moon is right, death is coming for me. At this moment I know there is no more hiding my thoughts. She is pulling the truth from me.*

And so I said: "This should be you, DeDe." I pointed to the left side of what remained of my face. "You should be sitting here wanting to die, wanting to hide from the world. *You* did this to me."

Wind creaked and hissed along the windowpanes.

DeDe didn't reply. Her hand felt wrong in mine, and I let it go. Her hand fell like a rope to her side, dead, lifeless, her shoulders trembling as she laid her forehead on the table.

A rattle—the sound of a doorknob turning—made me jump. The gold curtain was the only thing separating us from the short hallway to the door with the jangling doorknob—the door to the alley.

The curtain had a certain amount of transparency, like a fogged-over window, yet it was impossible to see if the knob was genuinely moving. Still, the distinct click and rattle moved back and forth, faster and faster with frustration. Someone, or something, wanted in.

I held my breath; my arm hairs prickled and stood on end. An intense desire to back into a protective corner gripped me, yet I couldn't move. No music, nothing except the continued doorknob turning back and forth, banging against the frame, straining to push the door free.

My mouth turned dry, my tongue thick.

The wind picked up. A loud thud hit the doorframe, once, twice, three times along with the incessant up and down jiggle of the doorknob.

I released a slow, strangled exhale.

A final bang rang out, and the door clicked open with a loud, drawn-out creak.

Cool air wound around my neck. No figure or outline of anyone in the hallway. No one yelled out 'hello,' or 'how are you.'

"What was that?" I asked.

The psychic's head popped up, her eyes no longer brown but clouded over with milk-colored pupils, her chin pointed in the direction of the curtained hallway. "Death," she said. She shook her head no, as if scolding me. "You may think you want death; you may think it's the answer."

I snatched my hand back from her grip, asking "Isn't it?" with a smallness to my voice.

"We're about to find out."

My sister lifted her head from the table, unrecognizable. Unearthly. She smelled just like those overpowering flowers, the suffocating stench. Exactly how I believed death smelled. As if death was so full of itself, so justified, I could choke on it.

The psychic lowered her voice and leaned into my ear. "You worship death as if it will save you. It will only take all that you love."

"You can't mean—"

My sister let loose a cackle I'd never heard before. "She wants something greater; she wants a new face." DeDe spoke with a fierceness I'd forgotten she had. DeDe had once been bold, before the accident. But, since the fire, she'd changed, half alive, like me.

I leaned away, taking her in. "DeDe, your face. How—" *She has half a face.* The left side swollen, red, raw, cracked, and stretched out with fresh burns. Her upper lip gone, exposing her front teeth. The fleshy part of her nose dissolved. Her left eye vacant and glassy, cloudy, sunken, and lifeless. Her good eye reflecting overwhelming loss. The other side of her face perfectly smooth and supple. The starkness between both sides was unsettling and unnatural.

Is that what I really looked like to others? I was uglier than I ever realized. Not a human being; a thing; a skeletal, unformed flesh-eaten beast that shouldn't be allowed to live.

I jumped from the table and the chair toppled over, banging against the hardwood floor. Backing away, I stumbled over the overturned chair until my back was against the wall, beside the mirror.

DeDe, or something that looked like her, rose from her chair and stepped closer to me.

"Stay back," I said, my arms out defensively.

She stopped moving, then spoke in a sweet, alien voice. "What happens when you get what you want, Lettie? No one to take it out on anymore. Would you rather it was me?" She paused to feel the burns and rough skin on her face, caressing her absent lip and defected nose. She laughed and cocked her head side to side, presenting every inch ear to ear. "Deep down, I've always known you wished I had burned that night, instead of you."

"Who are you?" I said, dropping my arms, trying to calm my breathing.

That voice again, now gravelly, said, "Don't you know? I know you do. Come on, say it."

Darkness had caught up with me. All I ever wanted. "You smell like Death," I said.

"Bingo. So nice of you to remember me. I've almost had you twice, three times now. Once when you were a small child. You remember the funeral, the flowers? In truth, the funeral was more of an indirect touch, you could say. I was there for your father. Ever since that day, though, I've yearned to pull you under the veil. And of course, how could we forget the fire." Death's voice sighed long in regret. "Oh, I was so close to having you then, but your sister got in the way. Always in the way. And, just recently, the alley. Oh . . ." Death groaned deep.

"I almost had your tortured little soul in the alley. You were ready to let go, to come to me." It cocked its head to the side. "I've been waiting a long time for you. If I can't have your beautifully depressed, traumatized soul, well I suppose your sister will do for now."

"What have you done with my sister?"

"She's in here somewhere, trying to fight back." Death winked its good eye at me.

I jerked back and my head connected with the wall. My hand shook as I grazed my face with my fingertips. Both sides felt smooth. I slowly removed my eye patch. No blurriness. I could see! My shoulders relaxed and a calm release filled my mind at what might be a new me. My thoughts raced with all the things . . . that I could do with a new face. Connect with anyone instead of locking myself away, or feel human enough, good enough, to look someone in the eye. And just like that, loneliness was a distant memory.

But, I needed a mirror to see for sure. My heart pounded in my throat. My stomach rolled. I reached out to the mirror's framing on the wall, testing it out, making sure it was really there. I turned on shaky legs. Slowly, I moved my face into view with the unscarred side first as I'd always done, timid and snail-like, until my whole face reflected a miracle.

My eyes widened and I leaned into my reflection. No burns! No scar tissue! I smiled and both tanned cheeks rose, my upper lip pink and full. Gingerly, I felt along the bridge of my perfect nose, even if slightly too large. Yes, that's right, I forgot that I had thought it too large. Freckles sprinkled across both cheeks. *How could I have ever hated my freckles or any part of me?*

I took a long shuddering breath. "I'm unmarked." *Maybe I am dreaming.*

Mother Moon spoke. "You want to turn back time, to undo, but it cannot be done; it can only be thus." She sat with her legs crossed and hands on her knees, relaxed, as if our turmoil wasn't playing out in front of her.

"What is going on?" I asked, entranced by my image. Then I turned to Mother Moon, reluctantly.

She continued, "Death has a strange sense of humor. It wants you badly, but your sister seems to always be in the way of saving you. Now, death has your sister, and you have your face."

The psychic stood and motioned for me, and I went willingly. She grabbed my hands and pulled me closer to the table. "A test for your soul, Lettie. Fail this and you will go where you wished you'd never gone. Win this and you will have a full life, a way forward, perhaps a new face of sorts. You can persevere. I see it."

She released me and spread her arms overhead. "I can feel it. Can't you? You will survive and make your life better. I see you overcoming anything."

I shook my head in frustration. "What can I do, how can I change this?" I said, nodding toward Death and my sister. *But I didn't want to change this, knowing deep in my bones I had what I wanted: a new face.*

"The door." Mother Moon pointed to the white door beside the mirror. "The door is your only chance to leave Death behind. You have an intact face now, but death will take your sister. Or, you can walk through that door, and go back to when you first happened upon my doorstep."

"What's behind the door . . . what will happen to me, to us?"

"That door has been many things to many people. It's for you to find out," she said.

I faced the door. "But I can't go back to half a face, watching people stare at me but not wanting to meet my eyes. To politely look away, to not know what to do, to not want anything to do with me. I'm not a person or a human anymore to anyone or myself."

Death walked toward the mirror, leering at me with longing in its eye. "Go live your life. You've got what you want. I'll play around for a bit in your sister's body before I take her soul. Play it by ear, as they say. Watch your sister's life fall apart, her mind spiral out of control, and find her wishing for the end. Won't it be fun?" Death smiled, and only the right side of its face curled upward.

The wooden door within the room suddenly swelled, bulging. Light slipped through the door's rectangular frame—bright as the sun, as if night had turned to day. The rest of the room went hazy and out of focus. Heat stirred under my skin. The closer I stepped toward the opening, the more my skin itched, like an allergic reaction. Vision blurred in my left eye. My bottled quietness returned within, building, seething, like a boiling tea kettle until I could no longer hold in the hot, scalding pain.

"Why does this hurt so much?" I rubbed my chest with both hands.

A sigh from Death. Death stood in front of the mirror, turning its head as if viewing every angle of the burns. "You're right, Lettie. Your sister should have let you die. I see why you wanted it so badly." Death's black eye met mine in the mirror, and the blackness of its eye shifted to blue, the color flickering back and forth like DeDe was trying to fight to survive.

As if Death knew my thoughts, it said, "Oh yes, your sister is fighting my possession. Perhaps you should say your goodbyes."

"DeDe," I yelled. *Could I really say goodbye?*

The room became hot as a sauna. I needed to get out of there. A strong wave of sickness punched through my stomach, and I couldn't catch my breath. Shaking, I stumbled back, away from the door, away from my sister.

A moan thrust through the room. DeDe. Her eye no longer black but full blue. She moaned as she rotated her head in front of the mirror and let out a scream. Her fists pounded the glass until it fell and shattered on the ground.

"I'll give myself over to Death," her strangled voice sobbed.

I approached her cautiously.

She turned away from the glittering shards of glass and walked toward the curtain, ready to give up and leave.

My first selfish instinct was to let her go.

Instead, I lunged for her, reached out, and grabbed a hold of DeDe's arm, screaming for Mother Moon. Looking around the tiny room, I saw that the damn psychic was gone.

DeDe put her hands in mine, and a warped haze took me back to the long funeral car and the flowers, and a forgotten memory. The pollen and roughness of the flower stems and leaves closed in on me, choking me; a small hand grabbed at mine—warm and familiar—steering me away from the black car, away from the flowers, and into the fresh air. Those hands dusted my face and patted my back as I coughed and spat. I opened my eyes for what felt like the first time, to see DeDe. Her hands had pulled me through. She had given me her stuffed bear to hold and asked me to sit with her for a while.

"I know you're scared," she had said. "I am too. Dad always told me to look after you." She smiled. "Seems more important now that he's gone. We'll wait together till it's over, Lettie." We held hands till our mom came and gathered us into the car.

I shook my head back to reality, still holding my sister's hands and holding onto the memory of what she had said last: "We'll wait together till it's over." I repeated the phrase until I realized DeDe had always held up her end, seeing me through life, saving me. She'd saved me that day long ago, from the fire, and even earlier today. And my spiteful hate was all she'd gotten in return.

The gold curtain, the sparkling mirror shards, the glittering chandelier, the light under the door—all glimmers of hope. It was my turn to save my sister.

"DeDe, come with me." This time, I held her tightly, supporting her. Feeling her body beside me, the drum of her heart offbeat with mine. Nevertheless, it beat with force and life.

"But it's not what you want," she said, hesitating, shoeing aside broken glass.

"It's not what I expected. Sometimes what we want isn't what we need. And I need you."

I focused on the door, knowing if I opened it with DeDe, I would find a way to understand my place in life.

I struggled with my sister's weight against mine as I reached for the handle.

The door widened, and my sweaty hand slipped off the knob.

DeDe's blue eye turned black, Death overtaking my sister once again. "But you'll have your face back," it said, as if pleading.

I needed to focus, and I reached for my new mantra, at first whispering and then crying out, "We'll wait together till it's over." I repeated it again and again, until I found the doorknob, the handle firmly in my grasp.

I twisted the doorknob, hearing its tumbler click with release, and pulled the door wide open. As DeDe and I stepped through, I said, "I never liked my freckles anyway."

**Amie DeStefano** enjoys writing short stories, poetry, blog posts, and anything else she dreams up and puts on paper, but especially fantasy. She writes as often as possible while living in Pennsylvania with her husband and two children. Amie revels in many things: sushi, coffee, a good book, but nothing compares to the Zen-in-the-moment feeling while writing.

**Author Website:** https://writingamie.wordpress.com/

**Social Media Handles:**
Blog: https://amiedestefano.medium.com/
Twitter: https://twitter.com/Amian2874

# EDITOR'S NOTE

Louisa May Alcott's original story, "Lost in a Pyramid, or the Mummy's Curse," was first published by Frank Leslie in *The New World* in 1869, one hundred years before I was born. Most people have no idea Alcott wrote thrillers, and this short was among her last. Her tale of a mummified sorceress points to her fascination with dark female characters, something she and I have in common.

In today's age, a reader may find this plot predictable. Keep in mind that she wrote "Mummy's Curse" in the Victorian age, and readers considered it highly original, though it didn't garner much attention through the twentieth century.

Noted Egyptologist Dominic Montserrat, upon rediscovering her story, believed Alcott the first to pen a "mummy's curse" narrative. Gregory Eiselein and Anne K. Phillips, authors of *The Louisa May Alcott Encyclopedia*, call Alcott's account "an unusually early and female-authored example of the Egyptianizing thriller later dominated by male writers such as Bram Stoker, Arthur Conan Doyle, and H. Rider Haggard."

Alcott, arguably the real-life Jo, wrote several Sensation fiction stories, a popular but short-lived genre in Great Britain during the mid-to-late 1800s, under the pen name A. M. Barnard. Why was Alcott drawn to the dark side with stories like *The Abbot's Ghost* and *A Whisper in the Dark*? Perhaps, like her character Jo in *Little Women*, the income inspired her (she received $25): "in those dark ages, even all-perfect America read rubbish." And no, Ms. Alcott, this humble American reader and author is not offended.

—Catherine Jordan, 6/27/2022

# LOST IN A PYRAMID, OR THE MUMMY'S CURSE

## LOUISA MAY ALCOTT

## I

"And what are these, Paul?" asked Evelyn, opening a tarnished gold box and examining its contents curiously.

"Seeds of some unknown Egyptian plant," replied Forsyth, with a sudden shadow on his dark face, as he looked down at the three scarlet grains lying in the white hand lifted to him.

"Where did you get them?" asked the girl.

"That is a weird story, which will only haunt you if I tell it," said Forsyth, with an absent expression that strongly excited the girl's curiosity.

"Please tell it, I like weird tales, and they never trouble me. Ah, do tell it; your stories are always so interesting," she cried, looking up with such a pretty blending of entreaty and command in her charming face, that refusal was impossible.

"You'll be sorry for it, and so shall I, perhaps; I warn you beforehand, that harm is foretold to the possessor of those mysterious seeds," said Forsyth, smiling, even while he knit his black brows, and regarded the blooming creature before him with a fond yet foreboding glance.

"Tell on, I'm not afraid of these pretty atoms," she answered, with an imperious nod.

"To hear is to obey. Let me read the facts, and then I will begin," returned Forsyth, pacing to and fro with the far-off look of one who turns the pages of the past.

Evelyn watched him a moment, and then returned to her work, or play, rather, for the task seemed well suited to the vivacious little creature, half-child, half-woman.

"While in Egypt," commenced Forsyth, slowly, "I went one day with my guide and Professor Niles, to explore the Cheops. Niles had a mania for antiquities of all sorts, and forgot time, danger and fatigue in the ardor of his pursuit. We rummaged up and down the narrow passages, half choked with dust and close air; reading inscriptions on the walls, stumbling over shattered mummy-cases, or coming face to face with some shriveled specimen perched like a hobgoblin on the little shelves where the dead used to be stowed away for ages. I was desperately tired after a few hours of it, and begged the professor to return. But he was bent on exploring certain places, and would not desist. We had but one guide, so I was forced to stay; but Jumal, my man, seeing how weary I was, proposed to us to rest in one of the larger passages, while he went to procure another guide for Niles. We consented, and assuring us that we were perfectly safe, if we did not quit the spot, Jumal left us, promising to return speedily. The professor sat down to take notes of his researches, and stretching my self on the soft sand, I fell asleep.

"I was roused by that indescribable thrill which instinctively warns us of danger, and springing up, I found myself alone. One torch burned faintly where Jumal had struck it, but Niles and the other light were gone. A dreadful sense of loneliness oppressed me for a moment; then I collected myself and looked well about me. A bit of paper was pinned to my hat, which lay near me, and on it, in the professor's writing were these words:

> "'I've gone back a little to refresh my memory on certain points. Don't follow me till Jumal comes. I can find my way back to you, for I have a clue. Sleep well, and dream gloriously of the Pharaohs. N N.'

"I laughed at first over the old enthusiast, then felt anxious then restless, and finally resolved to follow him, for I discovered a strong cord fastened to a fallen stone, and knew that this was the clue he spoke of. Leaving a line for Jumal, I took my torch and retraced my steps, follow-ing the cord along the winding ways. I often shouted, but received no reply, and pressed on, hoping at each turn to see the old man poring over some musty relic of antiquity. Suddenly the cord ended, and lowering my torch, I saw that the footsteps had gone on.

"'Rash fellow, he'll lose himself, to a certainty,' I thought, really alarmed now.

"As I paused, a faint call reached me, and I answered it, waited, shouted again, and a still fainter echo replied.

"Niles was evidently going on, misled by the reverberations of the low passages. No time was to be lost, and, forgetting myself, I stuck my torch in the deep sand to guide me back to the clue, and ran down the straight path before me, whooping like a madman as I went. I did not mean to lose sight of the light, but in my eagerness to find Niles I turned from the main passage, and, guided by his voice, hastened on. His torch soon gladdened my eyes, and the clutch of his trembling hands told me what agony he had suffered.

"'Let us get out of this horrible place at once,' he said, wiping the great drops off his forehead.

"'Come, we're not far from the clue. I can soon reach it, and then we are safe'; but as I spoke, a chill passed over me, for a perfect labyrinth of narrow paths lay before us.

"Trying to guide myself by such land-marks as I had observed in my hasty passage, I followed the tracks in the sand till I fancied we must be near my light. No glimmer appeared, however, and kneeling down to examine the footprints nearer, I discovered, to my dismay, that I had been following the wrong ones, for among those marked by a deep boot-heel, were prints of bare feet; we had had no guide there, and Jumal wore sandals.

"Rising, I confronted Niles, with the one despairing word, 'Lost!' as I pointed from the treacherous sand to the fast-waning light.

"I thought the old man would be overwhelmed but, to my surprise, he grew quite calm and steady, thought a moment, and then went on, saying, quietly:

"'Other men have passed here before us; let us follow their steps, for, if I do not greatly err, they lead toward great passages, where one's way is easily found.'

"On we went, bravely, till a misstep threw the professor violently to the ground with a broken leg, and nearly extinguished the torch. It was a horrible predicament, and I gave up all hope as I sat beside the poor fellow, who lay exhausted with fatigue, remorse and pain, for I would not leave him.

"'Paul,' he said suddenly, 'if you will not go on, there is one more effort we can make. I remember hearing that a party lost as we are, saved themselves by building a fire. The smoke penetrated further than sound or light, and the guide's quick wit understood the unusual mist; he followed it, and rescued the party. Make a fire and trust to Jumal.'

"'A fire without wood?' I began; but he pointed to a shelf behind me, which had escaped me in the gloom; and on it I saw a slender mummy-case. I understood him, for these dry cases, which lie about in hundreds, are freely used as firewood. Reaching up, I pulled it down, believing it to be empty, but as it fell, it burst open, and out rolled a mummy. Accustomed as I was to such sights, it startled me a little, for danger had unstrung my nerves. Laying the little brown chrysalis aside, I smashed the case, lit the pile with my torch, and soon a light cloud of smoke drifted down the three passages which diverged from the cell-like place where we had paused.

"While busied with the fire, Niles, forgetful of pain and peril, had dragged the mummy nearer, and was examining it with the interest of a man whose ruling passion was strong even in death.

"'Come and help me unroll this. I have always longed to be the first to see and secure the curious treasures put away among the folds of these uncanny winding-sheets. This is a woman, and we may find something rare and precious here,' he said, beginning to unfold the outer coverings, from which a strange aromatic odor came.

"Reluctantly I obeyed, for to me there was something sacred in the bones of this unknown woman. But to beguile the time and amuse the poor fellow, I lent a hand, wondering as I worked, if this dark, ugly thing had ever been a lovely, soft-eyed Egyptian girl.

"From the fibrous folds of the wrappings dropped precious gums and spices, which half intoxicated us with their potent breath, antique coins, and a curious jewel or two, which Niles eagerly examined.

"All the bandages but one were cut off at last, and a small head laid bare, round which still hung great plaits of what had once been luxuriant hair. The shriveled hands were folded on the breast, and clasped in them lay that gold box."

"Ah!" cried Evelyn, dropping it from her rosy palm with a shudder.

"Nay; don't reject the poor little mummy's treasure. I never have quite forgiven myself for stealing it, or for burning her," said Forsyth, painting rapidly, as if the recollection of that experience lent energy to his hand.

"Burning her! Oh, Paul, what do you mean?" asked the girl, sitting up with a face full of excitement.

"I'll tell you. While busied with Madame la Momie, our fire had burned low, for the dry case went like tinder. A faint, far-off sound made our hearts leap, and Niles cried out: 'Pile on the wood; Jumal is tracking us; don't let the smoke fail now or we are lost!'

"'There is no more wood; the case was very small, and is all gone,' I answered, tearing off such of my garments as would burn readily, and piling them upon the embers.

"Niles did the same, but the light fabrics were quickly consumed, and made no smoke.

"'Burn that!' commanded the professor, pointing to the mummy.

"I hesitated a moment. Again came the faint echo of a horn. Life was dear to me. A few dry bones might save us, and I obeyed him in silence.

"A dull blaze sprung up, and a heavy smoke rose from the burning mummy, rolling in volumes through the low passages, and threatening to suffocate us with its fragrant mist. My brain grew dizzy, the light danced before my eyes, strange phantoms seemed to people the air, and, in the act of asking Niles why he gasped and looked so pale, I lost consciousness."

Evelyn drew a long breath, and put away the scented toys from her lap as if their odor oppressed her.

Forsyth's swarthy face was all aglow with the excitement of his story, and his black eyes glittered as he added, with a quick laugh:

"That's all; Jumal found and got us out, and we both forswore pyramids for the rest of our days."

"But the box: how came you to keep it?" asked Evelyn, eyeing it askance as it lay gleaming in a streak of sunshine.

"Oh, I brought it away as a souvenir, and Niles kept the other trinkets."

"But you said harm was foretold to the possessor of those scarlet seeds," persisted the girl, whose fancy was excited by the tale, and who fancied all was not told.

"Among his spoils, Niles found a bit of parchment, which he deciphered, and this inscription said that the mummy we had so ungallantly burned was that of a famous sorceress who bequeathed her curse to whoever should disturb her rest. Of course I don't believe that curse has anything to do with it, but it's a fact that Niles never prospered from that day. He says it's because he has never recovered from the fall and fright and I dare say it is so; but I sometimes wonder if I am to share the curse, for I've a vein of superstition in me, and that poor little mummy haunts my dreams still."

A long silence followed these words. Paul painted mechanically and Evelyn lay regarding him with a thoughtful face. But gloomy fancies were as foreign to her nature as shadows are to noonday, and presently she laughed a cheery laugh, saying as she took up the box again:

"Why don't you plant them, and see what wondrous flower they will bear?"

"I doubt if they would bear anything after lying in a mummy's hand for centuries," replied Forsyth, gravely.

"Let me plant them and try. You know wheat has sprouted and grown that was taken from a mummy's coffin; why should not these pretty seeds? I should so like to watch them grow; may I, Paul?"

"No, I'd rather leave that experiment untried. I have a queer feeling about the matter, and don't want to meddle myself or let anyone I love meddle with these seeds. They may be some horrible poison, or possess some evil power, for the sorceress evidently valued them, since she clutched them fast even in her tomb."

"Now, you are foolishly superstitious, and I laugh at you. Be generous; give me one seed, just to learn if it will grow. See I'll pay for it," and

Evelyn, who now stood beside him, dropped a kiss on his forehead as she made her request, with the most engaging air.

But Forsyth would not yield. He smiled and returned the embrace with lover-like warmth, then flung the seeds into the fire, and gave her back the golden box, saying, tenderly:

"My darling, I'll fill it with diamonds or bonbons, if you please, but I will not let you play with that witch's spells. You've enough of your own, so forget the 'pretty seeds' and see what a Light of the Harem I've made of you."

Evelyn frowned, and smiled, and presently the lovers were out in the spring sunshine reveling in their own happy hopes, untroubled by one foreboding fear.

# I I

"I have a little surprise for you, love," said Forsyth, as he greeted his cousin three months later on the morning of his wedding day.

"And I have one for you," she answered, smiling faintly.

"How pale you are, and how thin you grow! All this bridal bustle is too much for you, Evelyn," he said, with fond anxiety, as he watched the strange pallor of her face, and pressed the wasted little hand in his.

"I am so tired," she said, and leaned her head wearily on her lover's breast. "Neither sleep, food, nor air gives me strength, and a curious mist seems to cloud my mind at times. Mamma says it is the heat, but I shiver even in the sun, while at night I burn with fever. Paul, dear, I'm glad you are going to take me away to lead a quiet, happy life with you, but I'm afraid it will be a very short one."

"My fanciful little wife! You are tired and nervous with all this worry, but a few weeks of rest in the country will give us back our blooming Eve again. Have you no curiosity to learn my surprise?" he asked, to change her thoughts.

The vacant look stealing over the girl's face gave place to one of interest, but as she listened it seemed to require an effort to fix her mind on her lover's words.

"You remember the day we rummaged in the old cabinet?"

"Yes," and a smile touched her lips for a moment.

"And how you wanted to plant those queer red seeds I stole from the mummy?"

"I remember," and her eyes kindled with sudden fire.

"Well, I tossed them into the fire, as I thought, and gave you the box. But when I went back to cover up my picture, and found one of those seeds on the rug, a sudden fancy to gratify your whim led me to send it to Niles and ask him to plant and report on its progress. Today I hear from him for the first time, and he reports that the seed has grown marvelously, has budded, and that he intends to take the first flower, if it blooms in time, to a meeting of famous scientific men, after which he will send me its true name and the plant itself. From his description, it must be very curious, and I'm impatient to see it."

"You need not wait; I can show you the flower in its bloom," and Evelyn beckoned with the mechante smile so long a stranger to her lips.

Much amazed, Forsyth followed her to her own little boudoir, and there, standing in the sunshine, was the unknown plant. Almost rank in their luxuriance were the vivid green leaves on the slender purple stems, and rising from the midst, one ghostly-white flower, shaped like the head of a hooded snake, with scarlet stamens like forked tongues, and on the petals glittered spots like dew.

"A strange, uncanny flower! Has it any odor?" asked Forsyth, bending to examine it, and forgetting, in his interest, to ask how it came there.

"None, and that disappoints me, I am so fond of perfumes," answered the girl, caressing the green leaves which trembled at her touch, while the purple stems deepened their tint.

"Now tell me about it," said Forsyth, after standing silent for several minutes.

"I had been before you, and secured one of the seeds, for two fell on the rug. I planted it under a glass in the richest soil I could find, watered it faithfully, and was amazed at the rapidity with which it grew when once it appeared above the earth. I told no-one, for I meant to surprise you with it; but this bud has been so long in blooming, I have had to wait. It is a good omen that it blossoms today, and as it is nearly white, I mean to wear it, for I've learned to love it, having been my pet for so long."

"I would not wear it, for, in spite of its innocent color, it is an evil-looking plant, with its adder's tongue and unnatural dew. Wait till Niles tells us what it is, then pet it if it is harmless."

"Perhaps my sorceress cherished it for some symbolic beauty—those old Egyptians were full of fancies. It was very sly of you to turn the tables on me in this way. But I forgive you, since in a few hours, I shall chain this mysterious hand forever. How cold it is! Come out into the garden and get some warmth and color for tonight, my love."

But when night came, no-one could reproach the girl with her pallor, for she glowed like a pomegranate-flower, her eyes were full of fire, her lips scarlet, and all her old vivacity seemed to have returned. A more brilliant bride never blushed under a misty veil, and when her lover saw her, he was absolutely startled by the almost unearthly beauty which transformed the pale, languid creature of the morning into this radiant woman.

They were married, and if love, many blessings, and all good gifts lavishly showered upon them could make them happy, then this young pair were truly blest. But even in the rapture of the moment that made her his, Forsyth observed how icy cold was the little hand he held, how feverish the deep color on the soft cheek he kissed, and what a strange fire burned in the tender eyes that looked so wistfully at him.

Blithe and beautiful as a spirit, the smiling bride played her part in all the festivities of that long evening, and when at last light, life and color began to fade, the loving eyes that watched her thought it but the natural weariness of the hour. As the last guest departed, Forsyth was met by a servant, who gave him a letter marked "Haste." Tearing it open, he read these lines, from a friend of the professor's:

> "DEAR SIR—Poor Niles died suddenly two days ago, while at
> the Scientific Club, and his last words were: 'Tell Paul Forsyth
> to beware of the Mummy's Curse, for this fatal flower has killed
> me.' The circumstances of his death were so peculiar, that I
> add them as a sequel to this message. For several months, as
> he told us, he had been watching an unknown plant, and that
> evening he brought us the flower to examine. Other matters of

interest absorbed us till a late hour, and the plant was forgotten. The professor wore it in his buttonhole—a strange white, serpent-headed blossom, with pale glittering spots, which slowly changed to a glittering scarlet, till the leaves looked as if sprinkled with blood. It was observed that instead of the pallor and feebleness which had recently come over him, that the professor was unusually animated, and seemed in an almost unnatural state of high spirits. Near the close of the meeting, in the midst of a lively discussion, he suddenly dropped, as if smitten with apoplexy. He was conveyed home insensible, and after one lucid interval, in which he gave me the message I have recorded above, he died in great agony, raving of mummies, pyramids, serpents, and some fatal curse which had fallen upon him.

"After his death, livid scarlet spots, like those on the flower, appeared upon his skin, and he shriveled like a withered leaf. At my desire, the mysterious plant was examined, and pronounced by the best authority one of the most deadly poisons known to the Egyptian sorceresses. The plant slowly absorbs the vitality of whoever cultivates it, and the blossom, worn for two or three hours, produces either madness or death."

Down dropped the paper from Forsyth's hand; he read no further, but hurried back into the room where he had left his young wife. As if worn out with fatigue, she had thrown herself upon a couch, and lay there motionless, her face half-hidden by the light folds of the veil, which had blown over it.

"Evelyn, my dearest! Wake up and answer me. Did you wear that strange flower today?" whispered Forsyth, putting the misty screen away.

There was no need for her to answer, for there, gleaming spectrally on her bosom, was the evil blossom, its white petals spotted now with flecks of scarlet, vivid as drops of newly spilt blood.

But the unhappy bridegroom scarcely saw it, for the face above it appalled him by its utter vacancy. Drawn and pallid, as if with some wasting malady, the young face, so lovely an hour ago, lay before him aged and blighted by the baleful influence of the plant which had drunk up her life. No recognition in the eyes, no word upon the lips, no motion of the hand—only the faint breath, the fluttering pulse, and wide-opened eyes, betrayed that she was alive.

Alas for the young wife! The superstitious fear at which she had smiled had proved true: the curse that had bided its time for ages was fulfilled at last, and her own hand wrecked her happiness for ever. Death in life was her doom, and for years Forsyth secluded himself to tend with pathetic devotion the pale ghost, who never, by word or look, could thank him for the love that outlived even such a fate as this.

# ACKNOWLEDGMENTS

I'd like to thank Lawrence Knorr for his support when I approached him about this anthology. Thanks to the Hive, and for your encouragement. Also, my appreciation for the edits and formatting from Jennifer and Crystal at Sunbury Press, and to Jack for his illustration.